Helen Phifer is the bestselling writer of twenty-seven books, including the hugely popular Annie Graham, Lucy Harwin, Beth Adams, Maria Miller and Detective Constable Morgan Brooks series.

She lives in the busy town of Barrow-in-Furness surrounded by miles of coastline and a short drive from the glorious English Lake District.

Helen loves reading books that scare the heck out of her and is eternally grateful to Stephen King, Dean Koontz, James Herbert and Graham Masterton for scaring her senseless in her teenage years. Unable to find enough scary stories she decided to write her own and her debut novel *The Ghost House* released in October 2013 became a #1 Global Bestseller.

You can find her over on Instagram @helenphifer, or on her website at www.helenphifer.com

Also by Helen Phifer

The Annie Graham series
The Ghost House
Secrets of the Shadows
The Forgotten Cottage
The Lake House
The Girls in the Woods
The Face Behind the Mask

Detective Lucy Harwin
Dark House
Dying Breath
Last Light

Beth Adams
The Girl in the Grave
The Girls in the Lake

Detective Morgan Brookes
One Left Alive
The Killer's Girl
The Hiding Place
First Girl to Die
Find the Girl
Sleeping Dolls
Silent Angel
Their Burning Graves
Hold Your Breath
Stolen Darlings
Save Her Twice
Poison Memories

Detective Maria Miller
The Haunting on West 10th Street
Her Lost Soul
The Girls on Floor 13

Standalone novels
The Good Sisters
The House on West 10th Street
Lakeview House

The Face Behind the Mask

HELEN PHIFER

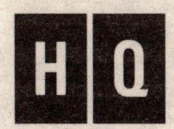

ONE PLACE. MANY STORIES

HQ
An imprint of HarperCollins*Publishers* Ltd
1 London Bridge Street
London SE1 9GF

www.harpercollins.co.uk

HarperCollins*Publishers*
Macken House, 39/40 Mayor Street Upper,
Dublin 1 D01 C9W8
This edition 2025

1
First published in Great Britain by HQ,
an imprint of HarperCollins*Publishers* Ltd 2017

ISBN: 9780008737214

Printed and bound in the UK using 100% Renewable
Electricity by CPI Group (UK) Ltd

For more information visit: www.harpercollins.co.uk/green

*This book is dedicated with much love to my adorable
Gracie, Laurence, Donovan & Matilda xx*

Prologue

Twenty-year-old Gordy Marshall was in the stuffy attic of his parents' semi-detached house admiring his reflection in the only full-length mirror. He'd found it hidden up here when he was a teenager. He had no idea why his dad hated mirrors. He had a thing about them and there were only two apart from this one in the whole house: one in the bathroom and one in the hall. He'd never been allowed one in his bedroom, which Gordy thought was just absurd.

He'd found this one hidden under a sheet one day when he'd come up here looking for something to make a clown costume out of. He knew that his mother kept an old trunk up in the dark, dusty attic full of costumes that she'd worn when she was a dancer for the circus. He'd found the trunk and sat for hours, looking at the shiny silk and sparkling dresses. There had been a photograph album full of pictures of when his mother was in the circus. She had photos of herself next to the lions, elephants, trapeze artists and clowns.

The clowns fascinated him the most. He was leaving to join the circus and become a clown. He couldn't tell his mother of his

1

dreams because she no longer seemed to have any of her own. She was a downtrodden, mean-spirited woman who did whatever her husband told her to. Gordy couldn't remember the last time she had laughed or joked.

He'd listened in awe to her tales of circus life when he was a kid. One day his dad had come home and heard her telling him all about the handsome trapeze artists and that had been it. The next morning his dad had taken him to school and when he'd come home his mother had been in the kitchen making tea while wearing a pair of dark glasses and a scarf around her neck – even though it was a warm autumn day.

She had stopped laughing and joking after that day. She didn't tuck Gordy in after that either, and the stories had stopped.

Today he was admiring the costume that he'd made himself, holding it up and standing in front of the mirror. He picked up the old satin washbag his mother had thrown away a few months ago and took the white greasepaint out of it. Gordy took his time applying it to his face. It had to be just right. He finished the thick coat of white and took out the red, drawing on the big, false, red smile. He drew the thick lines around his eyes and smiled as he stood as close to the glass as he could.

Turning his head left and then right he admired his skilful handiwork. He never heard the front door open; he was so fascinated seeing himself for the first time in full make-up. He stepped into the costume that he'd made out of some black and white stripy satin material he'd found in the bottom of the trunk. He pulled it up and smiled. There were three black pom-poms in the middle of his chest, which had taken him ages to make.

He pulled out the big, black ruffle that was to be fastened around his neck and lifted it up. Once that was secure he took the wig out of the suitcase next to the trunk. It was a bright orange curly wig from the haberdashery shop, which didn't look particularly spectacular until he cut away the curls, leaving just three tufts of bright orange hair sticking up. As he tugged it down onto his head he grinned at the reflection staring back at him. From now on he would be called Tufty the clown.

A loud bang, then a high-pitched screech, made him jump. 'Gorrrdy Marshall, what the hell have you got in here?' He grimaced at the way his mother shouted his name. For God's sake she needed to remember he wasn't some snot-nosed brat anymore. He was a grown man and the noise came from directly below him, which meant she was in his room. Going through his private stuff again. The last time she'd done that was under the pretence she was changing the bedding.

Anger filled his chest and he turned to run downstairs to see what she was screeching about. He ran into his room the same time as his father came running up the stairs. She was holding his old sweet tin in her hands, staring down at the contents. He muttered, 'Fuck.' As she held the open tin towards him she screeched.

'What the hell is in here? I feel sick. I don't know if I want to know or not.'

He shrugged at the selection of small bones from the animals he'd killed over the years then kept in there as keepsakes. 'Stuff, my stuff, that you have no right to be going through, you nosy cow.'

His father walked in behind him and shouted at him, 'Don't you dare speak to your mother like that – and what the hell are you dressed like a circus freak for? Do you know how idiotic you look? What if the neighbours saw you?'

Gordy felt the white-hot rage that he'd kept buried inside him since the day in the woods when he was twelve years old and had almost killed his friend Andrew. He had hit him across the head so hard with a tree branch that it had knocked him out cold. His anger had erupted that day because Andrew had laughed when Gordy had confided in him that he wanted to be a circus clown.

Luckily for Gordy, Andrew hadn't seen the rage coming. He'd spent three weeks in a coma and when he woke up he had no idea what had happened, so Gordy had escaped any blame. Then there was his teacher when he was fifteen: Mrs Goldsmith, who had made it her purpose in school to make fun of him. She hadn't thought it was as funny when he waited by her house one cold, dark January night. She had made him stay behind at school again and Gordy had known his father would go mad with him for being late.

He had found a rusty old axe in the bushes in the park and had taken it. He hid it behind the low wall of the park, which was opposite Mrs Goldsmith's house. He had retrieved the axe and waited in the shadows of the backstreet she had to walk past to get to her house. She hadn't even had a chance to scream as the anger had filled his chest when she came into view. The axe had hit her across the back of the head. She'd fallen and Gordy had run for his life.

He had felt no qualms about leaving her lying on the cold ground bleeding and all alone. He'd laughed to himself all the way home, thinking that he'd shown her. She wouldn't be making fun of him in class again. She hadn't died, but she never came back to school. He'd heard his mother talking about how she was barely able to talk and feed herself anymore.

Now he stared at his father. Once more the anger filled his chest. He didn't care if his mother saw him dressed this way. She knew what the circus was like, but he hadn't expected his father to be home. He was such a bigot and all he cared about was Gordy having a proper job, with prospects, and being respectable. His job working for his dad at Marshall and Marshall Accountants was about as exciting as watching paint dry and Gordy knew that he couldn't do it a day longer. The time had come to leave and he wasn't sorry in the least.

'I'm leaving to become a clown. I've been offered a position in the circus.'

His father's face turned the colour of beetroot. He spluttered as spittle flew from his mouth while trying to find the right words. 'You leave this house looking like that and you're never coming back.'

His mother had begun to cry, and then she let out a high-pitched scream as she ran at him. Her small fists pummelled his chest. He grabbed them in his huge hands to stop her. His dad bellowed at him to let go of her and Gordy lost it. Was he not allowed to defend himself? His father could punch and kick her yet this wasn't allowed? It was ridiculous!

Shoving his mother to one side he strode across the room, pushing past his father. He needed to get out of this suffocating house of misery. He had a suitcase packed already in the hall cupboard; he was wearing his most precious items of clothing. After running down the stairs he grabbed his case and walked into the kitchen where he had left his wallet.

His mother, who had found her second wind, was now running down the stairs, screaming at him. Without pausing, he picked up the sharp axe off the fire grate his father used to split the wood. Swinging it with full force he watched as, in slow motion, it hit his mother's neck and a fountain of red sprayed from it. Her eyes began to glaze over as she fell to the floor.

His father came charging at him, screaming Gordy's mother's name. Gordy knew he had no other choice now and swung the axe at his father. He watched as the fight left the huge bully of a man and he collapsed to the floor next to his wife. The spreading puddle of thick, red blood began to pool around both of their heads.

Gordy threw the axe into the open fire and the handle began to smoulder and burn. Flames jumped from it as the wooden shaft caught alight. He expected to hear sirens in the distance, but all he heard was silence. For the first time ever the house was truly quiet. After washing his hands in the sink, he dried them on the tea towel and picked up his case.

For the first time in his life he felt liberated; he felt free. He turned to take one last look at the crumpled, bleeding, dead humans he'd left behind – humans he had once loved, a very long time ago. He shrugged. He could get changed, but there was no reason why he had to. The circus was only a mile away down the road on the wasteland next to the park; he could walk there as if he belonged. No one would recognise him and he would finally be able to be himself after all this time.

Chapter One

The sea of black and white parted as if by Moses himself at the arrival of the horse-drawn hearse. Two lines of neatly formed police officers stood with their heads bowed, all wearing their number-one smart black dress tunics. Black boots polished highly enough to see their own reflections in. Pressed, crisp white shirts and the creases in their dress trousers immaculate.

Annie Ashworth stood at the back of the crowd of mourners; next to her was her friend and retired police sergeant Kav. She was still on maternity leave and thankful that she was, so she hadn't had to face the indignity of trying to squeeze into her too small uniform. She doubted very much that her tunic would fasten; neither would her trousers.

She hadn't wanted to come to Stuart's funeral and had forced herself to leave the house this morning because she felt partly responsible that he was dead. No, that was wrong. She felt wholly responsible that he was dead. If he hadn't turned up at her house that night, steaming drunk and being aggressive, then none of this would ever have happened. She wouldn't be here now, standing watching her husband, Will, leading the guard of honour and

7

trying to keep it together while looking distraught.

She'd only ever seen him cry twice: once when he thought she was dead at the hands of serial killer Henry Smith, and then at the birth of their son, Alfie. *Think about Alfie and how gorgeous he is. Don't look at the . . .* It was too late. Her eyes landed on the solid oak coffin with the Union Jack flag draped over it. Stu's flat cap and a beautiful display of white roses, lilies and gypsophila adorned the top of it. She felt her legs tremble, but Kav's strong hand gripped her elbow. He bent down and whispered, 'Don't even go there; this wasn't your fault.'

Her eyes filled with tears because, no matter how many times they told her it wasn't, she would always – every single day for the rest of her life – blame herself. As the officers saluted at the passing of their colleague she blinked and turned away. She'd come here for Will, who had worked with Stu and been his friend for the last five years; he'd supported her through so much and now it was her turn. Annie knew that what Will really needed was to get this over with, then go to the pub and get shit-faced with the rest of his team in CID. He could reminisce about the good old times, try to forget the bad and generally get it all out of his system.

She whispered back, 'I should never have come.'

Kav shrugged. Annie was aware that he felt just as awkward as she did because it had been him driving Stu home that night. He'd jumped out of Cathy's car and done a runner into the pitch-black along the wintry, desolate coastal road. Kav had set off a panicked search that had ended with Stu throwing himself in front of a fast-moving police car.

Debs, Stu's estranged wife, walked in between Stu's parents holding their hands. Annie admired her strength. She didn't know if she would have been able to do that. It was nice that his parents didn't blame her or Annie; in fact they hadn't blamed anyone and had accepted that their only son had made a reckless, drunken decision that had left him unable to feed himself, talk or open his eyes. As cruel as it was, it was kinder that he'd died. That was no way to live your life. Annie thought that Stu would have agreed with her wholeheartedly.

There were so many mourners that Annie was relieved they couldn't fit inside the small church and happily took her place standing outside. It was a warm summer's day, the kind of day that made you want to pack up a picnic and go sit on a blanket on the beach. It was far too nice a day for a funeral; the sun was certainly shining down on Stuart today. She just hoped he'd finally found some peace.

He hadn't been a bad person. He'd just completely fucked up and had paid the ultimate price. It could happen to anyone. Throughout the entire service Annie's attention kept getting drawn to one of the old tombstones in the churchyard. She couldn't see anyone standing around in that area, but she got the distinct impression someone was hiding and watching.

Elbow's 'One Day Like This' began to play and the coffin was carried out of the church. Annie bowed her head, waiting for them all to pass. She wasn't going to the cremation; she and Kav were going back to Jake's house. Jake's husband Alex was babysitting Alfie. Their fifteen-month-old little girl, Alice, was as besotted with her eight-month-old baby, Alfie, as Annie was.

Will passed her by, his eyes puffy and red. He smiled at her and she smiled back. Jake, who was one of the last out, walked straight over to them. Bending down he kissed her on the cheek. He looked at Kav and grinned.

'I may love you, Sarge, but I'm not kissing you in public; although I'm glad to see you bothered to have a shave for the occasion.'

Annie giggled; Jake was so good at being bad without even realising it and he always managed to cheer her up no matter how dark a day she was having.

Kav rolled his eyes at him. 'Thank fuck for that.'

'I'm not going to the crematorium. I'm bursting out of these pants and they itch like mad. My balls feel as if they're on fire. Should we head back now and have a drink?'

Annie and Kav nodded. Cathy wandered over.

'What are you three up to?'

'Nothing. I just asked these two reprobates if they were coming to my house. I bloody hate funerals.'

Annie smiled. 'Tell her the real reason you want to leave, Jake.'

He poked her in the side. 'Come on, who's giving me a lift?'

Kav pointed at Annie. 'She's the chauffeur today.'

'That's good. I get to be driven home in style by Miss Daisy. Bring it on.'

The four of them wandered towards the small lane where Annie had parked. A car went past with Will in the passenger seat. He blew her a kiss. No matter how many times she saw him her heart always did a little flip. She lifted her hand to wave. They got into her Mercedes: Kav and Cathy in the back, Jake in the front. She waited for the long line of cars to pull out and follow the funeral procession before setting off. Jake turned to look at Kav.

'Don't you two be getting up to any funny stuff in that back seat. You're both way too old for that sort of thing.'

Annie laughed as Kav's huge hand slapped Jake around the side of the head.

'You never learn do you, Jake? Always respect your elders, especially when they can still kick your arse.'

'Ouch, violence is never the answer.'

She edged the car out after the last of the mourners and began the short drive to Jake's house. She couldn't wait to give Alfie the biggest cuddle ever. She hated funerals. They were a painful reminder that no one lived forever, despite wanting to. Especially because she'd come close to dying herself a fair few times the last couple of years. It gave her the shivers just thinking about it.

She parked outside Jake's house and couldn't get out of the car fast enough when Alex opened the front door with her baby in his arms. Alfie was growing so much he wasn't going to be a baby for much longer. The last eight months had flown by so fast. She'd not had to think about much except looking after Alfie and she loved it. Although she was getting a little bored not having much adult conversation, she saw Jake a couple of times a week and Cathy kept in touch, as did Kav.

Jo – her new-found friend – even popped in whenever she wasn't busy. After surviving her husband Heath's almost fatal attack at their cottage, Jo had recovered well and got herself a job in the village café where they served huge cakes. Annie especially liked Jo's visits because she normally brought cake with her.

Annie needed to seriously consider if she was going back to her job as a community police officer soon. Before she knew it her twelve months' maternity leave would be up. Alfie reached his chubby hands towards her and his little face lit up when she smiled at him. She took him from Alex.

'Has he been good?'

'He's been a little angel, no bother at all.'

Jake sniggered. 'Thank God he doesn't take after his mother.'

'You're on fine form today, Jake.'

Jake patted Annie's back. 'Sorry, I promise I'll behave from now on. I think it must be funeral nerves. They make me want to laugh and joke to remember that I'm still alive.'

They all followed Alex into the kitchen where Alice was scooting around in her baby walker and stuffing cheesy puffs into her mouth. Kav shook his head. 'Bugger me, there are kids everywhere. How did that happen?'

Cathy laughed. 'Surely at your age you know exactly how that happens.'

Alice took one look at him and forced her little legs to manoeuvre the walker in his direction where she slammed straight into his shins. He bent down and tugged her from the walker.

'It's a good job I like you, kid; I wouldn't let your dad get away with that kind of behaviour.'

He winked at her and she giggled. Jake kissed both Alfie's and his daughter's cheeks then ran upstairs to get changed. Annie looked at Alex.

'Apparently his balls are on fire.'

Alex's laughter filled the room. 'Well, that makes a change.' He took some bottles of lager out of the fridge and offered them around. Annie shook her head. Both Kav and Cathy took one, opening them and drinking them in a couple of gulps. Putting Alfie down into the bouncer, she set about making herself a coffee.

'Was it bad?'

Annie nodded. 'Really bad – I hate funerals. Why do people have to die?'

Kav took hold of her hand. 'What did I tell you? That it's not your fault Stu decided to play silly buggers and made some terrible choices.'

Alex took hold of her other hand. 'How's Will?'

'I don't know. He's gone to the crematorium and then he's going to the wake for a bit. I said I'd meet him here, so I can drive him home. It will do him good to get it out of his system.'

Jake came back downstairs wearing a pair of cut-off denim shorts and a white vest top.

Kav started laughing. 'Bloody hell, it's George Michael in the flesh.'

Jake stuck two fingers up at Kav and took a bottle of lager from Alex and lifted it up. 'To Stuart: let's hope you're much happier up there than you were down here.'

They all lifted their bottles; Annie lifted her mug and everyone said in unison, 'To Stuart.'

Chapter Two

A loud knock on the door made Jake jump up off his chair. He managed to spill lager all down his front and stain his perfect white vest. He looked out of the living room window and laughed.

'Watch out, the rozzers are here. It's a raid.'

Annie peered out of the window and gasped to see Will being helped out of the back of the locked cage of a police van, which was normally reserved for criminals.

'Oh shit.'

The two young policemen who were standing at the back of the cage both had their arms out ready to catch Will. It was a good job they did because he stumbled, missed the step and landed in their arms. He tried his best to straighten up then saluted them both. Jake, who was standing at the front door, watched the scene before him with a huge grin on his face. The two policemen took an arm each and walked Will up Jake's path. They were both red-faced. Jake shook his head.

'Now then, William; we give you a couple of hours' freedom from your everyday life and look what happens! You're completely shit-faced.'

Will nodded his head in agreement. 'I can't argue with that.'

Jake took hold of his arm so the other two could let go. As

they did, Will stumbled forwards, almost taking Jake down with him. Annie, who was standing behind Jake holding Alfie, moved out of the way.

'I better get him home. Help me to get him in the car, please, Jake.'

'Wouldn't you be better letting him come in and have some water? You could stop here tonight.'

Will chuckled. 'Bloody water – are you having a laugh? I want whisky on the rocks, you pack of pussies.'

Annie was mortified at the state he was in. She wanted to throw a bucket of cold water over him to sober him up. She hadn't seen him this drunk for a very long time and she didn't like it. One of the coppers coughed.

'Erm, are you all right now, Sarge? Do you need anything else or is it OK if we get on?'

'Course it is, thanks for the lift.' Will saluted again, making them both smile. They nodded at Jake who waved his hand at them.

Annie passed Alfie to Alex. 'I want to get him home. I haven't got enough stuff for Alfie to stop here and I want to sleep in my own bed. Thank you for the offer, though, Jake.'

'Well, leave him here. Me and Kav can stick him in the spare bed and you can pick him up in the morning or I can drop him off on my way to work at twelve.'

The look of horror that passed across her face must have made Jake wonder if there was something wrong.

'I can't. I don't like being left on my own now there's Alfie. Please, just help him into the front seat. I'll be OK getting him home. I can manage.'

'Your choice. What if he pukes all over those nice leather seats?'

'Then he'll clean it up when he's sober. Shit. How have you got in this state, Will?'

'No breakfast; felt sick. Lots and lots of whisky.'

'You don't even like whisky.'

She shook her head. She wasn't angry with him for getting in such a state because she understood completely; she just didn't like it. He'd wanted to blot it all out and who could blame him? Jake and Kav led him to her car. She ran inside to get her keys, which Alice had been playing with. Clicking the car open she watched from the window as Jake and Kav manhandled Will into the front seat and strapped him in. Jake turned away, waving his hand in front of his nose. He came back into the house.

'Keep the windows down because you're likely to get drunk off the fumes radiating from him. He stinks like a brewery.'

'Thanks, Jake.'

She grabbed Alfie's changing bag and carried him to the car. Kav, who had been watching Will to make sure he didn't vomit and choke on his own sick, stepped back. He took the changing bag from her and opened the door so she could put Alfie into his car seat. When she'd strapped him in he shut the door.

'Would you like me to follow you and help you get him to bed?'

'No, thanks; anyway, you've had a drink. If I can't get him out of the car I'll chuck a duvet over him until he's slept it off.'

'If you're sure?'

She nodded and he bent down to kiss her cheek.

'Don't be too hard on him. Sometimes a man's got to blow off a bit of steam and he's been guilt-tripping over Stu since the night it happened. Maybe now he'll be able to put it to one side and stop beating himself up over it.'

'I'm not mad with him; I know he blames himself. Christ, I blame myself. I'm just shocked to see him dressed in his Sunday best and drunk as a skunk in such a short space of time. Thanks, Kav.'

He walked away and went back inside Jake's house. Jake and Cathy waved her off, Jake mouthing: 'You know where I am if you need me.'

She nodded and lifted her hand to wave goodbye.

She looked at her husband. 'Will, if you're going to be sick, make sure you let me know so I can pull over.'

'Urgh.'

Fifteen minutes later, as she got out of Ulverston, she heard him begin to retch.

'Hold on, don't you dare.'

Managing to pull into a lay-by, she got out of the car and ran around to his side, throwing his door open just as a stream of projectile vomit came her way. She couldn't get him out of the car. They were parked on a busy road and if members of the public saw him in full police uniform puking everywhere there'd be a complaint in before they got home.

She waited until he wiped his sleeve across his mouth and stuck his thumb up at her, then she slammed his door shut. Getting him through the winding lanes and back to their home in Hawkshead was going to be fun. Thankfully, by the time she'd got back to her side of the car, Will was snoring. She looked back across her shoulder at Alfie who was also fast asleep, his thumb in his mouth and his blanket pulled up around his chin. She felt her heart surge. There was no better love than a mother for her child. Every time she saw him her heart filled with joy.

She looked at Will – her handsome knight in shining armour – and was thankful she had such an amazing family, even if she was annoyed with her husband. She drove the rest of the way home listening to Will's gentle snores. When she pulled up outside their secluded cottage he opened his eyes and looked at her.

'Sorry.'

'Don't be daft. I love you.'

Alfie was still fast asleep so she opened the front door of the house then went back to help Will out of the car. He was slightly better than when Jake had put him in. Wrapping her arm around his waist she helped him inside, leading him to the huge corner sofa in the lounge. He stumbled towards it, but she kept hold of him.

'We need to get you undressed, Will. You'll ruin your tunic if you fall asleep in it.'

He winked at her. 'Any excuse to see me naked – admit it, you can't resist me.'

He fumbled with his tunic buttons, but failed. Annie deftly undid them and tugged it off. She pulled his tie over his head and unbuttoned his shirt. He fell onto the sofa and lay down. She ran outside to bring Alfie in, locking the car and then the front door behind her. He was still asleep. She was so lucky he hadn't woken when she transferred him from the car.

She went back to Will who was now snoring loudly. She untied his laces and pulled his shoes off, followed by his trousers. His muscular, tanned legs looked good in just a pair of white Calvins. Even though it was a warm day outside, it was much cooler inside the house. It always was, so she ran upstairs to get a duvet from the spare room, which she threw over him. Alfie opened his eyes and began crying. She picked him up and rocked him.

'Shhh, don't wake Daddy. Come on, it's me and you. Let's get some tea.'

She carried him into the kitchen and put him into his high chair. After feeding Alfie and making herself a sandwich and mug of coffee, she turned the television on and saw the news headline flash across the screen: 'Body found in house on Roose Road, Barrow-in-Furness.'

The camera panned to the front of a freshly painted white house and Annie felt her blood run cold as it zoomed in on the bright blue front door with the white plant pots either side that were filled with lilac and purple pansies. The mug of coffee slipped from her fingers. It smashed into pieces all over the breakfast bar, sending hot liquid and pottery everywhere.

She paused the television and looked at the mess she'd made, relieved it had landed on the worktop and nowhere near her baby. That house, she'd had a bad dream about it last night. She had been tossing and turning in her sleep then woken up in a cold sweat feeling sick and breathless. Alfie had begun to cry, which in turn had made her forget all about it until now.

Surely this was just a coincidence; there must be hundreds of white houses with blue doors. *But how many have the identical plant pots and flowers from your dream either side of the door?* Mopping up the mess she'd made she wondered what it all meant. The inside of the house had looked lovely through the window, very shabby chic, and everything inside was white with touches of colour. It reminded her a little of this house – her home – and she shuddered.

She left the television paused, not able to watch what the gory details were. She didn't want to know, and if she didn't, then it should have nothing to do with her, should it? It was a huge coincidence, nothing else. Annie set about checking all the doors and windows were secure. She was going to put Alfie to bed then have a long, hot soak in the bath. An early night with the bed all to herself would do her good, as long as Alfie slept for a few hours, that was. He hadn't been settling well of a night lately and she didn't know if he was teething or just going through a phase. She picked him up and carried him upstairs where she laid him in his cot while she ran a bath for herself.

Will opened one eye and turned his head to look where he was because he couldn't remember. The movement made him groan. His head was pounding and moving it made him feel sick again. For a minute he panicked. The last time he'd woken up in this state he'd almost lost Annie. He'd woken up next to Laura – one of his colleagues – after a drunken fumble. Annie had found them together.

He reached out beside him, glad there was no one next to him. The dirty grey light that was coming through the blinds was just enough for his eyes to adjust to his surroundings. He was at home, on the sofa, thank God. He remembered Stu's funeral. He'd felt so bloody guilty about it all. He'd gone back to the wake where he and Debs had sunk shots of whisky at the bar, both of them comparing their guilt: Debs because Stu had caught her having an affair and Will because he'd come home that night to find a drunken, angry Stu straddling his very pregnant wife.

He wondered if Annie was mad at him and how the hell she'd managed to get him here, because he didn't remember any of it except for the whisky at the bar. Christ, he must have been hammered. He lifted his arm out of the duvet to see his shirt was gone. His mouth felt like a sewer. He needed water.

Forcing himself to slowly sit up, he felt his stomach lurch. He was never drinking again. He stood up and stumbled into the coffee table, banging his shin. The glass of water Annie had left there for him tipped over and he cursed as the cold liquid ran down his legs and feet. Holding his head, he managed to make it into the kitchen where he got a bottle of water from the fridge and also found three paracetamol.

The television was still on and he wondered why Annie had paused it, then gone to bed. Picking up the remote he pressed play and watched the news clip, his heart sinking. Bollocks, another murder. It had been a while since there had been one in Barrow and he'd kind of liked the break. The last murders had been in Hawkshead.

He wondered where his phone was and if anyone from work had called him. He'd put a day's holiday in for yesterday, so technically they should have left him alone and called whoever the duty DS was. The kitchen clock told him it was four a.m. Thank God he still had time to go to bed for a few hours before he had to get up for work. Today was going to be a ball-ache if he was still feeling like this, not to mention he wouldn't be able to drive himself in to work. At times like this he missed Stu the most. He would have just phoned him to come and pick him up. Fuck, what a mess.

As he got upstairs he tried his best not to crash into the walls or doors and disturb either his wife or their baby. He went into the bathroom where he splashed cold water all over his face and brushed his teeth, then he sprayed some aftershave on so he didn't stink of eau du whisky. Alfie began to cry and Will went into his bedroom to pick him up. A bleary-eyed Annie met him on the landing.

'Sorry, I don't know how I got into such a state.' He pulled her towards him and hugged her. 'Are you really mad at me?'

Rubbing her eyes she laughed. 'No, I'm not, although if you'd have puked inside the car and not outside of it this episode would have a different ending.'

Will groaned. 'I'm such a disgrace.'

She nodded in agreement. 'Yes, you are, but you smell much better now and I'm lonely in that big bed on my own so I forgive you.'

He kissed her and Alfie let out a scream.

'I swear that kid knows when I want you to myself for a bit.'

They both walked into his bedroom where the night light had gone out. Annie walked over to his cot and picked him up. Alfie immediately stopped crying as he snuggled closer to her. Will led the way back to their bedroom where he got into bed and sighed. Annie sat down in the big, squashy armchair that doubled up as her reading and nursing chair. She began to feed Alfie. Grabbing a blanket off the radiator she wrapped it around them to keep them warm.

Will was asleep again as soon as his head hit the pillow and she envied him a little. When she'd insisted on breastfeeding, she hadn't really thought about the night feeds. Still, Will was the one working and she was at home, so it didn't really matter. And Alfie was having fewer feeds now that he was on solid food. As Alfie suckled, she closed her eyes and drifted off. It wasn't long before she was dreaming.

She was back inside the house with the bright blue door and she wondered why. This time she let herself go inside. She felt as if she was the first officer at the scene. Trepidation about what she was about to find filled her. The downstairs was pristine. The smell of lemon furniture polish filled the air, but it was tinged with something that smelt much darker. An underlying smell of copper lingered in the air. As she got closer to the stairs the coppery smell was much stronger.

Annie knew what blood smelt like. She'd been in her fair share of violent scrapes. The only sound in the house was that of a tap dripping. It was coming from upstairs. Annie looked down to see if she was wearing her uniform and had her baton and CS gas, but she was in her pyjamas. As she climbed the first step she knew she should try and wake herself up. What if this wasn't an ordinary dream and it was dangerous? She had nothing to protect herself with.

Her feet ignored her brain and carried on walking up until she reached the top step. She heard a door slam and heavy footsteps heading in her direction. Pressing herself against the wall and trying to blend in, she held her breath as someone came towards her. It took all her might not to let out a scream at the clown who came running towards her. She'd never been fond of clowns and to see this one in this strange house where she could smell blood wasn't good at all.

It was dressed in a black and white stripy outfit with the scariest clown mask she'd ever seen. Thanking her lucky stars it hadn't seen her, she watched as whoever it was ran down the stairs and out of the back door. Annie was torn. She didn't know if she should follow the scary clown or carry on towards the open bedroom door where the smell was coming from.

Relieved when her feet began to move towards the door and not in the direction the clown had gone, she found herself looking straight into a scene from one of her worst nightmares. There was blood everywhere, which was where the awful smell was coming from. Lifting her eyes to the ceiling, she saw it was even sprayed on the once-white light shade. She looked down to the floor and saw a foot sticking out from the other side of the bed.

A cry made her jump and she felt horrified that whoever was

lying there was still alive after losing so much blood. As she tried to force herself to go and help them, a much louder wail pierced her dream. Her eyes fluttered open and for a minute she wasn't sure where she was; then she felt the weight of Alfie in her arms and breathed a sigh of relief that she was at home. She blinked, looking around the room to make sure there was no scary clown standing watching her in the corner. Relief flooded through her body to see it was the same as it always was. The early morning sun was breaking and she had to take deep breaths to try to calm herself down.

Why was she dreaming about that house? It had already been on the news that a body had been found. The police were dealing with it. Will would probably end up working the case when he went in tomorrow. She wondered if she'd just been dreaming and surmising about what had happened or whether it actually had happened and she had somehow witnessed the killer fleeing the scene.

Will would be so angry with her if she tried to get involved or even mentioned it, so she wouldn't ask him. It was as simple as that. If she wanted to know, or had to know, then she would ask Jake to tell her the gory details. He wouldn't care; he thrived on doom, gloom and drama.

She lifted Alfie to her shoulder to wind him and he stopped crying. Will was gently snoring and she wanted to get into bed with him. She had no idea why, but Alfie didn't settle at all in his bedroom. He woke up at almost the same time every night. Maybe she should move his cot in here with them; at least she could have him next to her and she might get some more sleep. In fact, she was going to do it first thing in the morning.

Alfie was fast asleep again in her arms so she got up and went into his bedroom for his Moses basket. It was much colder in here than it should be and a horrible thought crossed her mind. What if he couldn't settle because he was getting ghostly visitors? It was all very well and good her having visions and seeing dead people, but surely a baby wouldn't be able to see any of those things?

She didn't want to speak her name; it was forbidden inside the house, but just what if it was her? What if Betsy Baker had come back? She'd had no qualms about killing children when she'd been alive. Why would she be bothered about scaring them when she was dead? Annie hoped to God that she wasn't around.

She would phone Father John in the morning to make sure her grave hadn't been disturbed. Just the thought of Betsy filled her stomach with a heavy, sick feeling. Placing the basket on its stand near to her side of the bed, she put Alfie in, kissing his forehead, then she climbed into bed. As she sank into the mattress she thought to herself what a horrible day it had been. Funerals were awful; they drained the very life from your soul.

As she lay watching her baby, her back resting against Will's and soaking up his body heat, she tried to clear her mind of everything. First she pushed the funeral to one side, and then the dream about the white house, until all that was left in there was an image of Alfie. Her eyes began to close. As she drifted off to sleep she prayed for God to keep her family safe.

Summer 1950

Gordy had walked out of his house, reached the garden gate, then remembered the safe his father had bolted to the floor in the storage cupboard on the landing. It would be foolish to leave all that money there. He turned and went back inside the house, stepped over his parents' bodies and ran upstairs. He didn't feel a flicker of remorse for what he'd done minutes ago.

His only regret was that his Uncle Bernard hadn't been here as well. Gordy would have loved burying the axe in his head. Out of them all he supposed it was Bernard who deserved it the most. The nights he'd babysat for Gordy, waving his parents goodbye as they went to a dance, eagerly waiting until he had him all to himself. Gordy hadn't realised at first that what he was doing to him was wrong. It was only when he got a little older that he understood it wasn't right for a grown man to want to do the things he did to him.

Before Gordy had the chance to tell him this, the man had collapsed one night and had a massive stroke. He was now a vacant, drooling wreck in a nursing home. He had to be fed and wore a nappy. Gordy supposed this was at least some kind of justice. Although not as satisfying as killing him would have been.

He opened the bedside table drawer and pulled out the small, black velvet pouch where the master key was kept. Then he opened the safe and took the wads of cash out. His dad had always been very cautious with his money, which really, come to think about it, had been a complete waste of time because he was dead and hadn't spent any of his hard-earned savings.

Gordy stuffed the notes into his suitcase and pockets. This would see him right for the next year or two if he was careful, and he could be very careful. If there was a legacy his parents had left, it was not to squander your hard-earned money and to keep it for a rainy day.

As he left the house once more, he closed the kitchen curtain and locked the door behind him, just in case any of his mother's nosy friends came around. It would be wise to make sure he had left town before their bodies were discovered. As he walked along the empty streets towards the circus he wondered where everyone was.

A poster tied to the park fence railings answered his question for him. The last matinee was now in full swing and then the circus would be leaving town, moving on to the next one to start all over again. This time they would have an extra clown with them and he couldn't wait to start his new life. He saw the peaks of the striped tent and his heart raced. Walking faster now, he wondered if he could catch the end of the show. He'd already been to all four evening shows, hanging around outside and chatting with the performers until the early hours.

He could smell the animals before he reached the waste ground where the circus was pitched. The smell seeping from the carriages was not for the faint-hearted. The animal cages made his eyes water with the piercing smell of ammonia, even though they were cleaned out daily. Gordy knew that being a part of the circus wasn't a job; it was a complete lifestyle. You didn't work the circus; you *were* the circus. You lived, breathed and ate the circus whether you were a trapeze artist performing in the centre ring or one of the many labourers who took care of the big top.

Everyone pulled together. They spent so much time in each other's company they were like one huge family. This was where you left your normal life far behind you and became a part of the greatest show on earth. It was the perfect place for Gordy Marshall to be. All his life he'd fought against the constraints of what society believed he should be, and now here he was, about to live his dream, knowing he would love every single minute of it.

As he reached the red and white striped big top he could hear the thunderous clapping of the audience and the loud cheers. He walked around to the office caravan where Betty – one of the trapeze artists – was sitting on the step nursing a badly bruised arm. The circus nurse was sitting on the floor with a pair of tweezers, trying to pull out splinters from Betty's leg. Her tights were in tatters.

'What happened? Are you OK?'

She nodded. 'The rope snapped, catapulted me across the bloody ring. I managed to grab hold of the pole and slide down it, but not before I'd almost crushed my arm and ripped my legs to shreds.'

'Do you need to go to the hospital?'

Both women laughed and Betty shook her head. 'Gordy is it?' He nodded.

'You'll soon learn that no matter what happens the show must go on. Even if you've got a broken leg, you carry on until you're out of the ring and the audience can't see you. I'll be right as rain tomorrow, new pair of tights, a bandage on my arm and a long-sleeved costume. I'll be good as new, won't I, Evie?'

Evie nodded. 'She will. No point telling her she won't, is there? She'll only go back up regardless.'

Betty grinned. 'So you're finally a part of the show? How long have you wanted to be in the circus for, Gordy Marshall?'

'All my life.'

'That, my new friend, is the right answer. When I've taken my final bow I'll show you where the clowns hang out.'

'Thank you, but it's no bother. I already know. I hope you feel better soon.' He smiled at the women and carried on walking to where the clowns' caravans were. As he passed the elephants he gave them a wide berth. They were huge and only had bits of rope and thin chains tying them to the outside of their cages. If they pulled, they would break free and be able to trample him. Until he knew them better it was wise to keep a safe distance.

As he continued he heard a loud roar and jumped at the three lions standing pressed against the bars of their cage. One of them had his mouth wide open and Gordy didn't know what would be worse, being trampled to death or having his head bitten off. Still, he smiled to himself because, either way, it would be better than being suffocated to death at Marshall and Marshall.

Chapter Three

2016

Walter Lacey sat on the threadbare chair in his cramped living room, the curtains drawn even though it was morning. He never opened them, preferring to leave them shut. It afforded him some much-needed privacy. He gently rocked back and forth – a coping mechanism he'd used since his childhood – trying his best to release the endorphins inside his brain to soothe himself.

He stared at the small bookcase stuffed full of his films: every horror film he could find at the second-hand stall in the market. He'd been obsessed with horror films since he was a kid. His mam blamed them for the voices he heard in his head back then. He knew that the films didn't help, but the voices had been there as long as he could remember; even when watching the kids' programmes he would hear them. She just found it easier to blame it on the movies and not the fact that her son was a fully legitimate schizophrenic.

He hadn't seen his mam for a very long time – not that it mattered. When he'd been taken into hospital for months when he was fifteen she hadn't come to visit him. He didn't really blame her; he shouldn't have tried to strangle her new boyfriend.

She'd come in and seen him straddling her latest man and gone mental. She'd rung the police who had rung an ambulance. Wally had ended up being dragged out of his house screaming that the clown on the front of the *Poltergeist* DVD had told him to do it.

He glanced at the clown suit that was hanging from his picture rail. When he'd found it in the trunk in the attic at the last house they'd cleared out he'd stashed it down his jumper. He knew that he should have left it where it was and boxed it up with the rest of the stuff, but he hadn't. The voice he hadn't heard for a long time had told him to take it, so he had, and now look what had happened.

Walter looked away from it. He found it fascinating yet terrifying. It was telling him what he needed to do; only today he didn't have time. He had to be normal; well, as normal as he could be. He stood up and went to the tiny kitchen to get a glass of water to swallow his pills with. He'd been on Largactil since he'd been in hospital, not that it was helping. He wondered if he'd become immune to it because he'd been taking it for so long.

After he swallowed the orange tablet he took the sun lotion off the windowsill and rubbed it on his face and arms. He was fair-skinned anyway, but the medication made him burn even quicker if he left the house without it.

A loud hammering on his front door made him jump, his heart pounding. The palms of his hands felt slick with sweat. *Surely not – they couldn't have found him so soon, could they?* He crept to have a look through the spyhole, hoping to God it wasn't a bunch of huge, hairy coppers on the other side.

As he bent his head forward to peer through the small, glass hole he heard a voice bellow, 'What the fuck you playing at? I've been waiting five minutes for you. Get your arse out here now. Jacko said if we didn't get that house cleared by dinnertime neither of us is getting paid.'

He stepped back, releasing the breath he'd been holding and hoping his trembling knees would hold his body weight.

'I'm coming now; sorry, I never heard you.'

He didn't particularly like Jacko, his boss, or Stevie who was waiting impatiently outside for him, but the job paid him cash in hand, so putting up with the pair of them was a small price to pay. He opened the door and waited for some arsy comment about what a state he was in from Stevie; instead he shook his head at him.

'You know, if you opened your curtains and windows to let some fresh air into that shithole of a flat you might see what life was like on the other side once in a while. Not to mention hear me when I beep the fucking horn.'

'Sorry, slept in. I was dead to the world.'

'Well, you can go brush your teeth. I'm not sitting in the front of that van with you breathing all over me if you've got bad breath.'

'Don't be stupid. I've cleaned my teeth and had a shower.'

Stevie peered at him with one eye then turned and walked off. Walter grabbed his door key then shut his door, locking it behind him. The house had been a fancy Georgian townhouse once upon a time until whoever owned it had died. The current owners didn't give a shit about the state of it and had turned it into far too many flats, letting it go to rack and ruin.

The smell of an assortment of herbs and spices filled his nostrils as he stepped into the communal hallway, making his stomach rumble even though it was only eight-thirty. Mrs Batta was always cooking no matter what time of day or night it was. He tried to think when the last time he'd eaten was and couldn't remember. It might have been last night, but he wasn't sure because he'd felt so sick before he'd gone out to that house that it was all a bit of a blur.

As he went out into the bright sunlight he squinted. His face was too white. He looked like a ghost at the best of times. He couldn't afford to get sunburnt, though. Stevie was already back in the van with the engine running. He was the complete opposite of Walter. Stevie was so tanned he looked like he'd just come back from three weeks in Tenerife.

Walter hadn't any inclination to do what Stevie did and pose in the gym every day after work and then go lie on the sunbeds. Each to their own, he supposed. If he did that he'd be burnt to a crisp in no time. He climbed into the van, which smelt of greasy McDonald's, and his stomach groaned loudly. Why was there food everywhere?

'Bloody hell, Wally, have you eaten lately? You look like a walking ginger skeleton!'

He shook his head, no point in lying.

'How are you going to do a day's work shifting boxes and furniture without anything in your belly, lad? You'll be no good to me if you pass out. Come on, I'll go back to the drive-through and you can get something.'

'Thanks, if that's all right.' He began to scrabble in his pockets to see what change he had and if he had enough to pay for a sausage and egg McMuffin. He pulled out his last crumpled five-pound note and hoped that after today's job Jacko would pay him what he owed him for the last two weeks. Stevie drove back round the drive-through, ordering the full works including two lattes. Walter felt sick. He didn't have enough to pay.

'I've only got a fiver, mate.'

Stevie waved his hand away.

'Someone's got to look after your sorry arse. You either need to find a woman or a man – whatever floats your boat – to sort you out, mate. You can't carry on like this. You look like some waif. This one is on me.'

He had to turn away for fear of Stevie seeing the gratitude on his face and the tears in his eyes; no one ever did anything nice for him. He couldn't remember the last time they had – definitely not since his gran had died two years ago anyway. He thought about the suffering she'd been through and then he thought about the woman he'd killed last night. He'd seen her coming out of the newsagent's and recognised her. She went to the same hospice that his gran had. He didn't know why he'd followed her home the night before; he just had.

That wasn't strictly true, though, was it, Wally? The voice that belonged to the suit told you to. You stabbed her like she was nothing last night. How many times did you need to stick that knife into her? He shrugged his shoulders; he'd had to make sure she was dead, hadn't he? He told the voice inside his head to shut up and took the bag of greasy food and the cardboard drinks carrier off Stevie.

As he bit into the hot, juicy muffin his stomach groaned in appreciation. He couldn't help but wonder who the clown stuff in the box he'd found at the last house had actually belonged to. He didn't have any internet or a decent mobile phone to try and search for some information. What he could do was go to the library at the weekend and do some digging there, maybe ask at the records office or use a computer there if he had a spare couple of quid to pay for it. It would be interesting to know more about the person it had belonged to. There was something so mesmerising about it.

When he'd pulled the costume out of the trunk there had been a wig and a big, black thing that went around your neck. He'd found a couple of black and white photographs in the bottom of the trunk, tucked into a faded yellow envelope. One was of a man sitting in a cage with three huge lions on his own; the other had been a small picture of three clowns – all different shapes and sizes.

He'd recognised the suit that he'd pulled out of the box. The clown wearing it had the strangest hair – just three tufts – and a huge red mouth. It was the kind of clown that would give anyone a phobia of clowns, not to mention nightmares. He didn't imagine the kids who visited the circus would want much to do with him unless he was really funny and kind. Then again, if he'd been kind, why had he felt such overwhelming feelings when he'd tried the costume on? And then that rage towards the woman had been nothing like he'd ever known. It wasn't as if he knew her and she'd upset him. It was as if someone else had taken over his body. Was that possible? He wondered if the clown suit was haunted. It might even be possessed.

Then he shook his head. He knew that the suit probably had nothing to do with it. The problem was him; it always had been. Stevie started the engine, waking him from his daydream.

'Right, that's enough of me being nice to you to last for the rest of the week. Don't you dare tell anyone. I don't want them thinking I'm going soft in my old age. We've got a shithole of a house to empty today and Jacko wants it done by one 'cause he needs the van back, so you better be ready to work your arse off.'

He nodded; at least it would keep him busy for the next few hours. Take his thoughts off the guilt that was seeping into the cracks that were opening all over his already delicate mind.

Chapter Four

When Annie opened her eyes to see Alfie's Moses basket empty her heart almost jumped from her chest. Then she realised that Will was no longer in the bed either. Reaching out for her phone she was surprised to see it was almost twenty to eight. How had that happened? She got up, pulling her dressing gown off the back of the chair and wrapping it around herself.

She went downstairs to the smell of grilling bacon. A small spark of anger flared inside her. Obviously Will had woken up hangover-free if he was making himself a bacon sandwich. By rights he should have a stinking hangover and be feeling as if he was dying. If it had been her who had consumed all that whisky on an empty stomach she probably would have died.

She walked into the kitchen to see Alfie strapped into his bouncer, which was balanced on top of the breakfast bar. Will was leaning down feeding him. Alfie was smiling and cooing at his dad and she felt her anger melt away. Damn, he did that to her every single time. She could never stay mad at him for long. He looked up and smiled at her. She was pleased to note it wasn't his normal, ridiculously happy smile. Good, so he did have a conscience after all.

'Morning, beautiful; I'm so sorry about yesterday. I've made us some bacon bagels and fresh coffee. I hope you're not too mad at me.'

She inhaled then shook her head. 'Well, I was until you mentioned the bagels. You know I'm a woman who likes her food.'

This time he did grin. 'Alfie was hungry so I've given him his breakfast. Did you manage to get back to sleep?'

She considered telling him about her ridiculous fears that there was something wrong with Alfie's bedroom and her dream about the white house, then stopped herself.

'Yes, eventually. He wouldn't settle in his own room. I think maybe we should move his cot in with us while he's teething. It just makes it easier for me if he wakes up, and if you can't sleep because of him you can always go into the spare room.'

She waited for him to give her a list of reasons why it was a bad idea, but he nodded.

'I think you're right. He's so unsettled through the night; maybe it will be better for all of us. I'll move his cot in when I get home. I have to go to work soon. Adele is picking me up on her way through to Barrow.'

Annie sat down on one of the high stools and bit into her bagel. Cream cheese squeezed out of the side and she wiped it with her finger then licked it.

'Steady on, you'll be getting me all excited.'

She laughed. 'I wish. I mean how long is it since we've . . .'

A horn beeped outside the gate. Will turned to look out of the window and waved. 'Well, maybe when I get home we might get a bit of time to ourselves.'

He walked over and kissed her forehead.

'Who's Adele?'

Annie tried to make the question sound casual, not like she was being a paranoid wife, but a small flutter of panic had formed in her chest when he'd first said her name.

'Adele Dean – she's transferring from Carlisle to Barrow. I suppose she's Stu's replacement although it hasn't been officially said. I did my training with her; she's lovely and very happily married with two grown-up kids. Does that answer your questions?'

Annie felt her cheeks burning. 'Sorry, it's just I'm stuck at home all day and I kind of miss my old life a little bit. I've just never heard of her and wondered, that's all.'

Will almost choked on the last bit of his bagel that he'd shoved into his mouth. 'You miss your old life? You mean the one where demented killers were following you and kidnapping you every couple of weeks?'

'Don't be daft; you know what I mean. I miss the going out to work and stuff, keeping up with the gossip and general banter. Of course I don't miss that other stuff.'

'Phew, that's a relief. Look, why don't you come outside and say hello to her? Then you can meet her and know what she's like instead of sitting here worrying over nothing.'

'And look like some crazy, jealous wife? No, thank you. I'm not worried at all. Have a good day and I'll see you later.'

Will smiled. 'You know how much I love you both, right?'

She nodded.

'Well, don't be worrying yourself over nothing.'

Annie lifted her hand and waved. 'Bye, Will.'

He blew her a kiss, grabbed his suit jacket off the back of the chair and took one last mouthful of coffee. He waved at her as he went out of the front door to the woman waiting in the car outside for him. Annie couldn't help herself and walked across to the window to take a peek. The woman was talking to Will as he got inside her car, then, as if she knew she was being watched, she turned and smiled at Annie, giving her a wave.

Annie waved back and let the curtain drop, mortified she'd been caught. Bugger. Today she was going to move some things around in their bedroom to make enough room for Alfie's cot, which was a bit of a monster. Then she would take him for a walk into the village for some fresh air. See, her life was about as exciting as watching paint dry. Then she remembered about phoning Father John. Scrap that; she might go and visit him and move the furniture around later.

Pleased she had something slightly more exciting planned for the morning, she picked up Alfie, who was wearing more of his breakfast than he had consumed. She took him upstairs with her so she could get them both ready.

Will clicked his seat belt in.

'I could get used to this being chauffeur-driven to work.'

'Well, don't bother. I'm not travelling every day; I can't be bothered. It's far too long and will cost a fortune in diesel. Aaron's agreed we can move back to Barrow. His mum still lives in Holbeck so we're going to move in with her until we find a place of our own. Was that the famous Annie Graham I just saw looking out of the window?'

Will looked at her to see if she was taking the piss, but she seemed genuinely interested.

'Yes, it was. Well, she's Annie Ashworth now. I think she's still a bit annoyed with me.'

'Because of yesterday? I should bloody well think so. I heard you were pissed as a fart and had to be escorted into the back of a van because you were that drunk. How did you manage that in less than two hours? I'm impressed.'

She winked at him and he laughed.

'How the hell did you know that?'

'News travels fast in this job, my old friend; you should know that. Actually it was Kav. He rang Aaron about something last night and happened to mention it. In fact it was Kav who suggested I offer to pick you up this morning. That bloke was as hard as nails back in the day when he was our sergeant. Now he's retired he's turned into a right old softie.'

'I guess seeing the stuff he's seen over the years has made him appreciate family and friends a lot more. And I think when you're not dealing with the shit day in, day out it makes you turn back into a relatively normal human being. It's certainly made me more grateful for every single day.'

Will's phone rang and he tugged it out of his trouser pocket.

'I'm on my way; well, we both are. Adele picked me up. Yes, I know. I saw it on the news last night.'

Will listened as the male voice on the other end related something to him.

'Be there soon, traffic permitting.' He ended the call and glanced at her. 'Did you see that murder on the news yesterday?'

She shook her head.

'There's a full briefing and they're waiting on us before they begin. Bollocks, my head's pounding and I'm not even at work yet. This is going to be a long day.'

'Aren't they all?'

The morning traffic wasn't as bad as Will had anticipated and before long they arrived at the brand-new, shiny police station that had replaced the old one, which had been deemed unfit for purpose. The only problem was that the shiny new one was crap compared to the old one. It was all open-plan and the sound carried. There were no private areas that you could go to have a good old slanging match with someone or to discuss just how much someone was pissing you off. Will would have moved back to the old station in the blink of an eye.

Adele whistled. 'I bet this cost them a pretty penny.'

He nodded. 'Yep, wait until you see our office. It's awful. Don't get me wrong, the canteen's handy and the chairs are comfy, but there's nowhere to hide from any of them now.'

'There's nowhere for anyone to be having a quick shag either by the looks of it. This building should do wonders for marriage survival. Divorces rates will be going down.'

He chuckled. 'I doubt that. Are you nervous?'

'Yes and no. I don't particularly like change, but I hated it at Carlisle. I wanted to come back, so it's on my terms, sort of.

I think I'm looking forward to it and, besides, there are much uglier bosses than you.'

'I take it that's a compliment?'

'You can take it how you want. I won't be calling you boss unless there's anyone around. I hate all that.'

'Good, I don't expect you to. I'm plain old Will. I only get Sarge when they want something anyway.'

'Excellent. Shall we?'

She'd parked her car outside the front of the building, instead of going into the secure car park around the back. Will got out, wondering if he was going to be able to stomach the crime scene photos. He felt like crap, although he'd not admitted that to Annie because he didn't want her to gloat too much. Hopefully, because he was off work yesterday, Max – who had been the duty DS – had already taken over the case.

They walked through the front doors of the huge building and Adele whispered, 'At least it smells new and not of sweaty boots and cannabis.'

Will nodded. She had a point. He swiped them in through the double doors that led into the atrium – as it was called – leading Adele to the spiral staircase in the middle of the floor. She followed him upstairs to the first floor and the major incident room where there was an assortment of bosses, detectives and OSU officers, all sitting around waiting for them. She went and stood at the back of the room, leaving Will to take the last seat at the front. The chief super began to talk. Will took his notebook out and wrote things down. He didn't realise his name was being called until the room went silent and he looked up to see that everyone was staring at him.

'Nice of you to join us, William; I was just explaining how you would be taking over the running of this. Max is going on holiday tomorrow and then he's on a week-long course at headquarters on his return, so you might as well take over as OIC.'

Will felt his heart sink; he didn't want to be the bloody officer in charge. It always fell on him whenever there was a murder or unexplained death. He'd had more than his fair share of murder cases the last three years. Why the hell couldn't they let someone else run with it?

'Don't look so happy about it. With your track record this should be a breeze. I'm hoping you'll have the case closed in the next twenty-four hours. Especially if we keep your lovely wife away from it.'

The super began to laugh at his own joke and Will felt his hands curl into tight fists as the blood rushed to his face. He'd never liked the pompous man standing in front of him. He wanted to stand up and punch him. The urge was so strong that he had to shake his head to get the image out of his mind. Instead he stood up, marched across the room to the Smart Board and stared at the super, eye to eye. The man was no longer grinning.

The room was silent as everyone watched the exchange between the two men. One of the response officers standing next to Adele whispered, 'A fiver on Will taking him out with one punch.'

Adele smiled, clearly hoping Will would. She could tell what an arsehole that man was and she'd only just seen him.

Instead, Will looked back at everyone and smiled. He could tell by their faces this was the most exciting briefing they'd ever attended because they wanted to see the super knocked on his arse. As much as he wanted to hit him, he wouldn't give him the pleasure.

'Well then, you might as well leave now, Chief. You normally do once the actual police work starts.'

The whole room exploded into laughter. It was the super's turn to bunch his fingers into fists and his cheeks flared red. He glared at them all, then turned to Will, who by now had realised, with some regret, that he'd just started the biggest pissing match of his career. But he didn't care. He was tired of the bullshit. What happened to coming to work and looking for the latest burglar who was doing the rounds? Why had this relatively quiet town decided to become the murder capital of England? And why was he always the officer in bloody charge?

'Seeing as how I was at my friend and colleague's funeral yesterday, I've missed out on what actually happened. So for now I want OSU searching . . .' He looked across at the grainy, faded photo of the woman who had been brutally murdered. Her name was there in bold black print underneath it. 'I want them searching Pauline Cook's house and garden, until I've caught up. I take it CSI have finished? Unless the search turns up anything that might have been missed?'

The OSU sergeant nodded.

'I want the whole street sealed off until we've determined how our killer arrived at the scene. Do we know if he was on foot or in a car?'

Everyone shook their heads.

'Tell the PCSOs to take over scene guard – they know the drill – and someone make sure that you rotate them. I don't want to find out they've been left there for hours without any breaks.'

The community sergeant nodded.

'Once the search has been done I want the house-to-house started. I'll draw up a map of the area I want checking. Then I want all the shops in the area visited to see if they have working CCTV, and I want the footage downloaded straight away, not in a week's time. If they can't do it immediately then seize the hard drives and bring them back for Barry to go through in the video imaging unit. That's it for now. We'll meet back here in a couple of hours and take it from there.'

Will was pleased to see everyone scribbling notes. Adele was standing at the back, her arms crossed. She nodded at him and he felt a little bit better.

'Before you go, I'd like you to meet DC Adele Dean. She's transferred from Carlisle and, although she hasn't replaced Stu – nobody could do that – she will be working from his desk. So if you need anything and can't get hold of me, speak to her.'

He walked out of the room before he had to look back at the super, who was still glowering at him. Will could feel the man's eyes burning through the back of his head. *Let the games begin.* He felt someone rushing up to him and turned to see Adele smiling at him.

'You know you would make an excellent chief super? What an idiot he is. How come he's still got a job? I bet he pisses people off on a daily basis.'

Will laughed; he looked down at his watch. 'Not bad, it took you less than five minutes in the station to come to the same conclusion as the rest of us. I have no idea how he still has a job, but I'd bet a hundred quid it's because he's part of the Masonic Lodge. If I give you the CCTV inquiries is that OK? I could give it to some uniform, but they're already short-staffed. Normally I'd use the PCSOs because they're really good at all this stuff, but I'm going to get them to do the house-to-house once the area's been searched because they're also very good at that.'

'You like your PCSOs then?'

'Like them? I bloody love them. They make my job so much easier because when you ask them to do a job they get off their arses and do it.'

'Ours were all right, but I wouldn't say they were amazing.'

'Well, mine are and I won't have a bad word said about them.'

'No, I wouldn't say a thing.'

Will led her across the landing to the large, open-plan office that he hated. There was no privacy whatsoever and it was right next to the canteen, which was a nightmare: having to smell sizzling bacon every morning when you were trying to still fit into your trousers.

'These desks are supposed to be anybody's, but we kind of tend to stick with the same ones.'

He pointed to an empty one.

'That one would have been Stu's had he moved here, but he

never recovered from his accident. So you might as well have that one because it hasn't got anyone else's crap on it.'

'Are you sure? It must be difficult for you all. I don't want to step on anyone's toes.'

'No, you're not. Stu's gone and, as hard as it is to believe or accept, we need to move on. No one will mind.'

Will walked into his office and shut his door. His head was banging. He was still fuming about the super's snide remarks, but he had a job to do and he would do it. He wanted to read the log as it had come in, read the reports they had up to now, go through the crime scene photos and decide how he was going to catch the murderous fucker who had broken into Pauline Cook's house and killed her in such a sick, violent frenzy.

Summer 1950

The huge red-and-white-striped tent had been erected on the field. Almost every person had helped to pull the guide ropes to lift it up and get it into place. It was something that needed as many of the labourers and performers as possible. Fresh sawdust had been scattered on top of the grass inside the tent, making it a softer floor. Gordy loved this part: when the centre ring was empty and the circus hadn't been tainted by thousands of men, women and children, all eagerly waiting to pay their money and file through the gap in the tent to take their seats.

Tomorrow, when it opened, the smell of popcorn and candy-floss would fill the air, mingling with the fresh sawdust and toffee apples. There was no better scent. The loud humming of the generators in the background was like music to his ears, blocking out the memories that were trying to fill his mind. It kept wandering back to his miserable childhood. The times he'd listened as his parents had argued, his mother's shrill voice carrying up the stairs until a loud thud would silence her.

More often than not his father – who liked to drink – would then come up and start on him, beating him for no reason. Gordy would go to school and make up the most intricate lies about the bruises. He hated his parents, but he hadn't wanted to go into a children's home. He became so good at telling lies that he almost believed them himself.

Then there were the incidents with Andrew and Mrs Goldsmith. Gordy didn't feel remorse for what he'd done to them. They had laughed at him and deserved what they got. It was life. Nobody had cared that his own father had punched and kicked him until he was black and blue, had they? He liked the feeling of being in control, of being able to inflict pain on others. This was what his father had taught him.

The circus was here for four nights and Gordy had an idea. Yesterday, as they'd arrived, there had been a group of kids waiting and watching their every move. They were almost as fascinated with the circus as Gordy himself was. One of the boys had looked a little bit slower than the rest of them; he'd stared at the lions, monkeys and elephants with a look of wonder etched onto his face. His jaw slack, his lips slightly parted as a line of spittle ran from them. One of the younger boys had elbowed him in the side and he'd closed his mouth, lifting a grubby sleeve to wipe his lips. Gordy had purposely gone over to talk to them, asking them if they liked the circus. All four of them had nodded in unison.

'Well, how would you like free tickets to come see it every night?'

'Really, mister? That would be ace. How would we get free tickets?'

'It's a big job setting this lot up; there's lots of work to be done. We could do with a hand setting up the chairs and putting fresh sawdust down each morning in the big top. I could square it with the ringmaster and see if he's willing to let you pitch in and help in return for some tickets.'

All four of them had shouted, 'Yes, please!' at the same time.

'I'm Gordy – well, that's my real name. When I'm working I'm Tufty the clown. You see that poster over there? The clown in the black and white? That's me.'

'Really, you're a proper clown? That's brilliant.'

Gordy smiled. 'I think so too. Wait there and I'll go speak to my boss, see if we can't give you lads some work to do. Of course you'll have to square it with your parents. They might not want you here every day.'

The boy who looked a little slower and older than the others laughed. 'My ma won't care. She's always telling me I should be in a freak show.'

The other boys laughed too. One of them said, 'Yes, she is. You could be a clown as well. We could call you Coco instead of Colin.'

The boy who'd elbowed him laughed so hard that tears rolled down his cheeks. 'Coco is a much better name than Colin. Shit on a stick is a better name than Colin.'

Colin scowled at them and his bottom lip trembled.

Gordy patted his arm. 'Well, I think Colin is a grand name, so why don't you go and see if you can all come back this afternoon and help out? Just come find me. I won't be far.'

The boys turned and ran off, leaving Colin lumbering behind. Gordy felt a spark of excitement; he had big plans for Colin. Since he'd killed his parents there was this feeling inside him that he wanted to do it again. No, not wanted – that wasn't strong enough. He knew he had to do it again. Only he didn't want to go after an adult. It would be easier to kill a kid. They were always wandering off and getting lost. He could make it look like an accident. Only he would know the truth. Colin was a lot bigger than he'd antici-pated, but it looked as if no one really cared about the lad so he would do nicely as a starter. Then if it all went to plan, he could carry on and no one would be any the wiser.

Gordy wandered off to help wherever he was needed. Betty and the two other trapeze artists were practising their twists and turns on a makeshift rope swing. He stopped to watch. She had done exactly what she said she would for the next show. Carried on as if she hadn't almost broken her neck. He had been fascinated; the strength she showed was admirable. In fact, the more he got to know the other performers, the more he liked them.

He was still wary of the lions. Marcus the lion tamer seemed to have them wrapped around his little finger. A loud roar made Gordy jump and he turned to see Marcus on the floor with Leo, the huge lion, standing above him. Gordy's heart raced and he thought he was about to watch Marcus get eaten alive. What happened next made him laugh so much a tear rolled down his cheek. The huge lion flopped down onto the floor of the cage next to Marcus and laid his head on his chest. He nudged Marcus until he gave in and rubbed his belly. Betty, who had paused mid somersault, giggled. She shouted, 'Marcus, that cat is more in charge of you than your wife. I bet you don't rub her belly like that.'

'Sweetheart, if I had a wife I most certainly would. Why don't you come over here and I'll rub yours?'

There was a loud eruption of laughter, which echoed around the field, and Gordy once more found himself glad that he'd finally had the courage to walk away from his old life so he could enjoy his new one.

Betty tutted and turned back to her rope swing. She looked at him. 'So, Tufty, how are you liking the circus?'

He fell forwards and tumbled to the ground, doing a forwards roll. As he stood up he pulled a bunch of flowers from his sleeve, handing them to her.

She giggled. 'That much, eh? Good, I'm glad you like it. I couldn't imagine living any other way. I've been part of circus life since I could crawl and I've been doing aerial stunts since I was five.'

He took a bow and nodded. 'I can't imagine anything else either – and that's amazing. You were born with circus blood in your veins. I feel as if I've finally found a place I belong, a place to call home.'

A loud voice shouted, 'Tufty, can you give us a hand?' He turned to see a group of men all unloading the wooden benches to go into the tent. He walked in their direction. For the next couple of hours he wouldn't have time to think about anything as they set up the seating for the audience.

Sweating and tired, he lifted the last bench into place, then straightened his back. It was lunchtime and he was going to take a well-earned break to eat a corned beef sandwich and drink a bottle of ginger ale. No sooner had he reached the shady spot he'd had his eye on all morning and sat down than he heard someone calling him. He stood up from the shade of the huge oak tree he'd taken shelter under from the burning sun and smiled to himself to see Colin walking towards him. Gordy waved at him and the big lad smiled. He was on his own.

'Hello, Colin, where's your friends?'

'Still talking to their mas. They don't seem to be having any of it and won't let them come to help you.'

'I see, I suppose I can understand that. What are you doing back? What about your ma?'

'She ain't bothered; said if I could get myself a job for four days it would be a bloody miracle. Glad to get me out of her hair.'

'Well, I'm sure I can find you a job.'

Gordy patted the grass beside him. 'Are you hungry?'

Colin nodded his head. 'Always hungry.'

He passed him half of his sandwich. 'Go on, take it. Big lad like you must have a big appetite.'

He took it from him, eating it in two bites.

Gordy laughed. 'I like you, Colin; I really do.'

They sat in silence for the next thirty minutes while Gordy rested his eyes. He wasn't asleep but he wasn't fully awake either. When he decided it was time to get back to work he took Colin with him to the trailer where he kept all his stuff. He pointed to his clown suit.

'What do you think about my costume, Colin? Do you like it? I made it myself.'

The seventeen-year-old boy reached out a hand, letting his fingers brush the soft, silky material. 'Nice. It's soft and smooth. I like it, Gordy.'

As he said his name, Gordy smiled at the image of Colin that had filled his mind – a very different picture to the one standing in front of him. He wondered if the boy would cry when he stuck his sharp knife into him and decided that, yes, he probably would, a lot. Then there was the fact that Colin didn't look like a normal, spotty, weedy teenager. He was tall and stocky; he was probably strong as well. He would have to be quick when he did it because if Colin decided to put up a fight, Gordy didn't know if he would be the one to come out of it alive.

Chapter Five

2016

Annie strapped Alfie into his car seat, put his changing bag on the seat next to him and then got into the driver's side. She loved this car more than words could say. She'd never thought another car would replace her beloved red convertible Mini, but after writing it off in an accident that had left her in a coma for a couple of days last year she'd had no other choice.

Will spoilt her; there was no doubt about it and it was nice that he did. It was reassuring knowing that he had more than enough money in the bank to cover the household bills and take them on holidays without having to scrimp and scrape like she'd had to when she was married to Mike.

She could live with the occasional treat from Will because she made sure she never asked for anything, preferring to earn her own money to buy what she needed. She didn't care if she wore Primark sunglasses or Dior; as long as they did the job it didn't matter, although the one thing she wouldn't compromise on was her perfume. It always had been and always would be Chanel.

Turning to check Alfie was OK before leaving, she smiled at him when he stretched his chubby hand out towards her. She blew him a kiss then turned back and drove away from her house. Since her niece, Matilda, had gone missing, she hadn't really had any visitors from the other side, which had been nice. Having a baby had taken up so much of her time, though, that she'd hardly even noticed.

As much as she wanted to help them, it still scared her every single time one put in an appearance. She'd spent the first thirty-one years of her life oblivious to the fact that the spirit world existed. Then, after that fateful night when her now-dead husband had tried to kill her, she'd woken up in the hospital with a huge wound on the back of her head and a new-found skill as a psychic.

As she took the narrow twisting road towards the car ferry to Bowness, she wondered how Will was getting on and if his hangover had kicked in yet. Adele had seemed nice and, if she was happily married with kids, surely she wouldn't be interested in Will. Still, Annie couldn't help worrying. The seeds of self-doubt that Mike had planted inside her during their marriage had left her with very little confidence in herself.

She knew she was being stupid; yes, Will had had quite a reputation for womanising before they got together, but he'd changed. They'd been through so much and, now they had Alfie, he wouldn't do anything stupid to risk jeopardising their marriage. She needed to stop worrying so much.

The ferry was quiet and before long she was loaded on to it and paying her money. As they reached the other side she drove off, relieved to be back on dry land. No matter how many times she used it the thought of its sinking always lingered in her mind. Even though it was only early, Bowness was starting to get busy. The obligatory coach full of Japanese tourists had debarked at the pier for the Lake cruises.

Annie smiled to herself. Passing the coffee shop where Gustav – her favourite barista – worked, she wondered if she should park up and pay him a visit; but a car pulled into the last parking space and she decided that maybe she would stop on her way home instead.

Driving up the steep hill, she passed the police station – her police station – which was now up for sale. All the staff now started and finished at Kendal, which was a pain in the arse. Jake had moaned about it for months, blaming her for making him transfer here from Barrow. The church came into view and Annie let out a small whoop of delight to see a parking space right in front of it. High five to Jesus or God.

She pulled in, then got out, taking Alfie, who was now fast asleep, from his seat. She decided to carry him to the rectory because she couldn't be bothered getting his pram out. She walked through the gorgeous garden, which was John's pride and joy, to the front door and knocked on it as loud as she could. It was a big house and – once a copper always a copper – she hated wasting time knocking on doors while at work so would always hammer on them. Disappointed that there was no sound of footsteps on the parquet flooring inside, she felt her shoulders deflate. She should have phoned to see if he was in. Shit. As she turned to walk back to her car, a voice shouted across the small wall that bordered the church and the rectory.

'Is that Annie Graham I see before me in the flesh? What a sight for my failing old eyes. It's been far too long.'

With much more spring in his step than Annie had, he briskly walked across to the wall and jumped over it. Father John was in his late sixties, but he was fitter than most men half his age. He pulled her to him, careful not to squash Alfie, and hugged her as best he could. He placed a kiss on her cheek. She grinned.

'You look younger every time I see you, John. Have you got a fountain of youth tucked away inside the baptism font?'

'Ah, I wish. I would be a much richer man than I am now. A humble servant of God relies on his faith and a little help from cheap moisturising cream.'

Annie laughed.

'So what brings you here, or am I lucky enough to be having a social visit?'

He raised one eyebrow and she felt bad. She'd dragged him into too much stuff the last couple of years and not once had he berated her for it.

'I'm looking for cake, if I'm being honest with you, and of course I wanted a hug from my very favourite priest in the world.'

John didn't miss the fact that her eyes were searching out the corner of the churchyard behind him where they had buried the bones of one Betsy Baker; but he didn't want to push her. She would open up and tell him what was bothering her in her own time.

'Well, if that's the case, come inside my house. I have a huge Victoria sponge cake that I've done my best to eat all on my own, but am failing miserably. Not to mention fresh coffee. Admit it, Annie Graham, you only came for the coffee.'

She pulled a face and he laughed.

'Sorry, I can't help it. You're so adorable to tease and there aren't many women around here that I get the chance to be myself with, if you know what I mean. The ladies of the flower-arranging club are still as bad as ever. It gets a bit embarrassing listening to them fighting over me like I'm a piece of meat.'

'You're so awful. Sometimes I find it hard to believe you're actually a priest. I often wonder if you just blagged your way into the priesthood.'

He clasped his hand to his heart, feigning a heart attack and pretended to stumble back. 'Why don't you just take my Bible, beat me around the head with it and be done with it?'

She laughed and his eyes lit up. There was nothing better than hearing this lovely, brave, amazing woman chuckle like a schoolgirl. His job was done; he could quit the fooling around now.

'Come on, don't you go telling that to the bishop. I'll buy your silence with a big slice of cream cake and a cappuccino.'

He led the way up the steps and she followed him. Alfie was

still asleep and getting heavier by the minute. John opened the door and she walked inside. He pointed to the lounge.

'Why don't you go and lay your young man on the sofa and I'll bring a tray through for us? We can be civilised for a change instead of slumming it at the kitchen table.'

'Thank you, he's getting so heavy you wouldn't believe it.'

John disappeared into the kitchen and she flopped down onto the big, squashy sofa. Moving the cushions she formed a bed for Alfie and laid him down. John came in with a tray with two huge wedges of cake and she looked at him.

'Did I ever tell you how much I love you?'

He chuckled. 'Ah, you're far too easily bought, and yes, I think you did mention that the last time I fed you.'

'Good, because you need to know this stuff.'

John passed a plate to her and let her tuck into her cake. He asked her about Will and how the funeral had gone. She relayed Will's antics to him and smiled to see him shaking his head with a grin on his face.

'I kind of understand, though. He's had to carry that guilt with him since the night it happened. As have you; you both have.'

'I know. That's why I couldn't be too mad with him.'

'Good, I'm glad you weren't. Now then, enough of the small talk. I couldn't help but notice you peering into a certain corner of the churchyard when we were talking outside. God forbid, but tell me is there something wrong at the cottage?'

'Sorry, John, I didn't come to upset you, but I did want to see you about something.'

'I know you did. You're very busy, what with your little prince there, but if something's wrong I want to know so I can help you. I value your friendship far too much to turn my back on you when the going gets tough, so don't worry about me.'

He grabbed hold of her hand and she squeezed his fingers.

'There's nothing obviously wrong that I know about. It's more a case of feeling as if there is something not right.'

'And you're wondering about our terrible friend, Betsy?'

She nodded. 'Just the thought of that horrible woman terrifies me. Alfie won't settle in his own room. He's started to wake up every night at a similar time, and I know babies do that – I'm not stupid – but it's always cold in there, even with the heating on. I just wanted to check her grave hasn't been disturbed and that nothing unusual has happened.'

'It hasn't, don't you worry about that. I don't even let them cut the grass by her with the lawnmower. I make sure they use the strimmer in that corner; believe me, I don't want a run-in with her again. Once was enough for any of us.'

'Well, I don't know what it is then. I used to hear the laughter of the boys she killed before I had Alfie, but since he's been here they haven't been around. I don't think that they would scare him either; they were good kids. There's something else: I had a terrible dream about a white house with a blue door where something bad had happened, and the next night the exact house was on the local news because a body had been found inside of it.'

'You're a very gifted woman, not to mention a very tired new mother whose hormones are all over the place. I don't think it's anything to worry about. If it was her in your house then I think you would know about it. She didn't like you being in there. She wouldn't stand in the background and do nothing; that's not her style. As for your dream, it was probably your sixth sense telling you about it, trying to forewarn you that Will was about to get involved in another murder case. Is he involved?'

She nodded. 'He will be, although he hasn't said anything yet.'

'Sometimes you have to switch it all off, which I think you have managed to do quite well since Alfie's birth. It's probably just bits and pieces sneaking in when you're not looking.'

'You're right. I'm so sorry to have bothered you, John. I'm letting it all get to me when really I'm just knackered.'

'You're never a bother to me – well, that time you and Jake turned up with a plastic box with the bones of that awful Betsy

Baker inside you were – but I've forgiven you for that one, just.'

They both laughed.

'Ah yes, that was very bad.'

'Come on, eat your cake and drink your coffee while you have five minutes' peace. I want you to tell me all about what you've been up to since I last saw you.'

They chatted and Annie felt as if a huge weight had been lifted off her shoulders. John would have known if that evil woman was back. She didn't like any of them and wouldn't leave him alone when he had been the one to inter what was left of her body in hallowed ground. She was being paranoid and overprotective of her son.

Stevie hadn't been lying when he'd said the house they were clearing out was a shithole. It smelt so bad inside, even Stevie had put a protective mask on, and he was normally hardcore when it came to stuff like this. Wally had a much weaker stomach and was sweating so bad he could smell himself through the mask.

The house was full of junk – nothing of any real value from what he could see. They hadn't started on the bedrooms yet, but they'd almost cleared the downstairs. If he was lucky, he sometimes found pieces of jewellery that he could stash and take down the pawnshop. As long as Stevie wasn't watching. He knew that Stevie did the same because how else did he afford the tidy white BMW that he drove when he wasn't in the works van?

He could hear Stevie muttering under his breath and he smiled. That bastard Jacko better pay him after this. They loaded the last boxes of ornaments and books into the back of the van and leant against it to take a breather. Wally lifted the mask away from his mouth, taking in gulps of fresh air. Stevie did the same and inhaled fresh air as well.

'Jesus, how can someone live like that? All those years of dust and filth. I mean, your flat's a shithole, Wally, but at least it's not that bad. Well, it wasn't last time I was in there.'

'Thanks, man, that's nice of you to say. Mine doesn't smell as bad as that; at least I hope not.'

'No, you're right – sorry. It's not quite that bad. I reckon we deserve a bonus for this job, me and you, Wally lad. What do you think?'

'Just being paid would be a decent start. That wanker hasn't paid me for two weeks. I'm on the bones of my arse. That's my last fiver I pulled out of my pocket.'

Stevie shook his head. 'Tight sod he is. Don't worry, I'll tell him when we get back to pay you.'

He went around to the front of the van and pulled out two bottles of water, throwing one at Wally.

'Here, drink this, then we can get the upstairs cleared. I'm telling you now, if we find a purse or money under the mattress, I'm not telling anyone. It's between you and me and we'll split it. Whoever lives here can't have any visiting family or they'd have sorted through the stuff themselves. You know how greedy folks are when someone dies; Aunty Wilma, who they haven't seen for ten years, was the best aunty anyone could ask for.' He pretended to cry and Wally laughed.

'Let's hope Aunty Wilma was a secret millionaire then.'

Stevie nodded his head. 'Yep. Come on, the quicker we do this, the quicker we can get out of here.'

He locked the van and headed back inside the rundown terraced house. Wally sighed, pulled his mask down and followed him. It was hard to concentrate when all he kept thinking about was the clown suit. The house they'd cleared where he'd found it had been full of circus memorabilia. The woman who lived there had been in the circus until it shut down. He'd read the articles in the scrapbook she'd kept on the sideboard, below the huge print of her hanging from a trapeze in the centre ring of a circus.

Wally would have liked to have brought the scrapbook and the print home with him to keep. They were nice, but he couldn't stash them like he had the clown suit. He couldn't afford to buy them and there was no way Jacko would have let him keep them. He sold everything on at the rundown auction house he owned. If he didn't come up with the cash he owed him, he could ask him for the stuff as part payment. It would be nice to start a little collection of his own.

Chapter Six

Detective Inspector Max Harper came into the office he shared with Will and shut the door.

'I see the super was his usual charming self at briefing.'

Will nodded.

'Are you OK to run with this one? I'm up to my neck in the Quigley case. Obviously I'll keep an eye on the investigation, but you've had far more experience with these sorts of cases than I have and I'm off to sunny Spain tomorrow.'

'Yes, I suppose so and, unfortunately for me, I have.'

'Why don't you put in for your inspector's, Will? You could run CID with your eyes shut.'

'Because I can't stand all the politics and the bollocks that goes with it. You know as well as I do, even if I passed the boards they'd probably ship me off to HQ for a couple of years and I can't be bothered with that. I'm quite happy being sergeant. At least I get to keep my hands dirty to a certain degree.'

Max almost threw himself into his chair and lifted his feet onto the desk.

'That's certainly true about the bollocks; they wouldn't dare ship you off to HQ, though. You're an absolute asset to this shithole. They'd be stupid to take you off CID.'

'Thanks, boss, that's kind of you to say. However, what they should do and what they actually do are two different things. You know how this place works. Everything is done back to front. Anyway, have you been sent in to give me a reprimand?'

'Ha-ha, for talking to the super like that? No, and if they'd asked me to, I'd have told them no. What are you going to do now then?'

'Well, I'm going to the hospital to see the esteemed Doctor Matt and watch the post-mortem for Pauline Cook. Nothing like watching someone get sliced and diced to set you up for the day.'

He didn't add the fact that he had a stinking hangover to his statement. There were some things that you didn't confess to the bosses – as much as you might like them.

'Adele seems nice. Are you going to take her with you? I suppose we might as well throw her in at the deep end and utilise her experience.'

Will nodded, thinking how pleased she would be to be so accepted into the team at such a grand level on her first day. No breaking her in gently, especially with two of his DCs on the sick and another on annual leave. They were pretty thin on the ground. There was a knock on the door. Will shouted, 'Come in,' and she opened the door.

'I've googled the shops in the immediate area and rang them all up to request their CCTV footage. I didn't ask them for it; I told them I would pick it up in a couple of hours. I find it better to just tell people what you want. If you ask, they can always say no.'

She winked at Will who laughed.

'True, I like your style. Are you all right to come up to the mortuary for the PM?'

'Of course, no problem.'

Will had to admire that she didn't once betray what she was really thinking because he'd have been swearing under his breath if he'd been her. He stood up.

'Come on then, let's get this over with. I've already spoken to Matt. He's ready to go as soon as we get there.'

Adele smiled and followed him out of the office. Brad, one of the younger detectives, rolled his eyes across the desk at Shona, who was staring at him, and whispered, 'The boss man has a new favourite. It didn't take him long to find a replacement for Stu.'

Will caught the last of what he'd said and turned back to him. 'Don't you be talking shite, Brad. Have you got nothing to do?'

Brad – whose face was redder than Shona's red patent leather shoes – nodded his head.

'Yes, boss; sorry, boss.'

'The only reason I'm taking Adele with me is because she has far more experience of post-mortems and won't pass out; unlike you, Brad, who drops like a sack of shit as soon as the doctor picks up his scalpel. I haven't got time to fan your face while waiting for you to come round today. There's a murder to solve.'

Brad looked away and Shona had to stifle a giggle. Will shook his head and walked towards the spiral staircase. Adele clearly didn't want to piss anyone off on her first day. She smiled at Brad and whispered, 'I passed out at my first PM, and honestly you won't do it again. Next time you'll be fine.'

Then she hurried after Will.

Brad glared at Shona, who was still laughing.

'Aw, come on, Brad; he does have a point. You went whiter than Casper the ghost and took ages to come round. I thought I was going to have to stick a toe tag on you and fill out a form 38.'

'Fuck off and I didn't think he'd bloody hear me, did I? He's got supersonic hearing.'

Shona nodded. 'Yes, he has, but he's a good boss so don't go pissing him off. He never moans if you need to finish early or swap a shift, so you'd do well to remember that. Do you really want to go and watch a post-mortem this time in the morning anyway?'

'I suppose not.'

'Nope, well me neither, so keep your mouth shut next time. Besides, Adele has been a detective almost as long as he has, so why wouldn't he want her expertise?'

'All right, bloody hell, Shona. Anyone would think you had a bit of a soft spot for our sergeant – sticking up for him like that.'

It was her turn for her cheeks to flush red. 'No, but he's a nice bloke, Brad. He's one of the good guys and there aren't many of them left.'

Brad shrugged. 'Yeah right, you well fancy him. Everyone fancies him. I bet it drives his wife mad and I suppose he has had a shit time. He nearly died, didn't he – last year? Forget I said anything.'

As the hospital loomed in the distance, Will's stomach lurched and his mouth filled with acid. He needed something to eat. A greasy sausage bun smothered in tomato sauce would do the trick. The only thing was, if he didn't digest it before he went into the mortuary, he would regret eating it.

'So do you think whoever did it knew the victim? I mean, it was a pretty violent crime and normally such violence is carried out by someone they know. Do we know if she was in a relationship or had recently ended one?'

Will shook his head. 'If I'm honest with you, I know jack shit. I've been thinking about the fact that there was no sign of forced entry. It looked as if Pauline may have known her killer – unless she regularly let strangers into her house.'

'What do we know about Pauline?'

'Not much at the moment. I'm hoping after this we can get some more information from her home address. The neighbour very kindly offered to do the ID; I want to have a chat with her as soon as we've finished up here. She doesn't think that Pauline has much family – said she was a bit of a loner.'

'And now she's dead and naked on a cold slab, about to be cut up in front of several complete strangers.'

Adele shivered. It made her feel ill just thinking about it. The shame of having to endure a post-mortem in a roomful of strangers was not one of the nicest things. It would give her nightmares for days, but she didn't say anything to Will. She didn't want him thinking she couldn't handle it because she could. It was just the thought of how desperately sad it all was.

The older she got, the more it made her contemplate her own mortality. Sometimes she wished she'd never become a copper, and then at other times the sense of pride she felt at solving some of the most horrendous crimes and taking those violent criminals off the streets made it all worthwhile. It had got much worse since she'd had children of her own; when they were little she'd been overprotective and had a hard time letting them gain their independence.

Some of her daughter's friends had been playing out in the backstreet and going to the corner shop on their own since they'd been six years old. Adele used to wonder what the hell their parents were thinking, but they didn't have to deal with missing kids who'd been snatched from their own front gardens and returned in body bags. Thank God for Aaron. He'd had a normal nine-to-five job and had been there to supervise when she'd finally agreed the kids could venture out onto the front street and gain their independence.

Will turned off the engine and she snapped herself out of her distant memories – time to focus on the here and now, not the past. It was time to do what was right for Pauline Cook and find the bastard who'd done this to her. What a way to spend her first day in a new station. She'd been hoping for a couple of simple cases, nothing too complicated, to ease her into it slowly. They got out of the car, which Will had squeezed into the smallest gap she'd ever seen, next to a portable MRI scanning machine in the hospital car park.

'Blimey, times are hard if you have to have your MRI done out in the car park.'

Will laughed and headed in through a small door, which led to nowhere. The only thing in the small entrance was a single knackered chair and a lift.

'What is this place?'

'No idea, but as long as you don't mind walking through the clinic on the next floor and looking like you know what you're doing, no one takes a blind bit of notice. Have you seen how full the car park is? You're lucky if you can get a parking space first thing, but this time of day there's no chance.'

He pressed the silver button to call the lift. The hum and clatter of the heavy machinery as the lift began its descent made Adele's eyes almost pop out of her head.

'Erm, I'm not really that fond of lifts and that one doesn't sound too healthy. Is there no other way to get into the hospital?'

Will shook his head. 'It's fine, I use it all the time.'

The double doors slid open and he stepped inside. Adele was hesitating, wondering if she should just go and find another way in, when the doors closed and he arched an eyebrow at her.

'It will take you ages to walk around to the front entrance.'

She shook her head and stepped inside, tucking her hands behind her back so he couldn't see that she had her fingers crossed. The lift juddered, made a squealing sound and then began to move upwards. Will laughed. No sooner had they started to move than it stopped again and the doors rattled open.

'See, what did I tell you?'

He led her through a set of double doors along a small corridor where there were various rooms full of machines and nurses; at the very end was a waiting room full of people. He pushed the next set of double doors open and the smell of grilled bacon and fried bread hit his nostrils. Will groaned.

'Do you mind if we make a quick stop at the canteen? I'm hungover and in desperate need of some greasy food.'

'Nope, I don't mind.'

'Good.'

Will tried not to think about the times he and Stu had come to the hospital canteen for their breakfast. It was still too raw. The dining room was busy with hospital staff and visitors, and along the back wall was a long row of response officers all tucking into plates of cooked breakfasts. Will raised a hand and was greeted by a chorus of 'Morning, Sarge'. The rest of the diners turned to look and Will felt his cheeks flush.

Adele giggled. 'Looks like you've been caught red-handed.'

'Yes, by that lot over there who are supposed to be protecting the good public.'

'We've all got to eat.'

It was her turn to arch an eyebrow at him and he grinned. He ordered a sausage, bacon, fried egg and mushroom bun. Taking a bottle of orange Lucozade out of the fridge, he asked her what she wanted.

'Black coffee.'

'They do lattes. Do you not want anything to eat?'

Adele didn't want to put her stomach to the test by eating a greasy bun filled with fried delights minutes before attending a post-mortem. She shook her head. 'I've already eaten, thanks.'

Will paid his money and carried the tray over to a table at the opposite end of the dining room, away from the rowdy bunch of coppers, who were laughing loudly at something.

'I'm probably going to regret this in twenty minutes, but all I can think about is food.'

Adele laughed. 'Well, rather you than me; my stomach's hard, but not that hard.'

Summer 1950

It took Gordy an hour to get ready for each performance, every single time. He didn't like to rush the best, most important, part of the process. He stared at the white face in the mirror. He liked

63

to make sure that every inch of his skin was covered in the thick, white greasepaint. His short black hair was hidden underneath a flesh-coloured stocking. He coloured around his eyes in thick, black paint. They had to be just right. If they weren't, even he wouldn't contemplate going out in public.

He heard a dry, hacking cough from behind him and paused. Colin had worked really hard the last three days, but he'd started coughing a lot today. His skin was almost the same colour as Gordy's face and he'd had a fine film of sweat on his forehead all day despite the temperature being much cooler today than yesterday.

Gordy hoped the kid wasn't coming down with something catching. The last thing he needed was to be laid up and out of action with some illness. He supposed if Colin was poorly he wouldn't be putting up much of a fight when the time came, but if Gordy was honest with himself he didn't really want to hurt him now. Colin had kind of grown on him – something he'd never anticipated. He was a hard-working lad and, from the tales he had told him, didn't have much of a life ahead of him with that bitch of a mother.

Gordy thought this might be his chance to do something good to make up for the bad. Plus, as he'd lain in bed last night, he'd thought about using Colin to help him with his plans. Colin had such a childlike manner about him; the kids seemed to flock to him more so than they ever flocked to Gordy, even when he was dressed in full clown regalia. It was as if the little bastards could tell what he wanted to do to them all – maybe they could.

He'd heard that kids could be perceptive. Maybe they knew he wanted to take them into the fields at the edge of the woods and hurt them so bad they would bleed to death. The urge was getting stronger; he didn't think he could hold off much longer. He'd never planned on killing his parents, but now that he had, it was hard to ignore the fire burning inside of him.

'How are you feeling, Colin? You look like shit.'

'I don't feel so good, Gordy. My throat feels as if I swallowed glass and my head hurts real bad.'

'Is your mother coming to the show tonight? Did you give her those free tickets I gave you yesterday?'

Colin shook his head. 'She sold them to the man in the pub. I saw her coming out of there last night. She was drunk and had some money in her hands. She don't care about this at all.'

Gordy felt his fingers clench into tight fists. He squeezed so hard he snapped the black crayon he was holding. The woman obviously didn't care about anyone but herself. He wondered if he should go and pay her a visit instead; maybe satiate his desire with her. He nodded his head. That was a marvellous idea. He would give Colin some of those strong pills the doc gave him last month when he hurt himself falling off the miniature car the clowns drove around the ring. They would knock him out for a few hours, leaving Gordy to go to Colin's house and speak to his mother, persuade her to let Colin join the circus – and if she wasn't agreeable?

A huge smile spread across his face. It was a perfect plan. She wouldn't be missed if she was as mean as Colin had said she was. He'd be doing the boy a huge favour. He stood up and went into the bag under his bunk that he kept his tablets in. After shaking three out, he got a glass of water and handed them all to Colin.

'Here – if you take these it will make your throat stop burning and you'll be able to have a little sleep before the show starts. If your mother arrives, I'll come wake you up. How does that sound?'

Colin nodded his head. 'Will they stop me hurting?'

'Yes, they will.'

The boy with the body of a man held his hand out and took the tablets from Gordy. He clumsily shoved them into his mouth then took a huge gulp of water from the glass Gordy had passed to him. Colin winced. Water splashed down his chin and he began to choke. Gordy slammed the palm of his hand across Colin's back, wondering if he'd inadvertently killed him. That would be just his luck: killing him accidentally when, in the first place, he'd wanted to skin him like a rabbit. The boy finally stopped coughing and wiped his sleeve across his eyes, which were watering.

'You OK?'

Colin nodded.

'Good. You lie down and, if I see your mother, I'll bring her to see you. Is that a good idea?'

Colin had no concept that Gordy wouldn't know what his mother looked like if he fell over her; he wasn't bright enough. But it didn't matter. Colin had told Gordy where he lived the very first day they'd met and it was only a five-minute walk from the circus. He could go in full clown regalia and if he took some leaflets with him to hand out to anyone he might pass, that would be a good enough cover story.

Gordy gave Colin a comforting pat and he lay back, closing his eyes. Taking a blanket, Gordy covered Colin with it then turned back to finish his masterpiece. By the time he'd painted the huge red grin across his mouth, exaggerating the corners, he was satisfied. Now he looked like his true self: Tufty. Taking the wig off the stand next to him, he tugged it over his head. He felt like he was invincible. Tufty took no crap from anyone.

He smiled at his reflection then turned from left to right to make sure it was perfect. He clapped his hands. Standing up, he took his precious silk suit from its coat hanger and stepped inside it, pulling it up over his vest and long johns. Shorty came in, took one look at him and laughed.

'Christ, Tufty, if you aren't the scariest-looking act in this whole miserable circus I don't know who is.'

Tufty gave a brief laugh. 'I'll take that as a compliment, shall I?'

'Take it how the fuck you want. I wouldn't want to meet you in a dark backstreet. Anyway, what's up with the kid? Have you worked him to death?'

He shrugged. 'He's got a fever. His mother is supposed to be coming. She can take him home with her. I don't really want him hanging around here if he's sick.'

Shorty nodded. 'Too true. We haven't got the time to be ill. It doesn't matter if we feel like shit because the show must go on, even if we're dying inside.'

He left and Tufty gave himself one last look in the mirror. He supposed he did look quite scary. Then again, what was a clown supposed to look like? They were all freaks when you came to think about it. Grown men prancing around trying to get the next laugh and wearing funny clothes and more make-up than any woman in the audience.

As Tufty bumbled into the middle ring of the big top, he nodded and clapped his hands at the audience, running around and getting them to clap back. He was very appreciative of such a good turnout for their last show. The next hour and a half went by in a blur; the atmosphere inside the tent was one of complete fascination, wonder and laughter. He knew his routine off by heart, not having to think about it, which was just as well considering he had much more pressing thoughts on his mind.

He wondered what Colin's mother looked like, whether she was pretty or a drunken old cow whose looks had been lost in the bottom of a beer barrel. It incensed him that she'd sold the tickets to tonight's show. She could have seen how hard Colin had worked and maybe appreciated how much potential her son might have if given the right opportunities.

The bucket of flour covered his face and for a second he wondered where he was, but the sound of thousands of people laughing snapped him out of his daydreams. He ran after Shorty, chasing him around in circles, almost catching him and shaking his fist at him, much to the audience's delight. The lights dimmed and the clowns made their way to the back of the ring and the curtains while the next act began to set up.

Within a matter of minutes there was a huge cage erected. The lights went out momentarily and a chorus of screams filled the air. Then they flickered back on and inside the cage were three huge lions. Alongside them was one of the stars of the show: the lion tamer. Although he disliked the man because of the way the dancers fawned over him, Tufty also had a grudging respect for him. Not many people would get in a cage with three huge man-eating lions every day.

This was his chance to make his disappearance and Tufty skipped, hopped and stumbled towards the exit the performers used to come in and out of the tent. The rest of the clowns were all standing in a circle, smoking and watching the lion tamer. He knew that every single one of them was waiting for the day it actually happened and the lions turned on him and ate the smug, snotty bastard.

Grabbing a handful of posters from the now-empty ticket booth he walked the short distance to Colin's rundown house. It was literally three streets away from the parkland where the circus was pitched. Tufty walked along the roughly cobbled pavements, his posters clasped in one hand, ready to give them to the first person he met – only the streets were deserted and he didn't pass a solitary soul.

The circus tent held over two thousand people so most of the locals must be there because he doubted the streets were normally so quiet. As he turned into the dark street he was pleased to see a single light burning in the upstairs front bedroom. He picked up his pace, not wanting to be seen. He stayed close to the wall across the street, which was overhung with large oak trees from the parkland behind it.

He crossed over and tried the front door handle, wondering if she'd left it open for Colin. It didn't budge. There was a small wooden door at the side of the house, which led to a narrow alleyway between both houses. He pushed this one and it opened. It was pitch-black inside the small passage, but less than thirty seconds and he was out in the open again with a gate to the small back gardens on either side of him.

The one to the left of him was immaculate. He inhaled the scent of the freshly cut grass. He wondered what these neighbours made of Colin and his drunken mother. The house Colin had gone into yesterday had a gate that was rotten and hanging off its hinges. Next door's house was in complete darkness and he would have bet that the nice family who lived there were at this very moment in time watching the lion tamer, their mouths open in fear and wonder.

He stepped into the overgrown, unkempt, weed-filled space and tried the door handle. This one went all the way down and the door opened. Grinning, he slid inside, pushing it closed behind him. The smell of lard and fried fish hit his nostrils, making him wince. Realising he had no murder weapon with him, he placed the pile of posters on the kitchen table and looked around the cramped room.

There were more dirty pots, pans and plates on the draining board than there probably were in the cupboards. Sticking out of the sink was a huge butcher's knife. It had some dark, sticky substance along the blade and he lifted it to his nose to smell. Strawberry jam. He would bet Colin had used this last to make himself a jam sandwich for his breakfast. Picking up a faded yellow newspaper from the table he wiped the blade down. A loud thud and the sound of raised voices from the room directly above him made him step against the wall and hold his breath.

Footsteps thundered down the threadbare staircase and he heard a woman's voice yell, 'Go on, fuck off out of 'ere. Run back to your wife and see if she'll let you stick your dick where you just did for free.'

The front door slammed shut and Tufty waited to see if the crude, horrible woman was about to come downstairs. He heard the sound of the mattress creaking as she moved around on it, but there were no footsteps. Removing his huge red clown shoes, he left them in the kitchen and made his way upstairs. His heart raced with both excitement and fear. Was it right to feel so confused, he wondered. He reached the top stair and stepped onto the threadbare landing carpet. The floorboard let out a loud creak.

'Who's there? Is that you, Colin? Decided to come home now, have you?'

Tufty didn't answer. She would know it wasn't her son's voice. He moved towards the bedroom that had the light on and the door ajar. At least she couldn't see him approaching.

'Colin, that better be you; stop messing around.'

Her voice didn't sound quite so harsh and cocky now. He detected a slight tremble. Two more steps and he'd be inside her room. He heard the bedsprings creak as she sat up.

'If you've fucking come back for sloppy seconds, Jack Sloane, you can do one. Get home to your wife.'

Her voice was definitely quieter. He took a deep breath and used the tip of the knife to push the door open. The look of horror on her face at seeing him standing there in all his glory with a huge, red grin on his white-painted face and the knife in his hands was one he would treasure until the day he died.

'What do you want? Who said you could come in and where's my Colin?'

She had pulled her knees up to her chin and her frail, pale arms were wrapped around them.

'Who the fuck are you? Are you the weirdo who wants my Colin to run away with him? Well, I've got news for you: unless you're going to pay him and me, he's not going anywhere.'

Tufty grinned at her and stepped into the room. He never spoke; instead he tilted his head and folded his arms across his chest, mimicking her. It was then that she saw the glint of the blade in the reflection from the bare light bulb and scrabbled to get off the bed, panic in her eyes. She looked around the room for something to protect herself with. As she spied the old cricket bat behind the chair that she probably kept for awkward men she brought home, so did he.

She tried to scrabble across the bed to reach it and he ran at her. Grabbing her spindly legs, he tugged her so hard that she fell onto the mattress. He sat on top of her, pinning her to the bare mattress that stank of sweat, cigarette smoke and sex. He was still smiling, even though she was trying her best to slap him and push him off. He lifted the knife and stabbed it down so hard it squelched straight through her eyeball and killed her instantly.

Her body twitched, but he wasn't finished. Now that her heart wasn't pumping the blood around her body, she wouldn't make so much mess. He stabbed her again and again until her body was unrecognisable. His hands soaked in her blood, he pushed himself up off the bed. His beloved clown suit was splattered with bright red spots. He looked in the mirror and smiled.

Leaving her body there with the knife protruding from her eye socket, he walked along the narrow hallway until he found the small bathroom where he washed his hands under the cold water. He didn't have much time. He needed to get back to the circus before the end of the show and the crowds flocked out of the parkland gates and the entire area was flooded with men, women and children.

He dried his hands on a threadbare towel and flung it onto the floor. Leaving to go into the next room, which was Colin's, he shook his head. It was sparse to say the least. There were a couple of toy cars on the floor and a one-eyed, tattered old bear on the bed. Pulling a battered suitcase off the top of the wardrobe he opened the drawers and stuffed what few clothes were in there inside. There were a couple of patched jumpers hanging inside the wardrobe, along with a pair of trousers and a winter coat. He stuffed those inside the case, shoved in the bear and shut the case.

He didn't look back as he ran downstairs and back into the kitchen where he slipped his feet inside the ridiculously too big clown shoes. He left through the back door and reached the passageway. Remembering the posters, he realised he had to go back inside to get them. *Stupid Gordy, you might as well have left a trail of breadcrumbs for the police to follow back to the circus.*

71

The street was still deserted and he jogged back to the small entrance he'd left through, hoping no one would see him. He was normally a good runner. He had to be to keep up with the clown routines, but the case, although not full, was weighing him down. A fine film of sweat underneath the greasepaint was making his head feel as if it was about to explode. He managed to get back to the circus just as he heard the final encore. He should be there now with the others taking his final bow.

He hadn't intended to go back inside the ring, but his ego – which was getting far too big – made him. The lights were bright and the audience members were all standing and clapping in time to the music. He threw the case under the nearest stall and cartwheeled into the centre ring of the big top. He loved the applause. If anyone wondered what was all over his suit, he would brush it off and pretend he had no idea what it was. He stood there next to Shorty and waved his hands, grinning from ear to ear.

The lights finally went down and he made his way out of the tent and straight to his trailer. As he opened the door he heard a gentle snore coming from the small bed where he'd left Colin. He tugged his wig off then pulled his suit off. Holding it up to survey the damage, he shook his head and tutted. He walked over to the small sink where he put the plug in; then, taking the box of soap flakes out of the cupboard, he shook them into the cold water. He immersed his suit in the solution and left it to soak.

He began to scrub his clown make-up off. He didn't think anyone had seen him in Colin's street, but it was better to be sure. When he started looking more like plain old Gordy Marshall he got dressed and went to retrieve Colin's suitcase. The sound of laughter and chatter from the different caravans and trailers filled the air.

It was always like this on the last night after a successful run. The circus hands were already dismantling the huge tent and would work late into the night. The animals were all caged up and eating their long-awaited meals.

He went to the small stall and tugged the case out from underneath it. Then he turned, whistling, and walked back to his caravan. He was tempted to put the case in and go and have a beer with the rest of the clowns, but he wouldn't be able to concentrate on their conversation. If they came looking he could say he was coming down with what the lad had. That would make them leave him alone so he could sit and revel in what he'd done.

Chapter Seven

2016

Annie fastened Alfie into his car seat. After shutting the door she turned to hug John, who was waiting with his arms open wide. There was something very comforting about being hugged by a priest. They broke apart and she smiled at him.

'You are officially the best hugger I know.'

'Well thank you; I'll take that as a huge compliment, especially considering the size of young Jake's arms – not to mention your dashing husband.'

Annie giggled. 'Don't get me wrong, they're both very good at it, but there's something extra special about a hug from you.'

He ruffled her hair. 'Ah, Annie, I like to think when I'm lying in my lonely bed, wondering what it would have been like to have children, that I could have had a daughter like you. I sometimes wonder if I've wasted my entire life.'

His pale blue eyes filled with tears and she felt fear inside her chest. Her heart tugged at the sight of him being upset.

'Are you OK, John?'

He nodded.

'I've spent the last hour blarting on about myself; we haven't talked much about you. Are you sure everything's OK? You're not ill, are you?'

'I'm fine – just being a soppy, sentimental old man. You know I keep thinking about what my life would have been like if I'd given up God years ago.'

Annie took hold of his hand. 'Let me tell you now that you would have made an amazing dad; there's no doubt about it. You also make one heck of a good priest as well. Look at how many people you've helped over the years. You saved me when I needed help. There aren't many men around who are as selfless and strong as you.'

He smiled and squeezed her hands. 'And you saved me, Annie, so we're quits; well, until the next time you turn up with some crazy old witch's bones stuffed into a plastic box.' He winked at her.

She blushed. 'I can honestly say, with my hand on my heart, I hope to God that never, ever happens again. Some nights I still wake up in a cold sweat thinking that she's there, scraping her long fingernails along the windows.' Annie shuddered.

John let go of her hand and stepped back. 'You and me both; now away with you and don't be standing around wasting any more of my time. I'm a busy man, you know. It will soon be time to go and speak to the old dears at the bridge club in the church hall who are all probably younger than me.'

She leant in, kissed his cheek, then walked around to the driver's side of the car and climbed inside. John made shooing movements with his hand and she turned the key in the ignition. It was time to go home. She looked in the rear-view mirror to take one last look and thought she saw a tall, dark shadow standing behind John. Turning around to look at him she felt a huge sigh of relief escape her lips to see there was no shadow.

She was tired. Her eyes were playing tricks on her. Lifting her hand, she waved, then set off. She hoped there wasn't some dark shadow hanging around John, draining his energy and making him feel so down. She'd never seen him anything but jovial, warm and happy, except for the two occasions when they'd been fighting to save themselves.

Alfie was cooing away in the back of the car and Annie smiled to herself. She didn't mind if Sophie or Alice had come to play with her baby, but she didn't want any other ghostly visitors. As she was driving through busy Bowness to get back home, she passed Jake, who was standing directing traffic outside the pier where there had been what looked like a minor road traffic accident.

She beeped her horn and he turned, his face a mask of anger until he realised it was her, and then he grinned. She blew him a kiss and he waved, then she was past and on her way. God, as much as she sometimes disliked being a police officer, she also loved it; well, she loved working with Jake. They had so much fun in between chasing serial killers and finding dead bodies.

She still had no idea what she was going to do. She knew Will wouldn't want her to be out working on the streets like she used to. But Annie knew she wouldn't survive if she was stuck in one of the stations working in an office. She could put in to do her detective's course, but what if she ended up working in the same office as Will? She loved him more than anything, but working with him might not be quite the same. She didn't know if she could take orders from him, and it would cause no end of hassle if she did.

He would never let her do anything more dangerous than boring inquiries and she would go insane if she couldn't get out and pitch in. She passed a boarded-up shop near the pier and wondered if she could do something with it: a bookshop, café, antique shop? Maybe a combination of all three; then she would see Jake every time he was working because he wouldn't keep away if there was coffee and cake on offer.

She would be able to keep herself busy. She had no end of babysitters for Alfie. Will's stepmum, Lily, had offered countless times, as had Tilly, her niece. In fact, she'd had a tearful Tilly on the phone a couple of days ago moaning about how crap and boring her life was. Although Annie didn't know if babysitting Alfie while Annie was working could be classed as exciting, Tilly could also work in the shop and maybe live with her and Will. They could take it in turns to open the shop and look after Alfie.

The more she thought about it the better the idea seemed. Will would be over the moon to think she wasn't out there working nights and putting herself in danger. She decided to pay Lily and Tom – Will's dad – a visit; see what Lily thought of the idea.

As the turn came up for their beautiful mansion set on the shore of Lake Windermere, an image flashed across her mind of the white house with the bright blue door. She blinked, shaking her head. That was the last thing she wanted to think about, especially when Alfie was with her. Annie had this strange, irrational fear that he would pick up on what she was seeing.

A few times when she'd watched Will pacing up and down with him, he'd look over Will's shoulder and smiled at no one she could see. What if Alfie had inherited her psychic gift? Annie hadn't known she possessed one until the days after Mike had almost killed her. Gosh, that seemed such a long time ago. So much had happened to her since then, most of it amazing, but some of it horrific.

She turned into the drive and was about to get out of the car and key in the code on the keypad for the automatic gates when they started to open of their own accord. Good, that meant someone was home. Since Will had been kidnapped by a half-sister none of them even knew existed, Tom had upped the security around the house. He had the same CCTV cameras Will had installed in their home and a very expensive burglar alarm, which went straight through to the police switchboard if it was activated. All of their lives had changed so dramatically over the last couple of years.

Before she could park the car, Lily was running down the concrete steps towards her. Tom was leaning on his wooden cane and waved from the top step. Annie waved back, feeling a rush of love for this kind, loving, forgiving, older version of her husband. They looked so alike. She knew that when Will was the same age, she'd still find him attractive.

Poor Will. Annie had no idea what she was going to look like, but he didn't seem to mind and there was always Botox. Lily had offered a couple of times to take her to meet her fixer-upper. Up till now Annie had declined, but give it a few years and she might feel a whole lot different. Annie released the lock on the door so Lily could lean in and take Alfie out of his seat. He waved his hands at Lily as she expertly released his seat belt, tugged him out and smothered him with kisses.

'Give the kid some air, Lily; you'll suffocate him.' Tom was laughing as she walked up the steps. Lily pushed Alfie close so Tom could kiss him.

'My, what a big boy you're getting. What's your mother feeding you on?'

Lily didn't hang around and went inside. Annie ran up the steps and kissed Tom's cheek.

'How are you? You look amazing.'

'Funnily enough, so do you. I'm all the better for seeing you two. Thank you for calling in. You might have just saved me from bankruptcy. Lily has decided that we need to redecorate.'

He winked and she laughed.

'You're welcome, but the house is beautiful as it is.'

'I completely agree, but I made the mistake of offering to take her for lunch at the newly refurbished Laura Ashley Hotel. Have you and Will been there? It's very nice. The only fault I could find was the catalogues on every table; it's a man's worst nightmare. Lily kept looking at the fixtures and fittings then pricing them up and making a very long list of what she'd like in here.'

'Oh dear, that's not a good idea, is it? Maybe I can talk her round for you. I think I've come up with a plan for what to do instead of going back to work. I was thinking of opening a shop myself. There's a boarded-up one near to that hotel.'

'Annie, what a wonderful idea – and you have my blessing. I

would much rather invest in a business with you than waste it on new chandeliers to replace the ones we have that aren't even twelve months old.'

They walked inside the hallway and Tom closed the door behind them, turning the key and locking it. Annie felt responsible that they'd had to change their lives so much since she'd come into it. Tom led the way through to the living room where Alfie was on a huge rug surrounded by every baby toy that Fisher-Price had ever made. Lily was playing with him. 'Was he moaning about my idea of decorating?'

Annie shook her head. 'No, but seriously, Lily, this place is beautiful. It really is. I was just telling Tom I'm thinking about opening a shop in Bowness. You could come and help me out on the days you're not too busy.'

Tom nodded in encouragement because he knew Lily was intrigued and he winked at Annie again.

'Well, I'll leave you ladies to discuss what you think. I'll go and make us all a drink.'

'Shout me when you're done. I'll come and get them.'

Tom nodded again, leaving them to it. He'd had a stroke last year. Luckily it hadn't been too serious and he'd pretty much regained all of the use of his arms and legs. He just needed the cane to stop him from wobbling too much. He set about filling the fancy coffee machine they used twice a week if they were lucky and made lattes. He would have loved it if Will and Annie had moved into this house with them. With little Alfie it wouldn't feel so big and empty.

Will had always been independent, though, and wouldn't hear of it – Annie even more so. It tickled Tom how she always insisted on working and paying her own way. Not that he didn't admire her for it, but he was glad she and Will were equals. Tom hadn't come into money until well into his forties and he'd worked hard his entire life to build up his business until he'd sold it so he could take it easy.

One day all of this would belong to both Will and Annie. Tom had left them equal shares as well as a trust fund for little Alfie. Tom didn't ever envisage Will and Annie getting divorced, but even if they did he wouldn't change his mind. He loved Annie like a daughter, which then reminded him of his daughter, Amelia, who he'd had no idea about and who was now locked up in a high-security mental hospital.

Tom had taken care of everything despite what she'd done to Will. It wasn't her fault he'd never known about her and it broke his heart to think of the life she'd led when it could have been so different. Before he knew it he'd made three lattes and filled a plate with freshly baked biscuits. Lost in his memories he'd been on automatic pilot. He shouted Lily, but it was Annie who came to get the tray from him.

'Oh my God, Tom, what are you trying to do to me? You know how much I love your biscuits and I've just eaten cake from Father John.'

He smiled. 'Well, someone has to eat them. There's only you and me. Lily is either carb counting or pointing or trying not to sin, so it's no good offering them to her.'

He bent his head towards Annie's ear and whispered, 'She gets so crabby when she's on one of her many diets. It drives me mad.'

Annie laughed. 'Yeah, I know all too well about that. I'm a member of every slimming club in South Cumbria.'

He shook his head. 'You women are mad. Why don't you just accept yourselves and enjoy your lives? It really is beyond me – the fact that you're both perfect as you are isn't good enough for you?'

Annie pecked his cheek. 'Aw, you are such a charmer, Mr Ashworth. I know where Will gets it from.'

She picked up the tray and carried it through to the living room. For the millionth time she asked herself what she'd done to gain such a wonderful family. There was one thing she did know, and that was that she would never take them for granted.

Chapter Eight

Adele snapped off her gloves, clearly relieved she'd been in charge of the exhibits so hadn't had to watch the entire post-mortem as closely as Will. He did the same and threw his gloves into the bin in the corner of the room. Matt had been thorough with his procedure; it hadn't taken a genius to work out that the victim had died from severe loss of blood due to the number of stab wounds inflicted on her body.

Amazingly, Pauline Cook's internal organs had pretty much been intact; her arteries had not, which had made her bleed to death in a matter of minutes. That was either a blessing in disguise or a curse. If anyone had found her in time, they might just have been able to put extreme pressure on the major wound and stem the bleeding.

They all agreed that whoever had held the knife had been angry enough to carry out a sustained attack, which was messy and violent. Will was grateful he hadn't regurgitated his greasy bun all over his shoes and the clean, shiny floor.

He met Adele outside the changing rooms and they left. Matt had promised to email his report over as soon as it had been typed up, and Will had made him promise to come and visit him and Annie soon because it had been too long. They left the mortuary, walking back the way they'd come. Will looked at the people who were walking along the corridors – either sick, injured or visiting someone who was. They were the lucky ones; they had no idea what it was like to watch what he'd just had to.

Despite how sad and cruel it could be, he wouldn't have changed his job for the world because he loved it – most of the time; but it did get depressing and downright terrifying sometimes. Sometimes he almost laughed aloud. Christ, sometimes it was almost deadly. This reminded him he needed to try and push Annie to come to some sort of decision on what she was going to do about work when her maternity leave was over. They couldn't go on as they had; not now they had Alfie.

The past eight months had been blissfully peaceful since he'd been born. Annie had been too preoccupied with the baby to get involved in anything she shouldn't. She hadn't even mentioned any ghostly visitors from the other side, which had been a relief for him because he really struggled to get his head around the whole speaking to the dead thing.

Now there was another murder. It had been a while since the last murders had happened in Hawkshead, and before that Bowness. This time there had been one in the lovely coastal town of Barrow. It didn't seem as though this had been some jilted lover, yet it was violent enough to be. There weren't any jealous family members around to be involved. Making this a stranger murder, which by rights in this quiet part of the country should be very rare.

Unfortunately for Will, they were more common than the reports would have you believe, and in his own experience they always led to more. The thought that there could be another serial killer on the loose glared in his mind. He tried his best to quash it, but it was no good. He had to take precautions and he needed to keep Annie as far away from all of this as possible. He made up his mind that he wouldn't discuss any of it with her. He wouldn't take an evening paper home with him or have the news on, and he hoped that she would be far too busy with Alfie to pay too much attention to it all.

There was only one flaw in his brilliant plan and that was Jake, who couldn't keep his mouth shut for love nor money. Will would ring him as soon as he was on his own. He didn't want Adele wondering what was going on or knowing too much about his private life just yet. He felt bad enough that he'd thrown her in at the deep end on her first day. He didn't want her worrying that she was going to end up dragged into something deadly. They reached his car and he began the drive back to the station, neither of them talking because they were both lost in their own worlds. The station came into view and Will didn't know whether he felt relieved to be back or not.

'If you don't need me for anything, I think I'll go and collect the CCTV from the shops I rang earlier.'

'That would be brilliant, thanks. If you come inside I'll sort you out with a car.'

They went back in and up to the first floor; Brad was sitting with his feet on the desk playing on his phone. He reminded Will a little of Stu, who had been addicted to that bloody stupid game Candy Crush and his mobile.

'Brad, what are you doing?'

At least he had the decency to look embarrassed when he realised Will was watching him.

'Nothing, boss, just catching up with stuff.'

'Well, do me a favour; take a plain car and drive Adele to pick up the CCTV, please – if you're not too busy.'

Adele pulled a face. 'I can actually drive myself, boss, and I know where I'm going.'

'I know you can, but Brad here is going to become Candy Crush King if we don't give him something to do and I'm not prepared to let him take that title just yet. We all know it belonged to Stu.'

The others, who were all watching the exchange, laughed, glad that Stu wasn't being totally kicked to one side and forgotten about. Brad stuck two fingers up at them all.

'Come on, Adele, I'll give you a grand old tour of Barrow. At least you won't have to watch dead bodies getting cut up with me.'

Will turned to him. 'No, but she will have to listen to your bollocks, which is probably worse. Take everything he says with a pinch of salt. He's a bit of a storyteller – aren't you, Brad?'

Brad shook his head. Turning, he grabbed a set of keys off the whiteboard. He walked off and Adele followed him. Will wanted some time on his own to sit down and think about what he was going to do.

Adele had to walk fast to keep up with Brad.

'Sorry, you don't have to take me. I'm quite capable of collecting the CCTV myself.'

'It's OK, I'm bored anyway. What was it like?'

'Crap. They always are. I hate them.'

'You should have told Will you didn't want to go.'

'It's my first day. I don't want to wind him up.'

'Suppose so; anyway, have you had your dinner yet? I'm starving. We can get some lunch. I know a right good greasy spoon that does cheap bacon butties.'

'No, I haven't eaten yet. Is there a sandwich shop on the way? I'd prefer a ham salad roll or chicken sandwich. My stomach's still a bit off after the PM.'

'Oh yeah, I forgot about that. There's one next door but one to the greasy spoon. So did you find out anything of interest? Like who the killer is? Let me guess, it's her nephew who is the sole beneficiary of her will or the man from the corner shop who had a bit of a crush on her.'

Adele looked at him to see if he was being serious, but he grinned at her and she felt her shoulders relax. He was just winding her up.

'Ha-ha, very funny; come on, take me to get my dinner before

I turn into a bear with a sore head. I don't cope well when I'm hungry. Women my age need feeding on a regular basis.'

It was Brad's turn to look at her and she started laughing. 'Got ya. I'm not some pre-menstrual monster. However, I am hungry, so food first and I'll not be too hard on you.'

They left the building by the rear exit, which led onto the car park full of an assortment of police vehicles and staff cars. Brad led them to a small Ford Focus that had seen better days. The key fob no longer worked and he had to unlock it with the key. She climbed in, brushing a pile of evidence bags and an empty cheese and onion crisp packet off the passenger seat onto the floor. This was a far cry from Will's tidy BMW with the soft leather seats that smelt of his expensive aftershave.

'Bit different from the boss's ride, eh?'

Adele nodded. 'Just a little.'

'Did you know that Will's loaded? He never talks about it, but his dad's rich. He lives in some big, posh house up the lakes. Can't understand why he comes to work at this shithole, to be honest. I know I wouldn't if I had a rich dad; still, suppose you'd have to do something with your time and he is pretty good at his job.'

Adele hadn't known about Will's dad. There was no reason why she should. It was nothing to do with her and it made her feel uncomfortable to hear Brad discussing Will's personal life so freely. It made her wonder what he'd be like down the pub after three pints. He'd probably sing like a canary, which made her decide to only tell him the bare minimum about her family life. She liked her privacy and didn't believe in mixing work and her family together.

'I've known Will a long time. We've never really discussed his private life.'

'Do you know his wife, Annie, then?'

Adele shook her head.

'You must have heard about her, though. She's a bit of an urban legend around here. Everyone knows about her, the stuff that's happened to her. She moved up to Windermere before I started down in Barrow.'

She shrugged, not wanting to get drawn into this conversation. She had heard all about the infamous Annie Graham and felt nothing but sorry for the horrors she'd had to endure.

'Come on, I'm starving.'

He followed the marked police van, which was heading for the huge sliding gates. A loud siren filled the air as the van's blue and red lights flashed, making Adele jump.

'Bloody hell, that's loud when you're so close up to it. I'd almost forgotten how bad it was. It's been a long time since I was a response officer.'

Brad laughed. 'Got to admit I almost shit myself then, and it's not that long since I was the one driving to the IRs. I don't miss it, though. I much prefer working in the office and going to more interesting stuff.'

The van screeched off, leaving them trailing behind it. Brad filled Adele in on the last six months of his life and his latest girlfriend – none of which she was remotely interested in. At least it wasn't gossip about her new colleagues, so she pretended she was listening and nodded her head every couple of minutes.

After ten minutes Brad pulled up outside a café, which was indeed called the Greasy Spoon. Adele smiled. Next door but one was the bakery, which was much more her style. Brad jumped out and she followed. She needed something to eat now she'd got over the shock of the post-mortem. She bought a ham salad baguette, bag of crisps and bottle of water, taking them back to the car. She didn't know how long Brad was going to be so she began to eat. She'd rather be finished before he came back with his greasy food, stinking the car out.

A battered old maroon transit van pulled up half on the kerb behind them, narrowly missing slamming into the back of the car. She stared into the rear-view mirror. If she hadn't been so hungry and the car such a piece of shit, she'd have got out and taken their details. A tall, muscular man got out of the driver's side and a skinny guy who looked as if he needed feeding up got out of the passenger side.

Adele didn't know if it was the fact that they'd nearly rear-ended her without so much as an apology or her copper's instinct kicking in, but there was something shifty about them. She made up her mind to get the registration when they drove off and check them out; she could run a PNC check and get the driver's details. She couldn't see the reg because it was almost parked up the arse of the Focus.

Brad eventually came out carrying a grease-spotted paper bag and a can of Coke. He got into the car and began munching on his huge bun. Adele looked in the mirror to see the two guys coming out of the bakery. They got back into the van and reversed. Taking a pen from her pocket she wrote the reg down on the palm of her hand.

'Do you know either of those two?'

Brad looked in the rear-view mirror then shook his head. 'Why?'

'Just wondered. I wasn't too keen on the way the driver almost rear-ended us.'

He laughed. 'Adele, looking at this car makes me want to rear-end it and I'm driving it, not to mention every criminal in the area knows this is an unmarked police car. Whatever you do, don't take it personally; some people just hate the police and what we stand for in general. Some of the crooks from around here can even reel off the number plates to you for all the plain cars. With brains like that it amazes me how they're not bankers instead of thieves.'

'Same thing, isn't it? Well, almost.' She smiled and carried on eating her lunch. She'd check it out when she got back to the station. Call it her internal radar, but something wasn't right with the occupants of that van. She and Brad ate the rest of their lunch in silence, wiping their hands on some tissues Adele pulled out of her handbag and shared between them.

'Right, where to first?'

She listed the shops she needed to visit in the area of the house where the body had been found. If she was going to be able to switch off when she went home tonight, she needed to focus and stop thinking about Pauline Cook as a person, which was pretty hard to do. Instead she needed to concentrate on the cold, hard facts. It took a bit of getting used to, but once she got into that mindset she found it highly productive. It was the getting into that was the difficult part, when every time she closed her eyes she saw a vision of Pauline's cold, dead body on the steel table in the mortuary.

Chapter Nine

When Wally and Stevie had arrived back at the rundown auction house there had been an auction in mid flow. Unable to unload the van straight away, Stevie had gone to the toilet and Wally had gone inside to watch. Jacko was holding up the contents of the box of circus stuff they'd found in the last house and Wally had watched with interest. If he'd had enough money he would have bought it all himself.

There were a couple of people bidding on it: a woman in her forties and a grey-haired man with a camera around his neck. The woman shook her head at twenty pounds, but the man nodded. Jacko had hit the gavel on the stand. 'Sold.' The man had looked happy with his purchase and Wally hadn't realised that he'd been staring at him until he'd turned around and smiled. Wally nodded then turned to go and empty the van. He wasn't a people person. He never had been. As he was lifting a box out he turned and saw the guy standing right next to him.

'Excuse me, sorry to bother you. Do you do the house clearances?'

Wally nodded.

'Well, I just bought the box of circus stuff and was wondering if you remembered what was in it?'

He stared at the man, wondering what he was talking about.

'Sorry, let me explain myself better. I saw the advert in the paper for the auction and knew I had to come and see it for myself. It's been such a long time since I saw this stuff. It used to belong to a friend of mine.'

Wally felt his stomach begin to churn.

'There was a black and white clown costume that matched the black ruffle and wig. Did you see it when you cleared the house? You see, it's sentimental and I'd really like to find it.'

'I didn't see any costume, mister. Just the stuff in the box; that's it.'

Wally turned away, trying not to betray the panic that was threatening to take over. Could the man tell he was lying? *How can he know you're lying, Walter? You need to stop being so paranoid all the time. You are your own worst enemy.*

'Oh, that's a shame. Never mind. Sorry to have bothered you.'

The man tucked the box under his arm and walked away. Wally felt a hand slap the back of his head.

'Come on, you goon, don't you go upsetting the customers. Let's get this van emptied and we can go home.'

Stevie jumped into the back of the van and began to throw the boxes at him, which Wally carried inside the hall and stacked.

As Stevie pulled up outside Wally's flat he nodded at him. Walter looked back at his dump of a flat and wondered if he really wanted to go back inside on his own.

'Look, thanks for today. You didn't have to buy my breakfast and I appreciate it. Things have been a bit tough lately.'

'Yeah, well, I'm sick of looking at you. Go spend your wages; get yourself some new clothes, Wally, and feed yourself. Go buy some food. I'll let you know if Jacko has any work on next week.'

He nodded. 'I will.'

Stevie drove off and Wally lifted a hand to wave at him. He turned and walked back to the communal front door. As he opened it the strong smell of spices and curry powder hit his nostrils once more – only this time his stomach didn't groan. He'd eaten more today than he had in the past three.

All day his mind kept having flashbacks to last night. He didn't think Stevie would have been so kind to him if he'd known what he'd done. No one would ever believe that it was him; he didn't look like your stereotypical killer. Then again, neither had Ted Bundy, and look at how many women he'd killed; but he'd done it for sexual gratification and that wasn't why Wally had done it. If he wanted to whack off he could do it with the latest copy of *Penthouse* – not over some middle-aged woman's dead body.

No, he was doing it for the right reasons: because the suit had told him to. It was talking to him. Not directly – he wasn't completely crazy. But it was telling what he had to do and he couldn't argue with it because it was right. He wondered what his community psychiatric nurse would say if he told him the suit was controlling him. He'd probably section him and he didn't want to go back to the hospital. He couldn't watch his horror films in there.

As he went into his dingy flat he could hear the couple in the flat above him arguing through the muffled beat of the music from the flat opposite. He wondered why they even bothered being together. They argued all the time. They would fight, throw things around and slam doors until one of them left. The other would chase them and drag them back, where they'd cry and beg each other's forgiveness until the next time, which by Walter's reckoning was usually every two days. Lately they were getting louder, which meant the music from next door got louder as they tried to drown out the sound of the fighting.

Some day he would grow a pair of balls and march up there to tell them to fuck off and pack it in. What would they do if he knocked on the door wearing his suit? Today, however, wasn't that day. Instead he shut and bolted his door, then walked into his bedroom and turned his knackered old CD player on. He turned it up until his music drowned out the sound of next door's and he couldn't hear the words of the arguing couple above him. He threw himself onto his bed. They'd worked pretty hard today and he needed some sleep. Not that he'd get much in this shithole. Still, he lay on his side and closed his eyes, pulling one of his pillows over his head to try and muffle some of the racket.

When he woke up it was dark and quiet, ever so quiet. The music had stopped; so had the couple upstairs. He lay there savouring the peace and quiet until he heard sirens in the distance. His stomach churned. What if they were coming for him? What if they knew what he'd done? He pushed himself up on his elbows. The sirens got louder and he got off the bed to peer out of the window through the yellow, stained net curtain. A police van screeched into the street and he felt his legs turn to jelly. *They knew; they bloody well knew. It was all over before he'd even got the chance to begin.*

Dropping the curtain he stepped away from the window. Thank God he had no lights on so they wouldn't be able to see inside. Panicking, he looked around for a hiding place. He could hide in the bathroom. They'd need a warrant to come inside, wouldn't they? The van came to a halt outside the front of the house and Wally felt every morsel of food he'd eaten earlier on lying heavy in his stomach. His hands were shaking and he was beginning to sweat.

The van doors opened and two big coppers jumped out, slamming them shut. The noise was so loud he thought they were coming straight in for him and he jumped onto the bed, pulling his duvet over him. The front door slammed open and he waited for them to put his door in with the big red metal battering ram any second. Only they didn't. The heavy footsteps ran straight past his door to the stairs and up to the second floor. The relief that washed over him was like a tidal wave. Someone must have reported the arguing couple; it was about time really. He could hear the voices of the coppers as they hammered on the door above him.

'Open the door! Police.'

There was nothing but silence from the flat above him and he was tempted to stick his head out of the front door and shout at them they were too fucking late, but he didn't want to draw attention to himself. Thinking they would leave because there was no one in he turned on his side to go back to sleep. Another van screeched to a halt behind the first and more coppers ran into the communal area.

Wally sniggered under his duvet. *How many fucking coppers does it take to knock on a door?* An almighty crack made him jump up. It was closely followed by another three and the sound of splintering wood. *Shit, they're actually breaking down the door. Hope they haven't got the wrong flat.*

'Would it surprise you if they had?' he said to no one and shook his head. Actually, it wouldn't. It had been in the paper the other year about them putting the wrong door through on a drugs raid, all brawn and no brains.

The door gave and suddenly there was the sound of footsteps racing around above his head. More sirens entered the street and he climbed out of bed. Surely not? An ambulance pulled up this time and he wondered what the hell had gone on upstairs and how he'd missed it. He watched as two paramedics carrying huge bags ran past his window and came through the front door. He was dying to go outside and ask someone what had happened, but he couldn't. He didn't want them to know who he was or why he was asking.

He listened to the sound of the voices above him shouting. There was one guy who must have taken charge because he was shouting out orders at the others. Crap, what the fuck had happened? As he was staring out of the window he saw the woman from the flat above hovering around by the ambulance. There was some shouting as the loud copper came running down the stairs and out of the front door towards her. She lifted up her hand and Wally watched in horror. Clasped in it was a huge butcher's knife. A red dot appeared on her chest. *Oh my God, they're going to taser the bitch.*

More shouting and the woman who was standing waving the knife around fell to the ground, twitching as the barbs from the Taser were fired straight into her. *Jesus Christ, what the hell is going on?* Wally felt as if he was watching some American television show, not staring out of his grimy flat window on a quiet street in Barrow town centre. All chaos broke loose then. There were police everywhere and another ambulance entered the street.

Wally felt his legs give way as he sat back down on his bed. Bollocks, they would come knocking and want his name. What if they could sense he was trouble and then arrested him, just in case he'd done something wrong? Some coppers had a nose for this kind of stuff. He lay down, pulled the duvet back across himself and decided he'd ignore the door if they knocked. That way he wouldn't have to talk to any of the nosy bastards and he wouldn't give himself away.

He heard the voice again. *Walter, you are too paranoid. You need to keep calm if you don't want to give the game away. You need to learn to play it cool.* The downside to having to lie in bed was that it meant he couldn't move around or put the lights on. He had to stay perfectly still. It was beginning to turn into a bit of a circus outside and he giggled. That was a great metaphor. He loved the circus.

There were police everywhere. The ambulance drove away with the girl, who also happened to be handcuffed to one of the coppers. A stretcher was carried down with what he assumed was the guy from upstairs. Something had happened and he'd bet a tenner that the girl had snapped and stabbed him. Which technically Wally thought he deserved, although he couldn't tell the police that because then they'd want to come into his flat and ask questions, too many questions.

It was a shame, though; he thought the girl had guts. Maybe the moron with the loud music next door to him would give a statement about the arguing every night. Mrs Batta would prob-ably tell them everything as well; she lived right next door to them. He was just drifting off to sleep when there was a loud hammering on his door. He felt his heart start racing as he lay there ignoring the noise. There was no way he was speaking to them, unless they didn't stop knocking.

He looked across at his clown suit, which was hanging up drip-drying. They would want to come in and then they would ask him about it. Well, he wasn't going to let them. He got off the bed and took the costume into the bathroom, shutting the door. There was more hammering that he couldn't ignore. Taking a deep breath he walked towards his front door, trying to slow his breathing down and trying not to look as if he was a murderer.

Chapter Ten

Annie kissed Alfie goodbye then turned to Lily.

'Are you sure you want him to stop over? He's been a bit cranky the last few nights.'

'Of course I'm sure. Would I even be asking if I wasn't? You've just fed him and I have everything I need for him. Get yourself home, have a long soak in the bath and a bottle of wine. Spend some time with Will, just the two of you.'

Annie must have looked wistful because Tom picked up on it. 'Is everything OK with you two?'

'Yes, it's fine. Well, apart from him being brought home stinking drunk yesterday after Stu's funeral and me having to put him to bed. We're fine; I'm just wishing he was going to be home on time, that's all. They found a body in a house yesterday and I know fine well they'll have put him in charge of the case. If it's suspicious he won't be home for hours.'

Tom hugged her with his good arm. 'Well, spend some time doing something you want to do until he gets home. Haven't you got some business plans to be drawing up?'

Annie squeezed him, kissed his cheek and smiled. 'Oh yes, I have plenty to do while he's not home.'

Lily gently pushed her arm. 'Good, go then before you change your mind. I want to take Alfie to see some of my friends and show him off. I'll ring you if he won't settle, so don't worry.'

Annie let go of Tom and kissed Alfie once more, then Lily. She left them while she could. She'd sworn she wouldn't be one of those obsessive mothers who never let her kids out of her sight, so why her eyes were filling up with tears was beyond her. She'd never imagined having children could turn a person into such an emotional wreck.

She ran down the concrete steps and got into her car before she changed her mind. The gates were already opening for her so she drove straight out and didn't look back. Once she was on the road back to her house she felt better. It would be nice to have a break from Alfie; as much as she doted on him, she was knackered. In fact she might have a soak in the bath and go to bed for a couple of hours. If Will came home early he wouldn't complain if she was already in bed.

By the time she got home she felt much better. She'd had the radio on full blast and had been singing along to the songs she knew. When her house came into view she smiled to herself. Home sweet home.

She parked the car and pulled out her phone to text Will.

Lily has insisted Alfie stops there tonight. It's just you and me. I'm going for a long soak in the bath and a couple of hours' sleep. Try not to work too late. I love you xx

She sent the text, hoping he would read it and rush home to her. In reality she knew that his phone would either be dead or on silent and he'd be too busy to read her message. Of all the days for a body to turn up, it would be when he was working. Then she crossed herself. *Sorry, whoever you are; that was mean. I'm sure you didn't want to die either. Please ignore that.*

As she went into her house it felt strange not having Alfie tucked under her arm. They'd been pretty much inseparable since his birth. She locked the door and went into the kitchen to get a bottle of water. There were several bottles of her favourite rosé wine on the wine rack and she was tempted to pour herself a large glass. What if Alfie needed her? *Stop it, for Christ's sake. Lily can bring him back. One glass won't hurt.* She pulled the bottle out, which was freezing cold because it had been in there for so long. After unscrewing the cap she took a glass from the cupboard and filled it half full. Taking a sip, she sighed. It tasted so bloody good.

As if it was a magic potion she felt her entire body relax as she sipped some more. She kicked her shoes off, went upstairs and began running a bath. Pouring a generous dollop of her Chanel No 5 bath gel in it she inhaled. She went into the bedroom, took a clean pair of pyjamas from the drawer and her Kindle off the bedside table. She went back into the bathroom where she was going to soak until the water went cold and she was out of wine.

Will felt his phone vibrate in his pocket. He was busy writing up his notes from the post-mortem. He wanted a full-scale set of house-to-house inquiries done in the area. He'd printed up a questionnaire and emailed it to Claire, who he knew would do the rest; she'd been a PCSO around the same length of time as he'd been a detective sergeant so she would know exactly what to do.

He still had no motive for Pauline's murder. There was no sign of a break-in. Her handbag had been undisturbed. When he'd spoken to the CSI they'd told him there were five hundred pounds in the chest of drawers so the money hadn't been a motive. He wanted to know why someone had decided to kill a middle-aged woman so violently and he wanted to know now.

He pulled out his phone and smiled. The thought of Annie alone in the bath made him feel as if he wanted to drop every-thing and drive straight home. In fact he didn't know if there was anything else he could do right now. Matt still hadn't sent his report over and they had no witnesses or a suspect to interview.

He stood up, looking around. It was getting late. Adele and Brad were in the video imaging unit going through the CCTV;

everyone else had knocked off. He'd told them to finish for the night; he wanted them all in bright and early to get a fresh start. His radio, which was turned down on his desk, rang. He looked down at it and groaned.

'Go ahead.'

'Sarge, we need someone from CID at this scene.'

'Which scene?'

'Abbey Road, the block of flats opposite the church. We have a stabbing and it's serious.'

He let go of the button so the officer on the other end couldn't hear him. *Jesus, no fucking way.*

'Right, is there no one else?'

'Nope.'

Will ended the call and looked at his watch; technically he still had two hours left of his shift. He would have to go and take a look. He wished they weren't so thin on the ground for staff. He might just have to pass it on to Kendal if it was serious. He had enough to do. Brad and Adele came out of the office.

'Brad, there's been a stabbing. You need to come with me. Adele, you can get off if you want. We'll go through everything in the morning. Did you find anything?'

Will looked at Brad, who looked like a kid who'd just been told he couldn't have a puppy.

'Boss, I have something on tonight. I can't really work late.'

'Why, what time are you on till?'

'Now. I'm due to finish at six.'

Adele stepped forward. 'I'm on till eight. I'll go with you.'

Will nodded. 'Thanks.'

He didn't bother to look at Brad, who was probably going to the gym or for a game of golf with his mates; his list of priorities was not what your average adult's would be. He walked off and Adele followed him out the front of the station. Adele looked relieved they were going in Will's car.

'Is Barrow normally this crazy?'

'Well, it's crazy, but more the Jeremy Kyle standard of crazy, if you know what I mean. Domestics over my boyfriend slept with my best friend's mother and now she's pregnant sort of stuff. There have been a fair few murders, though, and I suppose you've heard all about them. I think the whole world has heard about the murders in this town. If you don't count the killings, then no, it's not normally this violent. We have our fair share of drug-related incidents, though. Although I suppose it's a sign of the times – too many people watching horror films on Netflix and playing violent games on their Xboxes.'

'Carlisle has been like that for a long time. I suppose it was only a matter of time before Barrow caught up. There are definitely far more murders here, though, for a small town than there are back there for a city.'

Will nodded. 'Completely agree; you know one of the national papers called this the "Murder Capital of England". The rate is unbelievably high compared with most small cities.'

They got into the car and Will drove them to the address where the incident had taken place. An ambulance was just pulling away, as another was pulling up. He shook his head.

'What the hell's going on?'

Adele shrugged. She couldn't get a signal on her mobile tablet so she couldn't load the log to find out. 'These tablets are great when you're in a good area that gets a signal. The rest of the time they're a load of crap and weigh your pockets down.'

'They are very useful for checking your hair and make-up in, though, according to Shona, who uses it more for applying her lip gloss than doing any actual work on.'

Adele laughed. They got out of the car and Will approached the new acting duty sergeant who was looking flustered. The ambulance staff were loading a woman onto a stretcher. She had been lying on the ground.

'Smithy, what's going on?'

'You couldn't make it up, Will, honestly. Apparently she's

stabbed her abusive boyfriend. He's bleeding like a stuck pig and they've had to blue-light him up to the hospital, but according to the paramedics it's not life-threatening.'

He pointed to the stretcher. 'She left the scene then came back waving a bloody great big butcher's knife at officers, so they tasered her and she hit the deck like a sack of shit.'

'Another fine day in paradise then?'

'You can say that again. It's only my second shift as a sergeant. Parker has been a sergeant for three years and never had a day like this. What's going on? Murder scene and a stabbing in less than twenty-four hours. Jesus, I'm going back to being a plod. My life was so much simpler last week.'

'Ah, but think about it. You could have been the officer who tasered her and then you'd have to explain yourself and fill out all those use-of-force forms.'

'Suppose so. Should I leave this with you then?'

Will wanted to tell him 'no' but he couldn't because technically it was down to his department to deal with it.

'We'll take over once your prisoners have been discharged from hospital. Have you done any inquiries yet?'

Smithy shook his head. 'It's literally all just happened.'

'You don't need me to tell you what to do; you know the drill. Get CSI to attend and a couple of PCSOs to scene guard. We'll do some door-knocking while we're here to see if anyone witnessed it. As long as the hospital says he's going to improve and we don't have another corpse, then it should be pretty straightforward.'

'Thanks, Will, I really appreciate your help.'

Will nodded; he pictured Annie alone in the huge bath and groaned inside. He walked towards the front door of the flats followed by Adele. There was no blood around the communal area. The crime scene was contained inside the flat, which made life a whole lot easier. They both took their paper notebooks out of their pockets. Will's was immaculate, not a crease on it; Adele's was crumpled and scribbled all over.

Will took the door to the right and hammered. Adele did the same on the door opposite. There was loud music coming from inside the flat she was knocking on. Will knocked again and the door opened slightly. A pale-faced man opened the door two inches.

'Police. I'm DS Will Ashworth. Nothing to worry about, but there's been a serious incident involving the occupants of the flat above. Did you hear or see anything?'

The man, who was half hiding himself behind his door, breathed out and his shoulders relaxed, which made Will wonder what he was so uptight about. Adele hammered on the door again. The Meat Loaf was turned down and a voice shouted, 'Fuck off, no one's in.'

Will turned to her – a big grin on his face – and she rolled her eyes.

'Police. Open the door.'

There was a sound of heavy footsteps and several locks were unbolted. The door was opened wide. The world's oldest rocker was standing on the other side in a pair of ripped jeans, his stained white vest just covering his larger-than-life beer belly and his grey hair tied back in a ponytail.

'Sorry, love, thought you were those wankers from upstairs. What's up?'

Will had to turn back to hide the smile on his face. The man had opened the door a bit wider and Will couldn't help but compare the two blokes. This one was a skinny thing, with a shock of bright ginger, short, spiky hair.

'So, did you hear or see anything?'

The man nodded. 'Well, I didn't see anything. All I heard was them arguing, again.'

'Do they argue a lot?'

'Yeah, like every other day. I'm kind of used to it now, but I have no idea why they stay together when they obviously don't like each other.'

'Did you hear anything tonight, any threats?'

'Not really.' He lifted his finger and pointed across the gloomy hallway. 'Trev turns his music up really loud to drown the noise out, so I kind of block it all out. It's just normal behaviour. I'm used to it.'

Will nodded. 'What's your name – just for my notes?'

The man squirmed. 'Why do you need that? I didn't see anything and I'm not giving a statement. Have you seen the size of that bloke upstairs? I have to live here; you don't.'

'I don't need a statement. I just need to document that I've spoken to you.'

Just then Adele asked her bloke his name.

'Trevor Parks, love. Do you want my phone number as well?'

Will chuckled, shaking his head.

The strange man, who looked terrified, mumbled, 'Walter Lacey.'

Will scribbled it down and turned away. 'Thanks.'

Adele looked over her shoulder, immediately recognising the man as the one from the van earlier outside the bakery. The door shut and Will crossed to speak to Adele. Her guy had also gone back inside his flat and shut his door. The music started again and Will gave a brief laugh.

'Well, if you get fed up of Aaron, it looks as if Trev will be willing to show you a good time.'

Adele laughed. 'Thanks, I'm telling you, for me, that's about as good as it gets. I'll bear that in mind. Who was that you were speaking to?'

Will looked down at the name he'd scribbled onto his pad. 'Walter Lacey; why, do you know him?'

'Oh, it's nothing really, I just wondered. He was in a van earlier on today that nearly ran into the back of the car while Brad was getting his lunch.'

'Strange guy – if you ask me, he looked as if he'd done something wrong when he opened the door before I even told him what I was there for.'

Adele laughed again, but all the same scribbled his name into the back of her notebook. A white-suited and booted Debs walked into the hallway, her camera in one gloved hand and her bag of tricks over her shoulder.

'Is it really bad? My stomach's a bit off today.'

She directed her question at Will, who shrugged. 'I haven't been in yet. I was waiting for you to come do your stuff and tell me about it. I'm so hungover; I want to go home and collapse. How much did we drink?'

'Far too much, that's how much.'

'How come you're working today?'

'It didn't seem right asking for any more time off; I can't exactly say I'm grieving because I've got a guilty conscience. Besides, I'd rather be working with you on the goriest, bloodiest crime scenes you can find me, because I love it so much. Not.'

Will smiled at her. 'You just can't resist my charm, can you?'

She shook her head and walked off. 'If I chuck my guts up I'm blaming you, Ashworth. What were you thinking buying whisky shots like there was no tomorrow?'

'I've been asking myself that very same question all day.'

Will went outside. Adele followed.

'I suppose we better put some protective clothing on and go take a look when Debs has finished.'

'I suppose we'd better. Tell me, do you ever get any ordinary, run-of-the-mill kind of CID jobs or had I better prepare myself to be working all the violent crimes this town has to throw at us?'

He paused to consider her question. 'I could lie and make you feel good about your transfer down to sunny Barrow; but I can't, so you better prepare yourself.'

'I was afraid you were about to say that.'

Annie stayed in the bath until her skin was wrinkled and the water was too cold to be relaxing. She'd already let the plug out three times and refilled it. After drying herself she smothered her skin in her favourite body lotion and wrapped her dressing gown around her.

It wasn't late; in fact, Will officially didn't finish work until eight so she still had another couple of hours before he'd be home. She was hungry so she went downstairs to make a sandwich. She should really cook some proper tea, but she couldn't be bothered. Cooking was her least favourite thing, so she made a plate of sandwiches for her and one for Will. Covering his up and putting it in the fridge, she was hoping that he might have already eaten at work.

Often, when there was a murder case, he would work late. His team would stay on past their finishing time and get a takeaway. As she sat at the breakfast bar picking at her chicken sandwich and salt and vinegar crisps, she thought about the house with the blue door and shuddered. Why did it keep coming back to her? What was it about that door that kept drawing her in?

She knew that, sometimes, when a person was killed or died suddenly they got stuck and couldn't pass on because they didn't realise they were dead. Did the poor woman whose body had been found yesterday even realise she was dead? Annie hoped so. She couldn't get a fix on her at all. Normally she was quite good at making contact. Something was stopping her.

Closing her eyes, she tried to think about the inside of the house and the figure whose eyes she had been looking out of. It was a strange sensation. Why had she been dragged inside this house? She let out a loud yawn. Staring at her phone she thought about sending a quick text to Lily to see how Alfie was, but she didn't want her to think she didn't trust her, because she did.

Not having the energy to eat any more of her sandwich she pushed the plate to one side and stood up. Tucking her phone into her pocket she decided to go to bed. Hopefully sleep would come fast and when she next woke up Will would be there, next to her and naked. It had been too long since she'd had him all to herself without Alfie and his sixth sense making him cry out whenever they got any further than a quick kiss.

She left the landing light on, not scared of being in the house on her own, but something was unsettling her and she didn't know what. She turned off her bedroom light and left the door ajar so the light shone through. She pulled back the duvet and sank onto the soft mattress. It was unsettling having the house so quiet.

She peered at Alfie's Moses basket, which was next to her side of the bed. A feeling of longing filled her chest. She missed him so much. It was strange to be apart from him for any length of time. Her life had come full circle and she was now one of those mums who never let her child out of her sight, although she did have a very good reason for that. Before any bad thoughts could fill her mind she pushed them away. *Not tonight – Alfie is fine, Will is fine and I'm fine. Go to sleep while you can, Annie. You're getting wrinkles with all the sleep deprivation.* Turning away from Alfie's crib she snuggled up and closed her eyes.

Summer 1950

The caravan of circus trailers and trucks was finally packed and ready to begin the long journey north. The next stop was Manchester. Gordy had turned to take one last look at the site where the big top had been. The only reminder was the crushed patch of now-blackened grass underneath the trampled-in sawdust and the rubbish that was swirling around in the breeze.

They were some time into the journey before Colin stirred. He had begun to mumble under his breath and Gordy had sat with him, holding his hand until he'd sat up, confused until the realisation of where he was and who he was with sunk in.

'How are you feeling?'

Colin shrugged. 'Off. Where are we? Are we moving?'

'Well, I have some good news for you. I spoke to your mum

and she said it's OK for you to come with us and be a part of the circus. She even packed you a suitcase with your stuff in.'

He pointed to the battered case he'd stowed under the seat.

'She said you're to have a good time, to work hard and – when you're ready – to learn how to be a clown like me.'

Colin had stared at Gordy, not quite sure what he was hearing was true. He was clearly excited that he was going to learn to be a clown and was going away with the circus, but he looked worried.

'Are you sure she said that, Gordy? Because it doesn't sound like something she'd say. She shouts – a lot – all of the time at me. "Colin, get me fags; Colin, put the washing out; Colin, get me beer!" Who will she shout at now if I'm not there?'

Gordy thought back to the last image he had of Colin's mum lying on the bed like some broken, bloodied rag doll and smiled.

'She really did. She said she was sorry, that she knew she gave you a hard time and wanted to make up for it by letting you go.'

Colin accepted his explanation without further questions. 'I think that's why I'd like being a clown. No one would know I was dumb, would they? Underneath the face paint I'd be just like everyone else.'

Gordy nodded. 'You will, Colin, I promise you will.'

And he had every intention of keeping his promise. Gordy stole a glance at Colin who was staring out of the window. His mouth was open slightly and a dribble of saliva balanced on his lips, ready to begin the slide down them at any time. He knew this was the best idea he'd ever had.

When the circus finally arrived at the wasteland in Manchester, Colin was once more fast asleep with his feverish head leaning against the cool glass window. Gordy left him to it as he went and unhooked his caravan from the truck; first thing in the morning he was going to start teaching the lad how to be a clown. He was also going to try and bury the desire burning inside his chest that was telling him to kill someone, anyone. It didn't matter who it was; if the opportunity presented itself he would take it.

Until then he would focus on doing what he loved and teaching Colin what he knew.

The next few hours were spent in a blur of unloading trucks and trailers. The sounds of the animals filled the air along with the cursing from the men who were all working flat out. The more they did now while the sun was still setting, the less they'd have to do tomorrow when it was glaring down on them, burning their skin and making them sweat.

Colin and Gordy pitched in along with everyone else, working themselves into a sweat. Colin was feeling much better than he had the night before. When they'd finished and gone back to the caravan to get washed up and have something to eat, Colin had spent ten minutes standing in front of Gordy's clown costume, which was hanging up over the small bedroom door and was still damp.

'Why is it wet?'

'I had to wash it. Those bright lights in the centre ring make you sweat like a bitch. No good being a smelly clown. Kids won't like that, will they?'

Colin shrugged. He pointed to some rust-coloured spots that Gordy had scrubbed and soaked, but still hadn't been able to remove.

'What you got on it?'

'Oil off the generator.'

Gordy turned away. He'd been tempted to say 'your mother's blood', but he hadn't. Colin might freak out and start screaming if he thought the unloving, cold, hard bitch was dead.

'I'm hungry.'

'I bloody know you are. Jesus, give me a chance, kid. Your mother was right when she said you never stop eating.'

Gordy paused. He'd been careful not to strike up a conversation about Colin's mum in case he decided he no longer wanted to be in the circus and wanted to go home. 'Do you want to try the costume on when you've had some tea?'

Colin smiled. His whole face lit up as he nodded his head violently up and down.

The stench seeping through the gap in the open window was what had first made the neighbours call the police to the small terraced house. The constable who had been out walking his beat arrived. Mrs Turner – who had worked in the abattoir – led the big, burly man around to the back of the house and the opened back door.

'It's been open for three days now, just keeps blowing backwards and forwards in the breeze. The other night it drove me round the bloody bend, slamming every five minutes. I sent our Bobby round to tell Colin to sort it out, but there's no sign of Colin so Bobby just pulled it shut. No one's seen him since the day the circus left town.'

'And does this Colin live here on his own?'

'No, he's only seventeen, but he's simple in the head. He's got a head full of slamming doors.' She twirled her finger at the side of her head. 'His old slapper of a mother should be around, though. She only goes to the pub and back. I haven't heard her screeching for Colin either and she normally does that every half an hour. Something's not right. There's a terrible smell coming from that house. Something's died in there.'

Constable York took out his truncheon as he walked through the old, knackered gate to push the back door open. The stench of decay filled his nostrils and he gagged. 'Bloody hell, something's dead in there all right.' He stepped back.

'That's what I said. Aren't you going to go in and have a look?'

His ruddy cheeks had paled significantly in the last thirty seconds. He nodded. 'Yes, I suppose I should. You wait out here.'

'You can say that again; I'm not going inside there. It stinks bad enough from out here. I can't imagine how bad it will be in there. Poor Colin, I hope he's OK.'

The constable tugged his handkerchief from his pocket and wrapped it around his nose and mouth, then he stepped inside, trying desperately not to breathe through his nose. The kitchen was dirty – a sink full of unwashed pots – and there were big bluebottles buzzing around everywhere. He wafted a couple of them out of the way with his hand and walked through the living room to the stairs. As he stepped on the bottom tread he heard a humming, vibrating noise and paused to listen.

The smell was much stronger and, whatever it was, the answer to his question was waiting for him up there. The humming got louder the higher he climbed, and he reached the top landing, looking around to see what the source of the noise was. There were three doors: two of them were shut and one was ajar. A bluebottle flew out of the gap in the door and he headed towards that one first. The stench was horrific and his stomach heaved.

Forcing himself to move until he was outside the door, he paused and listened to the humming noise, which was much louder in there. He wondered if there was some kind of generator on inside of the bedroom causing the noise. Pushing the door open with his truncheon he shouted, 'Police.' And didn't speak again, when he realised what the sound had been. A huge black wriggling mass on the bed swarmed and filled the air.

Screaming louder than he'd ever heard anyone scream in his entire life, he let the door swing shut as he turned. His mouth filled with hot liquid and he ran down the stairs. Within seconds he was out of the back door, which he pulled shut behind him. Unable to hold it in any longer he bent over double and retched into the brown, shrivelled-up rose bush at the side of the back door. Hot vomit spewed everywhere and his legs turned to jelly. He reached out and relished the feel of the cold, damp, rough brick wall against his hand as he used it to keep himself upright. *What the hell was that?*

'What was it? Was it bad? Is Colin OK?'

The questions from the neighbour swam around inside his brain and he felt as if he was looking at her through a thick fog. He was going to faint; he needed to stop it now. The sergeant would have his guts for garters and he'd never hear the last of it. A small boy appeared with a glass of water and with a shaking hand the constable took it, nodding his thanks. Drinking the cold liquid down in one gulp to freshen his mouth and wake him out of the almost drunken stupor he felt as if he was in, he looked at the woman who was watching him with her hands on her hips.

'I don't know what it was – too many.' He retched once more; he would never get that image out of his mind ever again. Those bluebottles had been feasting on whatever or whoever it had been lying there rotting on the bed.

'I need my sergeant to come and take a look.'

'Bobby, make yourself useful instead of gawping at the constable. Go round to the station and tell whoever is in charge to get here now.'

The lad, who had been one of the boys teasing Colin the first day the circus arrived in town, took off running. He was scared for his friend. They'd been mean to Colin that day and he was scared in case something bad had happened to him.

By the time he'd returned with the sergeant and inspector, Constable York had got his bearings. His legs weren't as shaky and he tried to stand up straight. His sergeant, who was a right grumpy bastard, looked at him.

'Thank you for your concern, madam. We have everything under control now. If you would be so kind as to go back inside the house, we can do what we have to.'

Rita Turner tutted, shook her head and walked towards her house. She looked at York and muttered, 'We'll see how under control he has it when he's been inside.'

She winked at him and he smiled. Then she disappeared into her back kitchen and he heard her yell, 'Bobby, get yourself in here now! Let the coppers get on with it.'

Bobby, who had been peering over the fence, turned and ran to the back door before his mum dragged him in and gave him a clip around the ear.

Some hours later there was a knock on Rita's back door and she opened it to see Constable York, who was a much better colour than the last time she'd seen him.

'Can I come in, Rita? I need to speak to both you and Bobby.'

She stepped aside to let him in. 'Any news?'

He looked around to see if Bobby was anywhere to be found.

'It's OK. He's gone out to play down the park with his mates. I told them to keep out of the way for a couple of hours.'

'Good. Well, yes, there is news. There is a body in the back bedroom; it's badly decomposed so it's hard to tell, but we think it's probably Margery Lister.'

Rita nodded. 'What about Colin?'

'Well, there's no sign of him. We checked out his bedroom and his wardrobe door and chest of drawers were open. It looked as if he packed his stuff and left in a hurry. Do you know where he could have gone?'

Rita shook her head when Bobby came rushing through the door.

'I know where he is, mam.'

'No you bloody don't, you little fibber. How would you know where he is and who told you to come back already?'

'Everyone knows where he is – he's run away with the circus. No one's seen him since the circus left town.'

York, who was busy writing it all down, looked up at Bobby.

'I see – and do you know when the circus left town?'

He counted on his fingers.

'Sun, Sat, Fri, Thursday night was the last show. It had all packed up and left on Friday morning.' Bobby crossed his arms, smiling at his mam.

'You better not be fibbing or you'll be for it when your father gets home.'

'I'm not. I swear I'm not. Colin loved it. He kept hanging around with that clown called Tufty.'

'Thank you, Bobby, that's very useful. We need to find Colin and make sure he's OK and also to tell him about his mam.'

Rita shook her head. 'That's a shame, really. She was . . . Bobby cover your ears or go back outside.'

Bobby lifted his hands and covered his ears as he darted back out of the front door.

'Well, I don't like to speak ill of the dead, but she was a drunken old tart who would sleep with anyone for a packet of fags and some cider. Poor Colin is probably much better off without her.'

'I know, but we need to tell him. We don't know whether he's alive or dead. Until we find out, we need to know what happened and he might have been the last person to see her alive.'

Rita sighed. 'I suppose so, poor lad. Even if he did snap and kill her I don't blame him one little bit. She made his life a misery.'

York nodded, not sure he should be agreeing that the woman deserved to die because she'd been a crap mother. There were plenty of those around. Hell, if the bodies started stacking up because of that, there wouldn't be enough cemeteries to put them all in.

'Right, well, I'll be off. Oh, you don't know what that circus was called, do you? Or where it might have been going?'

'Darlin', I haven't got a clue. I don't agree with them myself, keeping those beautiful wild animals in captivity like that. The kids out the front will be able to tell you, though. They couldn't bloody keep away.'

Chapter Eleven

2016

Annie felt the bed creak and the mattress sink down as Will climbed into bed next to her. The smell of lemon shower gel and mint toothpaste filled her nostrils. She turned to face him.

'What took you so long? I've been waiting.'

He pulled her close to him. 'Do you have any idea how far away we live from Barrow when I need to get home to you in a hurry?'

She laughed. 'Yes, believe it or not I do. How are you feeling now?'

'Almost human – it's been a long day. Adele's been a great help although I feel a bit bad because I ended up completely throwing her in at the deep end.'

'Still short-staffed then?'

His lips found hers, signalling the end of talk about work. When she came up for air she gasped. 'Glad to see you still have it then.'

'What?'

'The ability to leave me breathless.'

He pulled her even closer and she closed her eyes as he softly kissed her throat.

***

In her dream Annie was in a confined prison cell. She looked around her, the panic building in her chest as she tried to breathe. She could hear a man's voice not too far away from her, praying. Through the bars she could see the outline of a priest she didn't know. She knew it wasn't Father John because it was a different voice that was reading from the black Bible. Standing in front of him were two prison guards. What was she doing in a prison? The guard standing to the left opened the cell door and she rushed towards him, glad to be let out. He grabbed her, pulling her hands behind her back. She felt the cold, biting metal as a pair of handcuffs snapped around her wrists.

'What are you doing? Get off me. Why am I here? I want a solicitor. I'm a policewoman not a criminal.'

Her pleas fell on deaf ears as she was dragged into a room directly behind the cell she'd been in. She had no concept of what was about to happen until a bag was placed over her head, obscuring her vision. Thick, coarse rope was thrown around her neck. She thrashed around, trying to free herself from her captors. There was an enormous boom as the trapdoors directly underneath her feet opened and crashed against the prison walls.

She woke up just before she dropped into the dark space below her and choked to death on the end of the hangman's noose. She sat up in bed, unable to breathe. Her throat felt constricted as if she'd actually been strangled. Her sweat-drenched hair was plastered to her head. Lifting one shaking hand she felt her neck to see if it was injured. Will opened his eyes and turned on the bedside lamp. He stared at her.

'Bad dream?'

She nodded, not trusting her voice to speak. Why was she dreaming about being executed?

'Want to talk about it?'

He rubbed her back with his warm hand, but she felt ill and pulled away from him. She needed to get her bearings. That wasn't just a dream; it felt as if she'd been there and was about to die.

She stood up and whispered, 'No thanks, you go back to sleep. I just need a drink.'

Will lay back down, closing his eyes. Almost instantly a gentle snore came from his direction. Annie envied his ability to drift off so fast no matter what; amazed that her voice still worked and her voice box hadn't been crushed, like in her dream, she went into the bathroom where she splashed cold water all over her face. Her hands were still trembling as she picked up the towel to pat her face dry.

Turning on the light she studied her neck. There were no marks or bruises, yet it was hurting her. Maybe she was coming down with a sore throat and her busy mind had turned it into a nightmare. She went downstairs to get an ice-cold glass of water. She couldn't shake the feeling that some impending doom was coming her way, which was ridiculous. *Get a grip, woman. It's just a bad dream, not the end of the world. Besides, we stopped hanging people in England in 1964, so stop it.*

Annie went back upstairs and climbed into bed next to Will. She didn't snuggle up with him because she doubted she was going to go back to sleep again and didn't want to disturb him too much. Picking up her phone, she checked to make sure there were no missed calls from Lily. Her screen was blank.

Closing her eyes she tried to block out the horror of that dream, but it didn't want to leave. It was there, in vivid Technicolour: the dirty grey walls of the cell, the hard mattress with the scratchy, grey woollen blanket on the low, cramped bed. She could even smell the rope that had been looped around her neck and then tightened. Annie lay on her side watching Will's chest rise and fall, hoping it would have a hypnotic effect and lull her back to sleep.

The vibrating of Will's alarm on his phone woke her with a start; she was surprised she'd dropped off and thankful there had been no more bad dreams. Will groaned and she leant over and kissed him.

'At least you don't have a hangover today and you can go fight criminals with a clear mind.'

He turned to look at her. 'I'd rather stay here with you; it's much less stressful.'

She laughed. 'Is that so? You don't normally say that – and look at that, are you pleased to see me?'

She pointed to his tight black boxer shorts.

'I'm always pleased to see you.'

'Rubbish, you need the toilet. You're not fooling me, Ashworth. Come back after you've been and we'll see how pleased you are.'

She jumped out of the bed before he could pull her back down. His phone vibrated.

'Bloody hell, I wish they'd bother someone else. Why does it always feel as if I'm the one on call?'

'Because you nearly always are, and because you're the best detective they have in the whole of Cumbria, thanks to my help.'

He swung his legs out of bed. After answering his phone he mouthed, 'I'd rather you didn't give me any more help.'

She shoved his back and left him to his phone call. She didn't want to know what it was about. That way she was avoiding any involvement on her part. Her throat was parched and still felt raw. She went into the bathroom to check no bruising had developed overnight. It wasn't black or blue – much to her relief. She would have no idea how to explain that one to Will and he'd only worry. He much preferred their life without any drama of the psychic kind.

She went downstairs and opened the fridge, taking out eggs, bacon, mushrooms and tomatoes for Will. Busying herself, she scrambled the eggs and grilled everything else. Her stomach rumbled. Thinking she wouldn't have much of an appetite after that horrible dream, she surprised herself as she plated up two huge helpings of breakfast.

Will came down dressed in his charcoal suit with a white shirt and grey spotted tie. He always looked smart for work; she loved that about him. He always took great care over his appearance. She could count the number of times on one hand when he'd been called out and actually gone in wearing casual clothes.

'You look sexy as hell. I love you in a suit; it does all sorts of things to my hormones.'

He laughed. 'You know they all say that.'

Annie picked up the magazine she'd left on the breakfast bar and threw it in his direction. 'Still think you're a lady-killer, eh?'

'I'd like to think I still had it, but I only have eyes for you and I'm not sure lady-killer is the appropriate term. More of a dashing bit of eye candy.'

Annie choked on the mouthful of coffee she'd just swallowed and he crossed the room to rub her back. He leant close to her ear and whispered, 'You know those days are long gone, don't you? I feel old and knackered and I'm sure I have more wrinkles today than I had yesterday. But you won't have to know about that for some time yet because you're far too young to have to worry about lines and feeling tired.' He kissed her cheek.

'You'll never look old to me and I don't care if you lose all of your hair and have a thousand wrinkles.'

He sat down to eat his breakfast and she tried her best not to ask, but she couldn't stop herself. 'Should I ask who was on the phone or do I not want to know?'

'There was a serious stabbing last night. Luckily the guy – who deserved it, to be honest, from what I've heard about him – is stable this morning, and it looks like he's going to improve. But it's just been made a lot easier by his partner, who we arrested after she'd been tasered for brandishing a knife at officers. She has made a full and frank confession an hour ago. So it's pretty much cut and dried. Hopefully the judge will look at the past history and take it all into account. I was thinking we were going to be tied up all day with that as well as looking for Pauline Cook's killer.'

'Any leads?'

'Not really. From what we know she wasn't a very social person.

The only thing she did was visit the hospice twice a week to sit with the patients to give their families a break. It seems as if she was one of life's nice people.'

'That's a shame. How awful; bless her. Well, I hope you find them soon.'

Annie wanted to tell him about her dream, how she thought there was some connection between her dreaming about Pauline's house and her murder, but she didn't. Instead she kept quiet as he finished his breakfast and put his plate in the sink, leaning over to kiss her cheek.

'I'll see you both later. I don't know what time, to be honest. I'll probably be late because I want everything taking as far as we can today and someone arrested before anything else happens.'

She smiled at him, waiting until the front door shut before she sighed. What was she going to do with herself all day? Her phone beeped and she looked at it, smiling.

Alfie's fine, been a good boy. He's playing with his granddad so I'll bring him home around one if that's OK? Xx

Good and thank you. That's brilliant xx.

After making herself a fresh mug of coffee she walked into the small snug, which was set up as a home office. First of all she searched the internet for any news about Pauline Cook. She'd wanted to ask Will about what had happened, but had been too scared in case he confirmed what she'd seen. Maybe she would tonight. Did she really see the clown figure or had it all been a bad dream?

Nothing much came up about Pauline Cook apart from the newspaper reports of her death. She didn't have a Facebook page or Twitter account. A local newspaper article about her helping out at the hospice and getting the bouquet of the week from the staff there was lovely. Annie felt her eyes begin to swim with hot, salty tears. What had she done to deserve to die like this? What was it all about? What was the connection to the man in the clown suit?

She pictured him in her mind. It didn't look like something a modern clown would wear. It almost looked faded and the white stripes had been yellowed as if the material was very old. Where on earth would you find a vintage clown suit? She did an eBay search, but all that came up were the tacky, cheap fancy dress costumes. Pages of them. That material had looked as if it was expensive – maybe silk or heavy-duty satin. Not some cheap, paper-thin, badly made costume.

Feeling frustrated she went to get some biscuits from the tin. As she sat nibbling on the custard creams she typed 'vintage clowns' into the search engine and watched as a page of images loaded before her. There were lots of black and white photographs of different clowns. As she scrolled down the page, one wearing a very similar costume to the one she'd dreamt about appeared.

Clicking on the image she felt her fingers grip the mouse while she inhaled at the headlines: 'Tufty the Killer Clown Sentenced to Death'. She clicked on the next link and a huge black and white news headline filled the screen with a grainy, black and white photo of a scary-looking clown who'd been caught on the run. He was wearing the exact same costume as the killer inside Pauline Cook's house.

The hairs on her arms stood on end. He'd killed the mother of a teenager who he'd befriended as well as his own parents. Was he still alive? Surely not. If he was, he'd still be in prison. She looked at the date: 1950. In the picture of the man without his make-up, he looked so young and scared. Annie shuddered at the thought of it all; she typed in 'Tufty Hanging' and was horrified when the headlines loaded.

The jury had found him guilty and within thirty days of his capture he'd been hanged in Strangeways Prison in Manchester. She put her hands together as if she was about to pray and pushed her chair away from the computer. There had to be some connection. That dream last night – she'd been there in a prison cell about to be hanged when she'd woken up. Oh dear God, she didn't want to be haunted by a creepy killer clown.

Sending the pages she'd saved to the printer, she waited for them to come out then slipped them inside one of the paper files in the drawer. She should tell Will. This could be really important to his case. The only thing stopping her would be the look on his face when she did. He would be so upset at her for getting involved. It wasn't her fault, though. What was she supposed to do?

For the first time in months she thought about Derek Edmondson, the psychic who'd first passed on the warnings from the other side when her life had gone to shit three years ago. She wondered if she should try and speak to him. The pair of them had ended up fighting for their lives against Henry Smith – inside the once-beautiful Victorian mansion that Jake had nicknamed the Ghost House.

Her phone rang in her pocket and she jumped. If it was Derek she would pass out with shock. Jake's name flashed up on the screen and she smiled for the first time in an hour.

'Hello.'

'Good morning, my little bundle of fun. How are you?'

'Erm, I'm OK, I guess. Why?'

'No particular reason. I'm on my own in the van and bored out of my tiny mind. Do you know what the new policy is, which, if you ask me, is a load of shite?'

'No, I don't, but I'm sure you're about to enlighten me.'

'Single crewed, single bloody crewed at all times. How fucking boring is that? Can't even grab a PCSO 'cause they've all been told the same. No point in you coming back to work ever again is there, really, if we won't be able to work together?'

Annie laughed. 'That's terrible. You'll go mad on your own for ten hours. Do you have half an hour spare? I have a bit of a problem that needs a nice friendly policeman to sort it out, if you're available?'

'Not sure your husband will be so agreeable about me sorting out your little problems, Mrs Ashworth. How many times have I told you I'm spoken for?'

'You have a filthy mind, Jacob; wash your mouth out with soap and water.'

'I'd rather swill it out with one of those coffees out of that fancy coffee machine that's sitting gathering dust on your kitchen worktop. Have you got any cakes?'

'No, but because I love you so much, I'll go into the village and get some from the café. Or you could just meet me there instead. I haven't seen Jo for a while. It will be nice to have a catch-up.'

'Now you're talking, as long as grumpy guts Cathy doesn't figure out what I'm up to. She's in a right foul mood today; either she and Kav have fallen out or she's hungry.'

'Throw her a Snickers, or even better, if you were to take her a slice of fresh cream cake back she'd cheer up no end.'

'God, I miss working with you. That's such a brilliant idea. We are such a great team!'

'Yes, we are. What time do you think you'll be here?'

'Providing no one gets killed – in half an hour.'

'See you soon.'

She ended the call, glad to have something to take her mind off the predicament she'd managed to get herself into yet again.

The briefing room was full. Will was glad to see the chief super sitting at the back, staring down at his phone and not standing at the front commanding everyone's attention. Maybe their little spat had knocked him down a peg or two – whatever his reason, it didn't matter now. What mattered was finding Pauline Cook's killer. He stood up in front of the rows of detectives and officers who had been assigned to his team.

'Right, let's get started. We have no close family members or disgruntled ex-boyfriends or even a current boyfriend to be exact. So everything is pointing to a stranger killing, which we all know are the hardest to solve. We need to figure out how she was picked out as his victim.'

A hand went up. 'So we know it's a him?'

Will shook his head. 'Not for definite; it's just a turn of speech, Brad. We've seen our fair share of violent females so we know exactly what they're capable of.' His mind flashed back to that day at the Lake House last year when Megan had plunged a knife into his kidney and almost killed him. The room was quiet as everyone waited for him to continue. He picked up his mug of coffee and took a sip, which gave him a few seconds to compose himself. All eyes were watching him.

'Brad, you carry on going through the CCTV footage that Adele procured yesterday. Adele, you and I are going to speak to the staff at the hospice and the neighbour who seemed to be the closest thing to a friend Pauline had. Gavin you and the rest of the search team can go through the house again now that CSI have finished. According to her neighbour, it doesn't look as if anything was stolen, but we need to see if there was something in there we've missed. Was there a wad of cash hidden under the floorboards in the bathroom?'

A chorus of 'Yes, boss' echoed around the room. Will knew they were clutching at straws because at this very moment in time they had nothing. No clues, no links, no failed romances. He was hoping that Matt's post-mortem report would come up with something, or that the forensic samples that had been taken would lead to a match.

What they needed was a bloody miracle because the pressure was on. The longer it took to come up with some sort of evidence or connections, the more difficult it would be to catch her killer. What really bothered Will was the fact that they could potentially have another serial killer on their hands and it filled him with dread. Gavin took to the centre of the room to brief his team and Will stepped to one side. His phone vibrated in his pocket and he pulled it out. He saw Matt's name and walked to the door, excusing himself.

'Morning, William; how are you?'

'Morning, Matt; I'll be a whole lot better if you tell me you found some damning evidence yesterday after we left and that you know who did it.'

'Ah, if only I did. I've been thinking about the injuries; in fact, I've been thinking about nothing but Pauline Cook's injuries. I think whoever did this was a virgin killer. They haven't done anything like it before, at least not on another human being anyway.'

'Why?'

'A lot of the wounds were . . . I don't know how best to explain it. They were messy. They weren't smooth like someone who was confident in what they were doing would be. I think that whoever did it was very scared and nervous, so much so that their hands could have been shaking with each fresh stab wound.'

'So this was their first killing?'

'Well, I can't say that officially, can I? Because I can't say they haven't killed at the opposite end of the country. This is more of a between you and me case study. I think that they were very scared to begin with and they might still be very scared about what they've done. I also think that the more they sit and think about it, the more the disgust and horror will eventually turn into a desire to do it again – and I think that they will do it again. Off the record, of course.'

Will walked into his office and shut the door. Sitting down at his desk, he sighed.

'I think you're right, Matt. I can't put my finger on it, but I don't think he's going to stop at this. We have no motive whatsoever at the moment and no suspects. It might take a while before he finds another victim and plucks up the courage to do it again, but that's both of us who think that he *will* kill again. Bollocks.'

Will leant forward on his desk, his head leaning on one hand to support it and the other holding the phone to his ear.

'We need to find out how he knew Pauline. How did he get into her house? There's no obvious signs of a forced entry. All the windows and doors were shut.'

'What's to say she didn't leave a window open? It's been warm of an evening this past week. He could have climbed through, waited for her and left through the front or back door.'

'I'll get the search team to check all the window frames again. Thanks, Matt.'

'You're welcome; that's what I'm here for. How are Annie and the baby?'

'Good, both of them are great to be exact. As long as she keeps out of this and any other murder case for the rest of our lives we should be just fine.'

Matt laughed on the other end of the phone and ended the call. Will looked through the glass partition at the whiteboard where Pauline Cook's picture was stuck up with a lump of Blu-Tack. Whoever had put it there hadn't even bothered to make sure it was straight. He walked out to peel it off and stick it back much straighter. It was all about respect.

He stood in front of her picture, staring into her kind green eyes. If she didn't go out or have many friends and the only place she worked was at the hospice, it had to have been there that she'd met her killer. A voice in his head whispered: *or on the bus, at the corner shop, in Tesco, at the petrol station. She could have met him anywhere.* He went back into his office, closed the door and sat down again. Adele knocked and he beckoned her in.

She came in and shut the door behind her. 'Morning, are you OK?'

He nodded. 'I think we should go to speak with as many staff at the hospice as we can. We need a list of all the families whose dying relatives she's sat with and the staff there. At least then Shona can check them all on the system and see if anyone rings any alarm bells, see if there's any previous.'

'It could have been an angry family member; maybe she told

125

them to have a break and the patient died while they weren't there.'

'Could be. Would be a line of inquiry worth pursuing, wouldn't it. Would a grieving relative be so angry they'd go and kill a good Samaritan for only trying to help them through their suffering, though?'

'Will, you know as well as I do there is no rhyme or reason to any of this needless violence. People can flip over the slightest thing. Come on, I'll buy you a decent coffee if you direct me to the nearest Costa on the way. There's no milk in the fridge and Brad is sulking because he said it was your turn to bring some in.'

This cheered him up and he smiled. 'Tough, I completely forgot. Brad's a big boy. He can cross the road and go to Asda without an adult now. I won't say no to a proper coffee, though.'

Chapter Twelve

Walter sat in his room, cursing the couple who lived above him. Because of their inability to live with each other like normal people, the coppers now knew who he was. They knew his name and address. *What else do they know, Walter? Do they know what you've done?* The voice from across the room was loud and clear. He didn't even look over at the clown suit, hoping that if he ignored it the voice would shut up.

He stood up and began pacing, trying to calm himself down. He was overreacting. They didn't know anything about him or what he'd done, did they? How could they? He'd never been in trouble with the police, although there had been times when his schizophrenia had almost landed him in it. But he'd always taken his medicine like a good boy so he didn't go completely batshit crazy.

He stole a glance at the suit. *Then why are you hearing the voices coming from it?* He shrugged; there was nothing to link him to Pauline. Apart from the hospice and the fact she'd been nice to his gran whenever he'd visited. *Yes, Walter, what on earth were you thinking? How could you do that to a lovely woman whose only crime was wanting to help?*

He lifted his hands to his ears, covering them up and trying to block out the sound of his gran's voice inside his head. She would be so disappointed with him; he saw his reflection in the small, cracked mirror on top of the chest of drawers and turned away. He didn't want to look at himself. He was a disgrace. He could feel the wave of anger rising in his chest.

He'd done it because it was the right thing to do. She was going to die anyway, wasn't she? He'd just given her a helping hand, saved her the months of misery. When that fat, ugly fuck from upstairs came home from the hospital he was going to finish off what his stupid bird hadn't for getting him into this mess. He was another waste of space and Walter would be doing the world a favour by getting rid of him. That would teach him a lesson.

He just hoped he was out of hospital before the coppers realised that he'd killed Pauline, because he was going to enjoy killing the wife-beating motherfucker. See how big and hard he was when he had a six-foot clown with a huge carving knife standing over him; see if he begged for forgiveness. Walter felt the anger and rage take over, blotting out the guilt that had been racking his body. He felt the shame slip away.

That was better. What he'd done was done. Maybe he wouldn't feel so bad about killing wankers – and if that bastard Jacko didn't pay him what he owed him tomorrow he'd be next on the list. Walter was so angry now that all the guilt had vanished.

He looked at the clown suit and once more wondered who had owned it. Maybe it was possessed; he'd watched countless reruns of *The Twilight Zone* and *The Outer Limits* when he was a kid. There were always stories on there about stuff that had belonged to people who'd done terrible things being passed on or bought by innocent people and turning them into killers.

He had no doubt that whoever had worn the suit hadn't been the sort of happy-go-lucky clown that paraded around in front of the circus ring. No, he knew for a fact that the man who'd worn this had been evil. He wished he'd never brought it home with him and tried it on. It was as if it had a hold over him; maybe he should get rid of it, but he didn't want to – at least not yet.

He'd see how things went. Hopefully the police wouldn't come looking for him. He'd been careful. He'd never been arrested for anything in his life; his DNA wasn't on any databases – or his fingerprints. He'd never even had his name taken when he was a kid for anything. They would have their work cut out looking for him. For the first time in a couple of hours he smiled, feeling much better about it again.

Lifting the suit off its hanger he undressed until he was in his boxers then stepped inside of it. It felt like a second skin and seemed to stick to him as if it was fusing with him, making the costume and himself one. He sat down in his chair, in the clown suit, and rocked himself backwards and forwards, soothing away the anger, which was threatening to disperse and leave him with the heavy burden of guilt.

Annie grabbed her phone off the table where she'd been charging it. Her new rule was never go anywhere without a fully charged phone. How many times had she needed one and had no battery? She bent down to turn the socket off and felt an icy cold blast of air cross the back of her neck, making all the tiny hairs stand on end and causing her to shudder.

She paused. Was that her breathing or was there someone standing behind her? The temperature had definitely dropped. Forcing herself to straighten up, she turned around, expecting to see someone there. She was on her own, but it was so cold. Blowing out, she saw the white fog as her breath clouded in front of her eyes. She held her hand out in front of her. Pretending that it wasn't shaking and that she could handle this, she passed her hand through the cold spot. She moved her hand from side to side. Either side of the spot was warm. It was just the space directly in front of her.

'Who are you and what do you want?'

It didn't matter how many times these incidents happened,

they still scared her until she knew who it was she was dealing with. The air felt as if it was full of static electricity.

'If you want me to help you, you have to tell me who you are or at least show yourself.'

If she could have kicked herself she would have. It was as if she just invited whoever it was to make themselves at home. The tension in the room was so fraught she wondered if something terrible was going to happen. A wave of helplessness washed over her and then it was gone. The temperature rose as fast as it had fallen and everything felt normal once more. She looked around, hoping to see there was no one standing in her house who shouldn't be, and then she ran to the front door and threw it open so hard it put a dint in the smooth, plastered wall.

Shit. What do I tell Will? Sorry, darling, we've got another resident ghost who just happens to be a bit shy. But don't worry – as soon as they introduce themselves we can all hang out together. She walked over to her car, not turning around to look back at her house. The last thing she wanted was to see the shadowy figure of a complete stranger inside her home.

Not realising how badly her hands were shaking until she tried to get the key in the ignition, she managed to start the car. Pressing the call button on the steering wheel she decided it was finally time to ring Derek Edmondson and see if he could help her. The phone rang through the speakers, filling the entire car with the sound of his voice.

'Hello.'

Annie paused. Should she drag him into this? Hadn't she caused him enough heartache in the past? Yes, she had, but she had to make sure her home was safe for Alfie. She couldn't put the most precious thing in her life at risk in any way whatsoever and she knew Derek would understand. Besides, she only wanted his advice. She didn't expect him to come and sort it out for her.

'Derek, it's Annie Graham. How are you?'

'Annie, how are you, my dear? Are you still chasing criminals?'

Guilt set in. She hadn't bothered to tell him about Alfie when she was pregnant, yet here she was expecting him to come to her rescue.

'I'm good, thanks. I've had a baby. Well, he's not so tiny now; he's eight months old.'

'Oh my goodness, has it been that long since we've spoken? Well, that's lovely news and congratulations to you both. I read about that dreadful man escaping, but not until it had all ended and he was dead. I was in hospital; I haven't been very well. My old ticker gave me a bit of a fright, but I'm on the mend and very bored. My sister won't let me do anything strenuous, which includes most of my favourite activities.'

Annie heard his sister muttering in the background and she smiled.

'Oh, Derek, I'm so sorry to hear you've been poorly. Why didn't you let me know? I would have come to visit you.'

'That's precisely why I didn't. You are a very busy woman and even more so now. You don't need to be worrying about an old bugger like me.'

Annie felt terrible and decided she wasn't even going to mention her house and what had just happened. Whatever it was, she would have to sort it out herself.

'Tell me, did you need my help with anything?'

'No, I wanted to speak to you and see how you are.'

'Well, that's very kind of you. I'm good and I'm glad to hear that you are.'

'I am, thanks. I'll let you go then. I won't leave it as long next time and please don't hesitate to call me if you need anything. I'm still on maternity leave and very bored so I can always come and visit.'

'That would be lovely; thank you, Annie. Oh, and Annie, before you go, if you need me I'm here. You know that, don't you?'

'I do. Thanks, Derek.'

She ended the call and felt bad. She'd been so self-absorbed

131

and wrapped up in her own world she hadn't even bothered to check if he was OK. She parked in the car park next to the police van where Jake was sitting, head bent down and typing away on his phone. He didn't even notice her until she'd got out of the car, fed her loose change into the machine to get a ticket that she'd attached to her window, and then walked around to his side of the van and slammed her hands against the glass. Jake swore, jumping and letting his phone fall from his hands into the footwell. Annie was laughing so hard at the look of shock on his face she had to cross her legs.

'What the fuck you doing? You gave me a heart attack.'

'Sorry, I couldn't help it. What were you doing that had you so engrossed?'

He held up a big black device that looked like a cross between a phone and a tablet.

'Trying to update this pile of shite. Cathy was on one this morning about us not keeping them up to date.'

'What the hell is it?'

'Your worst nightmare come true; that's what it is. It's our new pocket notebook. You can get the current logs up, search PNC and get your emails up as well as use the phone. It's brilliant when it works; only problem is, working around here with such shite coverage, it's a ball-ache. You are going to love it when you come back to work.'

Annie let out a groan. She was a complete technophobe.

'Great, so as well as not being able to pair up with anyone I'm supposed to use that thing on my own without supervision. You know you're not selling me on coming back to work at all, Jake.'

'Aw, don't say that, kid. We'll sort something out. By the time you come back these will have all broke and we'll be back to using pens and paper. Nobody can keep us apart. It would be like splitting up Morecambe and Wise. We come as a pair and they'll just have to accept it. Cathy won't let you out on your own anyway because you're too much of a liability, so I'll make her assign me to be your bodyguard.'

'I'm quite capable of working on my own. I managed quite well before I had Alfie and you know I did. None of what happened was technically my fault and a couple of times no one was there to save my arse anyway and I had to save myself. So thank you for the offer, Captain America, but I'll manage.'

Jake pretended to look as if she'd just mortally wounded him. 'Yeah, I suppose so. Come on, I need sustenance. I'm starving.'

Annie smiled. That was what she loved about Jake. He would put his foot in it and she would tell him off and then they'd be straight back to being best friends. There was nothing complicated about their relationship. It was simply friendship at its best and she was glad she had him in her life. A life without Jake wouldn't be worth living. She pushed his arm and he shoved her back.

'You're always starving.'

'And you always want coffee.'

'Aren't we just a match made in heaven?'

Both of them started laughing as they walked the short distance to the quaint coffee shop in the village. They looked quite a sight: the huge policeman in full uniform with the much shorter woman dressed in a pair of faded jeans and a black T-shirt. The tourists couldn't help themselves from looking at the pair of them laughing and chattering away, all of them smiling to themselves. It was refreshing to see a policeman who looked as if he was normal and not afraid to be himself.

As they walked into the shop they were greeted by the sight of Jo standing behind the counter, slicing up a huge chocolate cake. Jo looked up and smiled at them both.

'Well, what a glorious sight you two are.'

Jake winked at Annie. 'Thank you. I have to say you look pretty impressive yourself standing there.'

A faint blush rose up Jo's cheeks. She was much quieter than the pair of them. Annie nodded her head in agreement with Jake.

It was amazing to see the woman who had saved her life and almost lost hers in the process standing there, looking a picture of health. Jo wore a blouse, buttoned up almost to the top to cover the large, puckered, angry scar where her husband, Heath, had buried the axe into her neck, almost killing her. Unable to stop herself, Annie threw herself at Jo and hugged her tight.

'What was that for?'

'Because you're too cool and I'm always going to have to hug you for the rest of your life whenever I see you.'

'People will talk about us, Annie.' Jo laughed and Annie started laughing with her.

Jake unzipped his luminous yellow body armour and slipped it off his shoulders. 'The usual please, Jo.'

Jo nodded; she didn't need telling. These two were her favourite customers in the whole world.

Chapter Thirteen

Will squeezed into the small parking space on the street in front of the hospice. He didn't relish having to go in and disturb the staff. They were busy enough without having them intruding. As if reading his mind, Adele smiled at him.

'Come on, we don't have to put them out too much. We can ask to speak to the manager or whoever is in charge, and if they're busy we can make an appointment to come back another time.'

'Yes, we can. That's a good idea.'

He walked up the path, wondering why on earth someone would want to murder someone so kind and caring like Pauline Cook. It didn't make any sense. As they opened the glass-fronted door Will was expecting it to smell like a hospital and was pleasantly surprised that it didn't. He'd been expecting the smell of death to linger in the air and everyone to be walking around crying into tissues. Instead he was greeted by a friendly receptionist, who listened to his request and asked them to take a seat while she bleeped the manager.

He looked at Adele who nodded. Both of them sat in silence waiting until a woman who looked around the same age as Annie came rushing up the corridor and stopped in front of them.

'Hello, you must be the detectives? I'm Diane Porter, the

manager; would you like to come into my office? We're all in shock about Pauline. She was such a lovely lady. I can't believe it.'

They followed her along the corridor to an office, which was light, airy and smelt even nicer than outside in the corridor.

'Please take a seat. Can I get you a drink?'

Adele shook her head. Will sat down. 'No, thank you, but that's very kind of you. I'm sorry to have to disturb you, but we really need to find out as much about Pauline as possible.'

'Of course you do and I'll tell you everything I know. She was such a nice lady, but she was quite shy and kept to herself.'

'How did she manage to volunteer here then?'

'She was fine with the patients and families. She was fine with the staff as well on a one-to-one basis. I think she was quite lonely, though. She never talked about her life outside of here, which is really sad. I can't believe someone would want to hurt her to the extent that she died. It's unbelievable.'

'Did she have a next of kin on her contact details? It's just we haven't been able to find anyone except for her neighbour.'

Diane shook her head. 'I don't know what she did in her spare time apart from read. She would bring books in for patients when she'd finished with them. She didn't talk about going out and socialising. She came on the works Christmas dinner, but I think that was more out of us pressuring her to come along. It wasn't because she wanted to and she left after the dessert had been served. She didn't drink at all.'

Adele seemed to be trying her best not to cry, her heart obviously going out to this lovely lady who had done nothing wrong except to help others who were in need of comfort. Will was stumped; he didn't understand it.

'Do you know if she upset anyone at all? Were there any angry relatives who blamed her for being with their loved ones when they should have been?'

Diane shook her head. 'None at all; the patients she used to sit with and their families were so grateful to her for being willing to keep them company and give the family a much-needed break. I can't imagine anyone ever getting angry with her over anything. None of the staff has ever heard of any problems either and, trust me, if there were problems they would know. I have a fabulous team here, but they like to gossip as much as the next person. Anything remotely scandalous would have spread around this building like dry rot.'

Will ran his hand through his hair, then stood up. Adele followed suit.

'Well, thank you for your time; you've been very helpful.'

'You're welcome and I'm afraid that I haven't really, have I? It would be easier to accept if she'd been awful and had lots of enemies, but this wasn't the case at all with Pauline.'

Adele smiled at Diane. 'Yes, thank you for your time.'

They left and walked back to Will's car, neither of them speaking because they were both trying to figure out the motive for Pauline Cook's murder. Will was so angry. They had nothing to go on. Usually by now the cracks would begin to open and the dark secrets would start to surface. Once you found out some information about someone, suddenly the once-perfect husband or wife wasn't so perfect anymore. There was nothing like this and he could feel the frustration building inside his chest.

As he manoeuvred out of the parking space he turned to Adele.

'There has to be something. How can there be nothing at all on her? It's as if she never existed or lived a life beyond her four walls and the hospice. What kind of existence is that?'

'Well, your theory of a stranger killing is spot on then, isn't it? What we need to think about was how her killer came across her. How did she come to be on the top of the most wanted list for some psychopath?'

'You're right. Let's try and figure something out because the bosses are already pissed we have no leads. Only they're not as mad as I am because I don't like it. We're missing some link and I can't figure out what.'

He drove the rest of the way back to the station in silence. He knew Annie was really good at stuff like this. She would be able to do some digging and find him something on the internet. She might even be able speak to Pauline herself and ask her what happened. It would be great if she could put that weird talent of speaking to the dead to use; only there was no way he could ask her or tell her about it. If he did, that meant he was involving her too much in the case.

Even though she was still on maternity leave, everyone knew that there was a real possibility of it all going horribly wrong if she got involved. She had a habit of attracting serial killers and he couldn't afford to put her at risk, plus there was Alfie to consider now. After Annie, Alfie was the best thing that had ever happened to him and he wouldn't risk either of them. He needed to come up with some answers by himself. It was far less dangerous for his family that way.

Summer 1950

As Gordy sipped the cold bottle of beer, he couldn't get the way he'd stuck that knife into Colin's mother out of his mind. He'd enjoyed it far too much. It was such a satisfying feeling when it pierced the skin, cutting through the muscles and organs. He'd never felt so good, so in control. Colin had thrown himself into circus life and Barnard's Circus would wonder how it ever managed without the helpful, strong lad who never complained or wanted to stop for a rest. The caravan door slammed open, snapping him out of his daydream.

'God, those elephants stink. It took for ever mucking their cages out. You should see the size of the . . .'

Gordy held up his hand. 'I can imagine, thank you, Colin. Spare me the details.'

'Well, I've finished now, Gordy. Can you show me how to be Tufty now?'

Gordy looked down at the newspaper in front of him that he'd been trying to read. He felt his cheeks begin to burn when he saw the grainy, black and white photograph on the third page of Colin's mother. 'Woman Slaughtered in her Bed, Son Missing.'

He shut the paper, his mind filling with fear. Would they know it had been him? He didn't think so because he'd left no clues behind. Have you, though? Did you really leave nothing behind?

'Come on, Gordy, I been good like you said. I'm sick of cleaning animal shit. I want to be a clown like you.'

Gordy nodded and pushed himself up. Downing the rest of the beer, he wiped his mouth with the back of his hand. He stumbled forwards slightly but then caught his balance. He picked up the newspaper and tucked it under his arm.

'Give me five minutes, kid, and then I'll do your face. If you keep hassling me then I won't. Got it?'

Colin nodded, not daring to speak again in case Gordy classed it as hassling and didn't put the clown make-up on him. There was a breath of fresh air in the stuffy caravan as the door opened and Gordy went outside. Colin wondered where he was going. He heard the loud crash as the glass bottle smashed into the metal bin they kept in the middle of the caravans for them to put their stinking rubbish into. Colin smiled as Gordy came back up the steps. He felt a line of spittle beginning to form on his lips and wiped his arm across his face. He didn't want to get Gordy mad and he might if he was dribbling everywhere like a fool.

'Sit on the chair then, Colin; you're as tall as me. I can't reach your face that way, can I?'

Grinning, the lad sat down and closed his eyes, waiting patiently for Gordy to work his magic and turn him from being his slow, cumbersome self into a circus clown. It was the moment he'd dreamt about since that first night of the show. He'd sat at the ringside on his own, mesmerised by the performers, especially the clowns. He liked them because they made people laugh in a good way, not like the way the kids sometimes laughed at him and made him feel stupid. He wouldn't get laughed at like that when he was a clown – only in the good way. Everyone would want him to be their friend, just like he'd wanted Gordy to be his.

As Colin sat with his eyes closed, daydreaming about life as a circus clown, Gordy did his best to apply the clown make-up to his face; but it was difficult because his mind kept wandering to the newspaper article. If the police had found her body, they would want to speak to Colin and might even try and blame him for what had happened. He wouldn't let that happen. He would turn the lad into a clown and disguise him that way, keeping him safe. When he'd finally applied the bright red around Colin's lips, he stepped back and smiled to himself.

'Can I look now, please? Can I look?'

'Not yet, you're not finished. You need to look the full part, don't you? Wait there.'

Gordy went into his bedroom, taking the wig off the stand and lifting his costume down off the hanger. He carried them back into the cramped kitchen area where Colin was still sitting with his eyes squeezed shut. He tugged the wig down onto the lad's head.

'Right, don't look just yet. Here, put this on.'

He handed his costume to Colin who held out his hand, but didn't grab hold of it.

'Are you sure? Should I try it on? Can I try it on? Really?'

Gordy laughed. 'Yes, you definitely can try it on. Go on, it should fit you.'

Colin stripped down to his vest and underpants. He carefully stepped into the suit, as if he was afraid that he was somehow going to damage it. For a minute Gordy felt as if he was having déjà vu. It was like staring into the mirror almost. Granted Colin was stockier than him and his head was bigger, but in the costume he looked pretty convincing as Tufty the clown.

'Right, now you can go into my bedroom and take a look in the mirror to see what you think.'

Colin almost stampeded him out of the way to get to the mirror. Gordy heard a whoop of delight and clapping as Colin applauded himself and he couldn't help but smile. The boy was so easily pleased and he made a pretty convincing clown; maybe this could work out just fine. Who knew? Colin could become just as much of a famous circus clown as the rest of them. It would be nice for him to be accepted by his peers instead of teased.

'Well, what do you think?'

'It's the bestest thing I ever did see. I can't stop looking at myself. I mean, is this really me or is it you and am I having some sort of dream?'

'No, it's definitely you. I think you make a splendid clown. How would you like to go to the big top and practise some stuff?'

Colin didn't answer him. He ran past him out of the caravan and towards the huge red and white stripy tent. Gordy got himself another beer out of the fridge, unscrewed the top and followed him.

Chapter Fourteen

2016

Annie walked back to the car park with Jake, who was rubbing his stomach and groaning.

'Well, it is kind of your own fault. You didn't really need to eat every piece of your cake and then finish mine off, did you?'

'No, but then again, yes. Think of it this way: you paid for that cake. You didn't eat it all so it would have been thrown in the bin and that would have been a terrible waste. So I needed to eat it for you.'

She laughed. 'Oh no you didn't, and next time you're complaining to me that Alex is taking the piss out of you because you're getting love handles, don't expect any sympathy.'

'That's so harsh. Where's my Annie Graham gone? She would never have said anything so cruel. What have you done with my friend? I want her back.'

This made her laugh even harder. 'Jake, I don't care what you eat, just don't try and blame it on me if you feel sick. And your Annie's still here. You know I am.'

He leant down and kissed her cheek. 'I know you are, you mad woman. It's much easier to get rid of the guilt when you blame someone else.'

'I know all about that one. It's very true. So what are you doing now?'

He waved the yellow polystyrene box at her. 'Going to go back with a peace offering for the boss to see if it puts her in a better mood. She was so angry this morning and you know what a miserable cow she is when she hasn't eaten. Mind you, sometimes she eats more than you and me put together and is still a right grump.'

'I hope her and Kav are all right. I'd hate to think they were having a rough patch. They make such a great couple.'

'Yeah, who'd have ever thought that, but they do.'

Annie climbed inside her car and watched as Jake got into the van. He started the engine and put the window down. About to shout something to her, he paused and talked into the radio clipped onto his body armour instead. He leant forward to press the button, which illuminated the lights on top of the van. The siren wailed. He mouthed at her, 'Got to go,' and sped off to get to wherever the emergency was.

She watched him go, a part of her feeling envious that he was still living his life and doing what he loved. She missed working with him and the thrill of an immediate response call. What she didn't love was the fact that most of the IR calls were because of her. If they couldn't work together, she didn't think she'd be able to do her job as an officer to the best of her ability.

The fear of someone wanting to hurt her was always going to be there, in the back of her mind like some ticking time bomb. What if she froze in a situation that required fast thinking and put her own life or someone else's at risk? Although that wasn't really her style, she had so much to lose now that she didn't want to think about putting herself in any avoidable danger.

She looked down at her hands, which were trembling. She could feel her heart beating too fast – just thinking about what situation Jake was going to. And just like that her mind was made up. She couldn't do it; she couldn't go back to working as a response officer no matter how much she loved it. She was far too conscious of the risks and what she had to lose.

This must be how Will felt every time he thought about her going back to work. Until this moment in time it had never bothered her. She would talk it over with him when he got home if it wasn't too late. To say that he would be relieved when she told him her career as a police officer was finished was probably a bit of an understatement.

As she pulled into her drive, Lily arrived and parked next to her. The rush of love Annie got at the thought of seeing Alfie again was overwhelming. She couldn't believe how much she'd missed him in less than twenty-four hours. She jumped out of her car and ran to get him out of his car seat. He smiled at her and in an instant her heart melted. That kid was going to have her wrapped around his finger and she didn't care one little bit.

'Has he been good?'

'He has been a little angel; he always is. Well, except for helping me to break Tom's golfing trophy, but you did us both a favour, didn't you, sweetie, because it's a monstrosity.'

Annie laughed. 'Oh no, poor Tom. Was he angry?'

'No, how could he be when I've been telling him to move it for months? It serves him right. Anyway, I can't stop, darling. I have to go and meet some ladies for lunch to talk about the next fundraising event. It's all go, you know.'

Lily winked at Annie, who smiled. She hugged Alfie close.

'Thank you for the break. I hadn't realised just how much I needed one.'

'Any time and it was all my pleasure.'

Annie carried her baby, who was now snuggled close to her with his tiny arms wrapped around her neck, into her house. She heard the heavy car drive away as she shut the front door. 'Well, it's you and me, kid. What should we do?' His eyes were closing as she crossed to the sofa and lay down on it. No need to do anything, eh? Full from the coffee and cake, she sat down and pulled the throw over them both. It was cool inside the cottage, which was a bonus in the summer months and not so good in the winter.

Alfie was fast asleep and she felt her eyes begin to close. It was an automatic reaction. She had learnt fast that the minute a baby had a sleep, you did too, otherwise the days were long and exhausting. Content, she pulled her legs up and relaxed, her breathing slowing as she drifted off. Annie had no idea how long she'd been like that, until she became aware of the feeling of being awake. Only she wasn't fully awake; it was a dreamlike state of consciousness.

She looked across at her sofa to see she was still there, snuggled up with Alfie. How was this happening? How was she watching herself? It was freaky yet at the same time fascinating and she wanted to know how she was doing it or more importantly why she was doing it.

Turning to look the other way, she no longer recognised where she was. It wasn't her house. Instead she was in a huge house that had been turned into too many flats. The smell of curry and spice filled her nostrils. Where was she? A door opened and she almost screeched to see a man in a clown suit walk out of it: the same clown suit that the killer in that house had been wearing.

She held her breath, afraid to breathe out in case he heard her. She had no idea if he could see her, but she hoped to God he couldn't. He looked around then left his flat, closing the door behind him. He rushed out of the communal hallway, out into the front garden. Annie kept telling herself to find out where she was, where this house was. A voice in her head kept telling her to wake up, she had no business being here; but she couldn't. How could she walk away like that when this could be vitally important to Will? And she was dreaming. He couldn't see her, could he?

She followed him outside, realising she knew where they were. The house was one of the big ones along Abbey Road in Barrow.

The outside was as rundown as the inside. How was he walking down Abbey Road dressed as a clown and no one was taking any notice? Then she realised just how dark it was outside. There were no cars on the road and no pedestrians. The moon was high in the sky. It had to be the early hours of the morning.

She watched as the man ran across the normally busy road and clambered over the metal gates that locked the park off to the public after nightfall. Not that it stopped many members of the public from using it because there were lots of other ways to get access; but where was he going? She knew she should follow him and find out. After crossing the road she somehow found herself on the other side of the gates – much to her relief. The last time she'd had to climb over these when she'd got locked in, her trousers had split.

She looked around to see which direction he'd gone and felt a cold shiver as what little light there was disappeared. He was standing directly in front of her and she'd never seen anything more terrifying that was human. She let out a scream and wondered if this was it. He looked confused as if he thought he'd heard a sound, but couldn't be sure. Lifting her hand to her mouth she bit down on her knuckles, realising that he couldn't see her. He could sense her and knew someone was there, but he couldn't figure out who or where they were.

She stayed perfectly still in case any movement gave her away. He began to turn ever so slowly. *What if he can see you, Annie, then what?*

He stopped dead in his tracks, staring directly at her. Tilting his head to the side he tried to decide if he was hallucinating and then he whispered, 'I know you're there. I can't find you right now. I don't know how, but I will. I'm looking for you so you better start to run and pray that I don't catch up with you. Get out of my head now.'

Terror filling her veins, she watched as he lifted the huge butcher's knife and slashed at the air right in front of her. Her reflexes making her jump back, she started. She almost jumped straight off the sofa, nearly letting go of Alfie, who began to cry at his rude awakening. Annie could feel her hands shaking and her heart was racing so much. The coffee and cake from earlier threatened to come back up.

She laid Alfie on the chair and tucked a cushion behind him. Disorientated, she stood up and looked around the room. It was still daylight. She hadn't been asleep for very long. Alfie was crying louder by the second and she rushed across to the kitchen to grab a sharp knife from the butcher's block. She couldn't shake the feeling that the scary clown man was nearby. She ran to each window and door, checking they were secure, and then she checked every room to make sure there was no one hiding inside her house.

Alfie was almost at screaming point now; satisfied the house was empty she ran back downstairs and picked up her son. She did her best to hold him close while feeding him, despite her whole body trembling. She felt as if her insides were churning the contents of her stomach into butter. What was going on? It was freaking her out; she needed to tell Will when he got home, just in case.

Just in case what? *Just in case these dreams are some kind of fractured reality and it's all real. The clown man might come looking for you and then what are you going to do?*

She didn't know what she would do. She did, however, know that Will was going to be so angry with her for getting involved with something, even though it wasn't her fault.

Chapter Fifteen

Will decided to call it a day. He'd had a showdown with the bosses over what little evidence they had and he needed to go home and calm down. Spend some time with his family. Sometimes this was how it worked. You couldn't always solve a murder within the first forty-eight hours, and they needed to stop pinning their hopes on him and face reality.

Adele had left along with Brad and Shona an hour ago. All of them had been going to the Black Dog for a drink and some food before heading home. As tempted as he was to go with them he couldn't. The thought of drinking or smelling anything alcoholic made him want to puke. He was definitely off the drink for a couple of months.

He left the station, hoping that somehow something would come up and they would find the killer before whoever it was decided that they'd enjoyed it much more than they'd imagined they would and struck up the courage to do it all over again. As the huge Tesco superstore came into sight, he indicated to pull into the car park.

After he'd bought the biggest bunch of flowers they had for Annie and a toy car for Alfie, he grabbed a box of Indian takeaway and several bags of chocolate. He didn't know if Annie would have made tea yet, but if she hadn't, he would sort it out. He paid and went back to the car, the whole time racking his brains as to how much he should tell his wife when he got home. No doubt she would want to know how it was going.

The drive home through the lanes soothed his troubled mind. The views and the surrounding countryside along the road to Hawkshead never failed to make him feel better. He wondered what it would be like to not have to go to work, not have the pressure of being responsible for finding the sickest individuals this part of the country had to offer, and he realised that he'd be lost without it. As much as it sometimes got to him he loved his job. He couldn't imagine doing anything else.

He finally reached the small lane that led down to their cottage and smiled. He couldn't wait to see them. Parking behind Annie's car he watched as the front door opened and he felt his breath catch in the back of his throat. He could never have imagined how motherhood would make the most important woman he'd ever known even more beautiful than she already was. Her hair was in a messy bun, her tanned, freckled face bore no traces of make-up, and in her arms was the cutest kid he'd ever seen. He jumped out, strode across and pulled her close, kissing her on the lips and trying his best not to crush Alfie.

'Sorry, kid, your mum looks good enough to eat.'

Annie laughed, but he noticed it wasn't her normal hearty chuckle. She kissed him then pulled away, smiling.

'I'm so glad you're home now. It's been such a long day. I was terrified you were going to roll up much later.'

Will took Alfie from her, swinging him around a couple of times then planting a huge kiss on his forehead.

'Why would you be terrified? Is everything OK?'

'It's fine. I just get fed up and lonely.'

He nodded, passing Alfie back to her.

'I'll just grab the bits out of the car. Have you made tea yet?'

She shook her head. 'I wasn't hungry so I didn't bother. I would

149

have if I'd known you were on your way home, though.'

Will turned to look at her. Something was wrong. She seemed nervous, which wasn't really Annie's style, and he wondered if she had some bad news for him.

'Is my dad OK?'

She nodded.

He grabbed the flowers, holding them towards her.

'They're beautiful, thank you.'

She turned and went inside, leaving him to get the shopping. She put the flowers in the sink then took Alfie upstairs to their bedroom where she put him in his cot with his snuggle blanket. Leaning down to kiss him she whispered, 'Wish me luck.' His eyes closed and she watched him for a few minutes until he was asleep.

She turned the night light on even though it was only dusky outside. Pulling her bedroom door to, she left the landing light on. She wasn't sure why, but she didn't want him being on his own in the dark. Then she went back downstairs where Will had unpacked the box of Indian and was busy putting it onto trays to put in the oven. She sat on one of the bar stools and watched him. When he'd finished he looked at her.

'I'm going to get a quick shower. I won't be long.'

Annie nodded.

He wanted to ask her what was wrong, but he needed to get out of this suit. He was hot and sticky. He'd have a cool shower and put on his shorts and a T-shirt, then he'd make her tell him what was bothering her. When he came back downstairs with towel-dried hair and smelling much fresher she was still sitting where he'd left her. The house was so quiet. Normally the television was on or the radio, but tonight there was nothing. He climbed onto the stool opposite her.

'What sort of day have you had? Has Alfie been hard work?'

She shook her head. 'No, he didn't come home until one. I met Jake for a coffee this morning.'

Will wondered if her strange mood was because of Jake.

'Has Jake said something that's upset you? Come to think of it, have I? Are you still mad with me about the funeral?'

Annie looked at him and shook her head. 'Of course I'm not mad with you, and no, for once Jake was on his best behaviour.'

'Well then I'm stumped, Annie. You're going to have to tell me what's wrong because something is.'

She sighed: a heavy, weary sigh that made Will feel bad. He waited for her to speak. She looked at him then looked away as if she was trying to find someone to tell her it was OK. She finally turned back to him.

'That house the other day on the news – the white one with the bright blue door. I dreamt about it before I even knew about it. I dreamt I was inside watching through someone else's eyes. As soon as I saw it on the news I knew something terrible had happened there.'

'What do you mean, you were watching through someone else's eyes?'

'I don't know; it's hard to explain. I felt as if I was there. It was so weird.'

'Well, you're psychic; maybe you saw into Pauline Cook's future and didn't realise. It doesn't mean anything. I wouldn't worry about it.'

'I saw the killer run out of the house. He was dressed like a clown. The scariest damn clown I've ever seen.'

Will studied her face to see if she was joking and couldn't tell. He laughed.

'I'm not joking. This is serious, Will. I saw a clown wearing a black and white costume with a scary mask run down the stairs and out of the front door.'

'Stop clowning around Annie. Oh God, that's a good one. Ha-ha, clowning around.'

She stood up, her hands balled into tight white fists. She was so angry with him for not taking her seriously.

'Will, I'm scared. Today when I was sitting on the sofa with Alfie I drifted off and it happened again. I was there and saw him come out of a house on Abbey Road wearing that same costume. I followed him into the park. Only he knew I was there. He couldn't actually see me, but he knew I was watching him and he told me he was coming to get me.'

'For Christ's sake, Annie, it's just a dream. A bad dream. There is no clown man coming to get you. Have you been reading scary stories again? This is a serious murder case and it's not right taking the piss out of Pauline Cook with this bullshit.'

For a fleeting moment Annie looked as if she wanted to pick up the vase of flowers next to her and launch them at his head she was so angry. 'What's wrong with you? Why don't you believe me?'

He looked at her face and realised she wasn't joking. He felt the seriousness of the situation come crashing down on his shoulders. His laughter turned into anger. Why, for God's sake, was this happening to them? Hadn't they been through enough? He paced up and down, anger and frustration making it hard for him to concentrate.

'This has to stop, Annie; it can't go on. What is wrong with you? How many times have I almost lost you because of this stupid shit? I can't stand it anymore and now we have Alfie to think about. Why would you even consider getting involved and letting a killer know that you're watching him? I mean, Christ, is that even possible? Do you know how crazy this sounds? And what about Alfie? It's not fair dragging him into this kind of life. You have to stop it. Stop getting involved in things that have nothing to do with you.'

This time Annie did reach for the glass vase and threw it in Will's direction, her face a mask of fury.

'You stupid prick, do you think I want this? That I asked for this? That I want a stupid, fucked-up life? That I want to be scared shitless ninety per cent of the time? Get out of my sight, Will; you have no idea, do you?'

Unable to think straight and in shock that she'd actually thrown a vase at him he picked up his car keys from the table and stormed out of the back door, slamming it hard behind him. He was furious. He'd never felt so angry with her and he needed to go somewhere to cool off. He got into the car and reversed out of the drive at speed, not caring if a tractor was coming the other way he was so mad.

Annie watched him speed off, only realising it was dark outside when his headlights illuminated the country road that led to their cottage. Terror filled her insides along with regret. What had she done? Why had she got so angry with him? It wasn't like her; she wasn't a violent person. She looked at the mess of broken glass, water and flowers and began to cry.

She ran outside to see if he'd stopped further up the lane. She couldn't see anything except for the blanket of approaching darkness and she felt a cold tendril of fear snake up her spine. Alfie – she'd left him alone. He'd wonder what all the noise was. She ran to the front door, terrified it had somehow locked and she would be outside, unable to get in with no key or phone. The fear was crushing her chest, making it harder to breathe. She reached the front door and fell through it, she slammed into it that hard.

The house was silent; unbelievably their arguing hadn't woken the baby up. After locking the front door she ran upstairs to check on him. He was asleep in his cot. Annie felt her legs tremble. What was wrong with her? She wasn't acting like a sane person. Was she finally losing her mind? She'd wondered each time she'd ended up in hospital with yet another brain injury or life-threatening wound whether it would be the one to send her over the edge.

She couldn't shake the image of the clown who had told her he was coming to find her from inside her head. Even though she tried to tell herself it was just a dream, it was far too real to take a chance and now she was on her own. Will had left her on her own when she needed him. She'd never seen him so angry

153

either. They never argued like this. Of course they weren't perfect and had their ups and downs, but not to this extent.

What was she going to do? She felt safe when he was here and now she was on her own. She went down to the kitchen and took the two biggest knives out of the butcher's block. Then she went into the utility room and opened Will's toolbox, taking out a roll of silver duct tape. She taped one knife underneath the kitchen island; the other she kept with her. The whole time her hands were shaking and her legs trembling.

Taking the heavy-duty rolling pin out of the drawer, she placed it behind the silver dish on the sideboard by the front door where she could get it should she need to. She went back inside the utility room and came out with a handful of large screwdrivers, which she placed strategically around the house, pushing one into her dressing gown pocket. She felt better knowing she had weapons to use to defend herself with should she need them.

Next she carried the monitors and CCTV base system out of the utility room and put them on the breakfast bar so she could watch the outside of the cottage and see if anyone tried to creep up on her. Then she hid the rest of the knives so they couldn't be used as weapons against her; although she had a feeling that the clown liked to use his own, as an image of the huge, sharp knife he'd waved in front of her filled her mind.

She was either being paranoid and cracking up or she was being cautious. Whatever it was, it made her feel a touch better. There was no way she would take this without a fight. Will's voice echoed in her head: *for Christ's sake, Annie, it's just a dream. A bad dream.* She whispered aloud, *I hope you're right, Will, I really do. Please come home. I'm sorry.* She picked up her phone and tried calling him, but it went to voicemail.

After making sure she had a clear view of the perimeter of the house and that everything was locked up tight, she sat down and realised she could smell burning food. Jumping up she ran to turn the cooker off. As she opened the door the smell of burnt tikka masala and blackened naan bread filled her nostrils. She slammed the door shut again; the smell reminded her of the block of flats the clown lived in. That had smelt of Indian food. It made her feel queasy and she normally loved an Indian.

She felt the world's biggest fool. The anger she'd felt towards Will had subsided into cold fear and she hoped he'd calm down and come home soon. How had that escalated to that degree? Not knowing what to do with herself, she picked up her phone and rang Jake. He'd make her feel better.

'Evening, Annie, are you missing me?'

'Yes, funny you should say that. I just wanted to check you were OK. I'm bored.'

'Is he not home yet? Bless him, he's working far too hard. Do you want to come down here?'

'No, thank you. Alfie's flat out. I'm sure he'll be home soon.'

They chatted about the kids for five minutes. Annie realised that Jake had had a glass of wine – probably several – and it wasn't fair to drag him into her mess again. He deserved some peace as well. She told him Alfie was crying and she had to go.

'Goodnight, flower.'

'Night, Jake.'

She ended the call with a heavy heart. It was so tempting to get Alfie up and drive through to Jake's house in Barrow. After getting Alfie's pram out of the hall, she put it in the kitchen. Then she went upstairs and carefully lifted him out of his cot. If Will wasn't here, she didn't want him on his own up there. She wanted him where she could see him.

Chapter Sixteen

Alex came downstairs with a towel wrapped around his waist, his hair tousled. 'Who was that on the phone?'

'Annie.'

'What's wrong? Is she OK?

'Nothing was wrong; she just wanted a chat.'

'Really? That's strange. How often does she ring this late? Did she sound OK to you?'

Jake sat up. 'I think so. What do you mean, Alex?'

He shrugged. 'Nothing, I don't know. I'm probably being stupid, but it just seems strange. She's been through a lot lately and we both know how much hard work having a baby is. Was Will there? He works such long hours. Maybe she could do with a break?'

'Fuck me, Alex, why did you have to say that? Now I'm worried and I can't drive there because I've had a bottle of wine.'

Shaking his head, Jake picked up his phone and dialled her straight back.

'Are you OK? Seriously, tell me if there is something wrong because mother bloody hen Alex has it in his head that something is.'

***

Normally she would laugh and tell him to bugger off, but she couldn't and paused.

'Everything is fine. Tell him thank you, but I'm OK.'

'Are you sure? Because I can come up and see you; only I'll have to get someone to drive me because I've already drunk a bottle of wine.'

'Don't be daft, Jake. I just wanted to speak to you. Will's not home and it can get a bit lonely up here on your own.'

'Are you and the golden boy OK? Have you had an argument?'

Annie knew that if she said yes he'd get all protective over her and ring Will to have a go at him. She looked at the mess of broken glass and shook her head. She just wanted Will to come home. He'd never reacted like that before and he'd looked so angry.

'Honestly, Jake, stop worrying. I'm bored. I love you all and I'm going to bed now. Night.'

'If you're sure . . . We love you too, Annie. Night.'

She felt the hot tears fall from her eyes and ended the call before she let out a sob. What the hell was wrong with her? Once upon a time, Mike would have ripped her to shreds, punched her until she was black and blue, then left her for hours while he went to the pub. And now she was in a state because Will had shouted at her and driven away. *Seriously, Annie, you need to get a grip. This isn't normal.*

She sat down on one of the stools and studied the television monitors to make sure there was no one sneaking around the outside of her house. It was blowy outside. The weather had changed and it had been cooler this evening than it had all month. Scrutinising each monitor, she saw there was nothing out of the ordinary. Her eyes started to close and her head began to nod.

Jerking herself awake she stood up and made herself a mug of strong coffee. She was probably overreacting, or she hoped to God she was; but she couldn't shake the feeling that something wasn't right. She wouldn't be able to relax until Will had come home and she'd apologised to him. She just hoped it would be soon because she was tired and didn't know how long she would be able to keep her guard up for.

Will took the long way around Windermere to get to his dad's house on the opposite side of the lake. He would go there for a couple of hours to cool off. He'd almost reached the turn-off for the drive when he realised what a complete idiot he'd been and pulled over onto the grass verge, sticking his hazard lights on.

Why had he got so angry with Annie? She hadn't been sleeping properly and had black circles under her eyes. Whatever was bothering her must be serious for her to even mention it to him, especially when she knew how he felt. And what had he done? Acted like a complete prick, that's what. He knew why he had but it didn't make it any better. He wanted a nice, normal life like most other couples. Boring he'd take any day over what they'd had to endure up to now. He didn't know any other married couples who had been through anything like they had. The pain, suffering, heartache and worry about Annie was like nothing he'd ever known.

He did a U-turn, heading back in the direction of Hawkshead, his wife and their baby, his perfect family. He'd way overreacted and now she would never tell him anything again. He slammed his hand against the steering wheel. He was furious with himself. Putting his foot down he drove as fast through the winding lanes as he could so he could go home and tell her he was sorry.

When he finally turned into the drive he got out of the car and ran to the front door. Taking his key from his pocket he put it in the lock – it wouldn't turn. She must have locked it from the inside. He hammered on the door but there was no answer. His heart racing, he ran around to the side of the house where the kitchen light was still on and pressed his face to the glass.

He felt like a complete bastard when he saw her perched on a bar stool, her head resting on crossed arms on the island with the CCTV monitors in front of her. She was fast asleep. Alfie was asleep in the pram next to her. He knocked on the window, making her start from her sleep. She looked confused then turned to stare at the window when he knocked again. He waved at her, but the light from the kitchen made it hard for her to see his face.

Will knew that as long as he lived he would never forget the look of fear etched into his wife's face. She stood up, reached into the pram for Alfie and held him close to her chest with one hand. She began to back away, picking up the biggest knife they owned in the other. Will was horrified. This was far worse than he'd ever imagined. Taking out his phone he rang her and she jumped when her phone vibrated on the side table. Running to pick it up she breathed a sigh of relief to hear Will's voice.

'Open the door, Annie. It's freezing out here. I'm so sorry.'

'Where are you?'

'Staring at you through the kitchen window outside.'

'How do I know that's you? I can't see you.'

'Look at the monitor, Annie. It's me; please let me in.'

She glanced across at the monitor and saw Will waving at her. Putting the knife down she crossed to the back door and opened it wide enough for him to step through and then pushed it shut, locking it again. He didn't speak, pulling her close enough to kiss her. They would talk, but it would wait until the morning. He'd never seen her act like this. Not even when Henry Smith had escaped from the secure psychiatric hospital and was on the run. She looked exhausted.

'I'm so sorry. I shouldn't have snapped like that. All I want is for us to have our happy ever after. We deserve one after the last few years. Let's get you both to bed and we can talk in the morning.'

She nodded and pulled away from him, handing him Alfie. 'I need a quick shower.' She went upstairs, clearly relieved he was home.

Will reset the burglar alarms and then carried his son upstairs where he laid him back down in his cot next to Annie's side of the bed. He undressed and slid under the duvet, relieved to be able to finally relax. Annie came out of the bathroom, her black hair damp and in ringlets. She had on a pair of pyjamas that he'd bought her for her birthday and smelt of Chanel No 5.

She shut the bedroom door and crossed the room, climbing in next to him. It wasn't until he reached across to hold her close that he realised she was trembling. She was cold and he wrapped his arms around her, trying to warm her up and make her feel safe again. He loved her more than anything and he hated it when he got angry with her. She didn't deserve it – not after everything she'd been through.

'I'm so sorry, Will.'

'For what?'

'Being a complete fuck-up, that's what. I know it can't be easy being married to me. I'm sick of it as well, you know, but I can't stop it happening. I feel as if I'm on a roller coaster and the brakes are about to fail.'

'You don't need to be sorry. None of it was your fault. I was just being a complete dick. I'm stressed out with work and I love being married to you so don't ever forget that. We'll talk about it in the morning and see what we can do. Try and get some sleep.'

He kissed her damp, coconut-smelling hair and she snuggled into his chest.

Annie closed her eyes, hoping the tiredness wouldn't let the dreams come and that she wouldn't wake up in her dream life, watching the world through the eyes of a killer. She also hoped Alfie wouldn't wake up for a couple of hours, because she'd taken a good, hard look in the mirror and realised that she needed some beauty sleep now more than ever.

Summer 1950

It took three weeks before Colin was allowed to go in the centre ring for a performance. Gordy had worked him hard and he'd

160

done everything that had been asked of him plus more. The other clowns had pitched in and the rest of the performers had watched as the cumbersome teenage boy had been transformed into quite the performer. He was a natural and had a knack of making the smallest trick look easy. Gordy was impressed and a little bit worried that Colin would steal the limelight from the rest of them.

The circus had paraded through the town they were in today and the kids had flocked to Colin – much to his amazement and Gordy's annoyance. He questioned whether his protégé was going to be too good at this performing lark. After the parade Colin had been so happy that Gordy felt guilty. He'd taken away the lad's mother, although he wasn't aware of that yet and – so far so good – the police hadn't turned up looking for him.

There was a problem, though. He had the itch again and it was like a burning sensation inside his skin. He wanted to scratch it until it bled, but he knew it wouldn't make one bit of difference. The only way to satisfy this itch was to kill someone. He didn't care if it was a man, woman or child. If the opportunity came along he would take it. Just the thought of it sent him into a frenzy. He had to go for a walk to calm himself down.

Leaving Colin practising in the ring, Gordy walked along the perimeter of the circus then slipped through a gap in the fence to get into the park. He could see a playground in the distance and headed that way. As he got nearer he saw a solitary girl playing on a swing. Looking around he couldn't see her parents, or anyone else in fact. She was pushing herself backwards and forwards using her body to make the wooden seat move.

He crossed the playground in her direction. When the girl noticed him he did a hop, skip and then bowed to her. As he bent down he pulled a bunch of flowers out of his sleeve and handed them to her. Her surly face broke into a smile and she laughed. He grinned at her then sat on the swing next to her. He copied her and pushed himself back and forth until he was swinging at the same level. She looked around then turned to him.

'What you doing?'

'Swinging. What are you doing?'

'Swinging.'

He laughed. 'That's makes two of us. Why are you here on your own?'

'Why are you here on your own?'

Gordy tilted his head while he considered his answer. 'I'm here because I needed some peace and quiet. It gets very noisy over there.' He pointed in the direction of the circus.

'Me too. I ran out of Sunday School. I'm tired of listening to them talk about Jesus.'

'Do you think that was wise? Aren't they going to be worried about you?'

She shook her head. 'Who, the nuns? They don't care about anything except God. They'll want to hit me with a ruler or a slipper, though, when I go back. It hurts as well. You would think God wouldn't want them to hurt kids, but they do.'

Gordy absorbed the information the girl had just shared with him. She was either an orphan or at a boarding school. Technically she had no one to miss her. This was a very good sign.

'How would you like to come and have a look around the circus?'

She jumped off the swing. 'Really, like right now?'

'Yes, now; well, in a minute. You see that field over there? I have to go and collect some more flowers first. You could come and help me pick some, then we can go and I'll show you the lions and elephants. It's almost feeding time. You can watch. If you're good I might even get you some popcorn. How does that sound?'

She hesitated for a moment, wondering if she should be going with the clown. She didn't know him. He smiled at her and held out his hand. She looked over her shoulder at the circus not too far away, then she looked at him and reached out her fingers to grasp hold of his. He smiled to himself as he led her across the playground to the empty field in the distance.

As the sun was setting and a cool breeze fluttered the trees and flowers, so did the material of the girl's once-white, now blood-red dress. There were several policemen along with a handful of volunteers out searching the park and surrounding fields for little Ester White, who had run out of Bible class this morning and not been seen since. They were taking the task in hand very seriously and there was no sound as they beat the long grass and shrubs with wooden sticks. Sister Sarah at the orphanage had been left wringing her hands while the men were out searching.

'Bleeding hell, I've found her. Dear God, at least I think I've found her. Officers, over here.'

Sergeant Young blew his whistle to alert his colleagues and ran towards the park groundsman who was now bent double and heaving all over the grass. As Young covered the ground he saw the two white legs protruding from under a bush at the side of the scrubland. One shoe on; the other nowhere to be seen.

Crossing himself, he didn't want to go any further because, if he did, it meant it would be true. He couldn't think of anything worse than having to look at the dead body of a child. Knowing he had no choice he forced himself to carry on. The sound that escaped his lips was one of complete horror. The girl who he'd had cause to speak to on several occasions because of her insolent behaviour no longer sported a face that was recognisable and he felt his own legs give way as he fell to the ground.

Who would do such a thing? There was a monster out here somewhere; this town was not huge. The worst cases of violence that happened here were behind closed doors after husbands returned from the pub after one too many beers. He had never seen anything like this and prayed to God he'd never have to see anything like it ever again. Peters came running behind him, out of breath. Not looking in front of him, he was concerned as to why his sergeant was on the ground. Young pointed in front of him and he heard Peters' sharp intake of breath at the pitiful sight of the girl.

'What's happened? Is she . . . you know?'

Sergeant Young forced himself to stand up. 'Yes, Peters, she's dead. She has no bloody face.'

'How? Maybe an animal from the circus escaped and killed her.'

Young wished with all his heart it could be so straightforward. It would be far easier to accept and believe that a lion or bear had done this terrible thing. Only she didn't look as if she'd been mauled. There were distinct knife wounds all over her body and face. He doubted very much a wild animal would have tried to conceal her body under a bush either.

'Really – and you don't think the circus would have notified us if a lion escaped? You think maybe it killed her and strolled back in time for the evening matinee so it didn't get in too much trouble?'

'Well, now you put it like that, no.'

'No, you're right. An animal has done this to her, but it wasn't the four-legged kind; it was a two-legged monster and I'll bet my month's wages that whoever it is lives in that circus. Now go back to the station. I need a doctor and more officers. I want this field closing off from the public until we've moved her to the hospital.'

Peters nodded then turned and walked back to the car. Young forced himself to turn around to face the girl and whispered, *'I'm so sorry, Ester White. I'm sorry that you had to die like this. I promise you I'll find him and when I do he'll hang for his crimes. I give you my word, sweetheart.'* Brushing away the tears that were falling with his sleeve, he coughed as he imagined his own daughter lying there instead of Ester.

While Colin and Gordy performed their final act in the circus ring, they were totally unaware of the mayhem that was about to ensue. The crowds were loving it. They were clapping and singing along, laughing at their antics. Colin was such a natural even Gordy was impressed at the ease with which he'd filled his role.

As Gordy turned to run away from Colin he couldn't help but spot the two burly policemen who were at the sidelines, whispering in the ringmaster's ear. His heart skipped a beat and he knew that they'd found the girl. He should have hidden her better. He'd known it was risky leaving her only partially hidden, but he'd heard the sound of a dog barking and kids laughing in the distance. He'd panicked and now it was all over.

He could run, turn around now and get out of here. Slip out through one of the fire exits; but then what? His life was this place. Without it he would die anyway and, besides, they might not be here for him. He turned and waved at the crowd then walked over to where they were standing.

Colin wondered what he was doing. This wasn't in the routine. Tufty didn't just walk out of the ring and leave him on his own. He panicked, wondering what was happening. The lights dimmed, signalling the trapeze artist was about to start her show, and Colin followed Gordy, who was now deep in conversation with the ringmaster and coppers.

Colin panicked as they looked over. What if they'd come to take him home? His ma was probably fed up of having to go to the shop for her own beer and fags and had sent them after him. Well, he wasn't going back. He didn't care anymore. He didn't like her and she didn't like him, not how she was supposed to like her own kid anyway.

He turned and ran in the opposite direction. Gordy chased him along with the two policemen, but there was no way Colin was going back to that house. He ran through the curtains. Gordy was almost up to him when there was a loud shout as the men who were lifting one of the heavy poles up on a rope and ginny wheel to replace a broken one outside the tent heard the chaos of the police, ringmaster, Colin and Gordy. Their attention was taken away for a moment and the pole, which was far too heavy for the rope, pulled taut as the rope snapped. It fell to the ground, landing on the two clowns and pinning them both to the ground.

He woke up in hospital, not sure how long he'd been there. Turning his head slightly he looked to the side to see his friend in the bed next to him being examined by a doctor. There was a bandage around his friend's head and neck. His eyes were open, but he wasn't moving. He cried out and the doctor and nurse came running over to him.

'It's OK; you're fine. Just had a nasty knock to the head, unlike your friend, who took the brunt of the fall and has had his larynx crushed. He can't speak. So this is very important: can you tell me your name, son?'

He paused. What was his name? Panic set in. He couldn't remember, but then it all came back to him.

'Colin . . . I'm Colin and that is Gordy. Is he going to be all right?'

The doctor looked at the nurse who was staring at the two policemen standing by the side of his bed.

'Colin, is that man over there Gordy Marshall?'

Colin nodded then winced as pain shot through his head. 'Yes, that's Gordy. Why?'

The doctor turned to the policemen and nodded his head.

'We just need to know so we can get him sorted out.'

'Oh right. Why are the coppers here? They were chasing us. I haven't done anything wrong and I don't want to go home. I'm old enough to stay with the circus if I want.'

'Of course you are – you don't need to go home. I think these policemen will want to talk to you. Do you feel well enough to speak to them?'

He nodded. 'Good, that's a good lad.'

The biggest man of the two came across to his bed. 'Colin, why did you run away when you saw us?'

'You can't make me go home. I like it here. I got scared you were going to make me go back to my ma.'

'Were you with Gordy this afternoon?'

'No, he went for a walk on his own.'

'Do you know where he went?'

Colin paused. He didn't want to get his friend in any trouble – and what was a crushed larynx?

'It's all right, son; I just need to know if you saw where he went.'

'He went into the park. I think he was mad at me and I was going to follow him to tell him I was sorry, but he was talking to some girl in the playground so I left him and went back to the caravan.'

The policeman was nodding his head as he tried to write down everything the lad was telling him. He had been right. They had their monster and he had been dressed as a clown. Of all the dirty, rotten tricks. Everyone knew that kids loved circus clowns and wouldn't think they were evil hiding behind a smiley face. They knew it had been a clown because when they'd moved Ester's body there was a crushed bunch of silk flowers – the kind that clowns pull out of their sleeves – underneath her.

Young had everything he needed. The bastard in the bed opposite couldn't move his head or speak because of his injuries, but it didn't matter. He would keep one of his lads with him until he was fit enough to be moved to the prison. That sick bastard wouldn't be hurting any more kids because as soon as he was well enough they would be hanging him. It was a waste of good hospital care in his opinion.

Chapter Seventeen

2016

Walter Lacey didn't feel very well. He opened his eyes, wondering where the hell he was. He knew he wasn't in his bed; that much was for sure. He tried to move and heard the groaning creak of the springs in the knackered old sofa. He groaned even louder. He didn't remember getting on the sofa; he didn't remember going to bed. In fact he didn't even know what day it was or what time.

He felt in his pocket for his crappy pay-as-you-go brick of a phone and felt the smooth, cool, silky material of the clown suit underneath his fingertips. *What have you done, Wally? Why are you dressed in this suit and why don't you remember?* Panic filling his chest, he tried to get off the sofa, but he felt hot and dizzy. He must have picked up some kind of bug in that old woman's house yesterday. It had been pretty grotty in there.

Rolling until he fell off the sofa onto his hands and knees, he let out an even louder groan. He felt as if his head was about to explode everywhere and leave brain juice and matter on the walls and furniture. His body was soaked with stale sweat. He could smell the mustiness whenever he moved as it permeated the air around him.

Pulling himself to his feet he stumbled forwards, afraid he was going to fall over and not get back up. He managed to just keep on his feet and made his way in the direction of the cramped bathroom. As he threw open the door and turned on the light he gripped the cracked, grubby sink and stared into the broken mirror. His face was white. There was a big red smudge across his cheek. He leant in closer. *What is that?* He rubbed at it with his fingertips. He licked them, rubbed at the mark, then licked them again and gagged.

Blood. It was dried blood. There was no mistaking the metallic taste and it was all over his face. Looking down he saw his hands were stained the same colour. Fear filled his entire body; he'd done something really bad. He knew he had, but what and to who? When he looked down at the clown suit he let out a scream. The white of the silky material was stained dark red.

He tried to get it off him, dancing around in the confined space and praying it wasn't fused to his skin like it felt it was. Stripping it off he kicked it to one side and looked at his skinny arms and legs. They were stained red. Whose blood was that? He didn't remember getting dressed and going out of the flat, but then it came back to him. He'd gone into the park and then what? Yes, he'd gone into the park out of sight of anyone, but he hadn't been alone, had he? Someone had followed him; he remembered feeling as if someone was breathing down his neck as they watched his every move.

He'd turned around and there was no one there. Some invisible man was watching him. He laughed, which sent shock waves through his head. He lifted both hands to clutch the sides of his head, pressing his hands against his ears to drown out the sound of his own voice because it sounded like the voice of a madman.

Turning on the shower he forced himself to step under the luke-warm spray. He'd have given anything for a scalding hot shower to rid himself of the blood that had dried all over his body like some kind of war paint. Wally had given up asking the landlord to sort his heating out. It cost him too much credit on his crappy phone to ring the number and try and get through to him.

Squeezing the last of his shower gel over his hands, he scrubbed away at his skin, raking it with his nails. He didn't like the fact that he had no recollection of what happened after he'd left the park. He was going to have to venture out later on and buy a newspaper to see if there was any mention of a body being found. As he stepped onto the cold tiled floor – which was a death trap with wet feet – he towel-dried himself.

He felt a bit better than when he'd woken up now he was clean and didn't smell as if he'd been rolling around in an abattoir. His head was still hurting when he moved it. Pulling on a pair of clean boxer shorts and a T-shirt he went and climbed under his bed covers. He might as well try and sleep off this awful hangover-type thing he had going on inside his head. He wouldn't have minded if he'd been drunk last night. He knew he wasn't because he didn't have any alcohol in the house.

It was something to do with that clown suit. He should throw it away, get rid of it. He'd never wanted to kill anyone before he'd brought it into his house. It was as if it was cursed. The voices in his head had always been muted until now. Someone had turned the volume up and he didn't know if it was him. He threw back the covers, pulled on his jogging pants, slipped on his trainers and got a carrier bag from under the sink. He walked into the living room, expecting to see it hanging up on the back of the door and exhaled with relief to find it still in a crumpled mess on the floor where he'd kicked it off.

Using the carrier bag he picked up the suit then tied the handles in a knot. He left his house swinging the bag and trying to keep it as far away as possible from himself. He crossed the road and went back into the huge public park where he walked until he found a bin. He stuffed the carrier bag inside. He made sure no one was watching him and then walked away.

He felt much better. His head still ached, but not like it had when he'd opened his eyes this morning. He felt lighter, better, as if he'd done the right thing for the first time in his shitty life. A couple of hours' sleep and he could go out for a paper. If he kept his head down this might all blow over and no one would be any the wiser about his murderous spate of killings. He didn't think he'd be able to cope in prison. He'd rather die than be locked up for the rest of his life. He might have a crappy life at the moment, but he could make an effort to do something and change it, couldn't he?

Will heard Alfie stir and got out of bed, taking him downstairs with him so Annie could have a bit more sleep. He'd forgotten about last night until he walked into the kitchen to see the monitors on the island. He also saw the empty knife rack, which reminded him he needed to ask Annie where they were. He would give her another half an hour and then wake her up; they needed to talk about what was going on and why she was so scared.

Like an expert he changed and fed Alfie, then sat him in his bouncer in the kitchen so he could watch him put everything back. He disconnected the monitors, carrying them back into the utility room. He never heard Annie come downstairs.

'What are you doing?'

He tried to dismiss the high pitch of her voice, not wanting to believe she was still upset that much.

'Just putting everything back to normal for you.'

'Well, don't bother; I want them out here – where I can see them at all times, not stuck in there out of sight. I can't sit in there all day and watch them. There isn't enough room for all Alfie's stuff.'

He stopped and turned around, putting the monitor he was carrying back down. 'What's wrong, Annie? This isn't like you.'

'I don't know. I feel scared being here on my own with our son.'

Will's phone started ringing. He ignored it.

'I don't want anything to happen, but I don't know if I can stop it this time.'

His phone rang again and he picked it up. It was work. He wanted to ignore it, but he couldn't. It might be important.

Annie glared at him, daring him to answer it. He did his best to not press the green button, but at the last second he did.

'Ashworth.'

He shrugged and mouthed *sorry* to Annie who didn't see because the tears that had filled her eyes had made her turn around.

Annie didn't know why she was acting like this. She did know that she wouldn't let him see her crying just because he'd had to answer his phone. She bent down to pick Alfie up and take him into the living room to sit on the sofa with her. She turned on the television and the screen filled with the familiar sprawling green lawns and the bandstand in the middle of the park in Barrow.

Her heart missed a beat. What had happened? She had been there in her dream last night. Could she have stopped it if she hadn't got so scared by the clown man and run away? Will walked in saw the television screen and bent down to kiss her cheek.

'I have to go. There's been another murder.'

Annie nodded. What could she say? This was his job and she knew that when she married him. Just because she'd had a couple of scary dreams, she couldn't expect him to not go to work and stay here.

'I promise I'll phone you after when I get a minute and we can talk. Why don't you go and stop with Jake and Alex for the day? At least you won't be up here on your own.'

'I might do. I'll ring you if I do.'

'Everything's OK, Annie. We're OK, aren't we?'

'Of course we are. Go find that killer.'

'I'll try my best. If you don't want to go to Jake's, why don't you go to my dad's?'

She forced herself to smile. She adored Tom and Lily but she didn't want to be stuck there all day. Tom always knew when

172

something was wrong with her and she didn't want to burden him with anything.

'I'll find something to do.'

He turned and walked away and it took every ounce of strength for her not to scream at him to stay, that if he walked out she'd never forgive him. The front door shut behind him and she heard his car start. She couldn't move. She was frozen to the sofa because she felt the raspy cold of someone standing behind her and breathing down her neck. The thought that the clown from last night had found her exploded inside her mind.

She grabbed Alfie and jumped off the sofa, spinning around at the same time as backing away. There was nobody there; well, no one that she could physically see. She looked around the room to make sure he wasn't hiding anywhere and was grateful they had decided on an open-plan layout downstairs so they didn't have lots of hiding places. There was only the utility room and cloakroom that had doors.

She backed up to where she had a knife hidden and pulled it free. If that creepy fucker was in her house then she wouldn't go without a fight. She ran to the kitchen window to see if Will was still outside and felt her heart sink to see the empty space where only minutes ago his car had been. She could ring him; tell him to come back – and then what? He was going to think she'd cracked up and lost her mind, which was exactly how she was feeling. Everything was out of her control.

Not wanting to put Alfie down while she searched, but not wanting to have to fight with him in her arms, she didn't know what to do. She ran outside and strapped him into his car seat, then typed a quick text to Jake. *Can you come to mine as soon as you can? Need to speak to you.* She sent it. If there was someone in her house and they got the better of her, at least Jake would be on his way and would be able to take care of Alfie.

She let out a pent-up sob. The thought of being murdered in her own home with her baby outside was too much. She couldn't not go back in. Whoever it was could lie in wait in there for her or Will to come home, and if she left and Will came back, oh God, the thought of a killer lying in wait for him made up her mind. She'd almost lost him once at the hands of a killer; there was no way she'd let it happen again. She ran into the house and checked the utility room, cloakroom and then made her way upstairs. It was so quiet; the television was still on pause. As she checked each bedroom, she felt a little better until she reached Alfie's. It was so cold in there she could feel the goose bumps that covered her arms.

'Who are you and what do you want? I want to know what you are doing in my baby's bedroom!'

Peering out of the window she could see Alfie in his car seat, gurgling away. Suddenly she felt a small hand slip into hers and she looked down to see the faint outline of Sophie standing there.

'Sophie, is it you? Have you been breathing in my ear?'

The ghostly girl shook her head and Annie felt her voice inside her mind.

'No, it's a man. He's scared and wants you to help him.'

'Where is he, Sophie? I can't see him like I can see you.'

'He's standing in the corner. He said he's sorry if he scared you. He doesn't know what to do. He didn't want to die and it's happening all over again.'

Sophie let go of her hand and crossed to the corner where she'd pointed moments ago. Annie heard Sophie's soft, soothing voice whispering in the corner and looked out to check on Alfie, who was now fast asleep. Squinting, she stepped closer to the window. It looked as if his baby chair was being rocked ever so slightly and she smiled. *Alice.* She turned and faced the corner.

'You don't have to be scared; you were very brave to come and find me. I'm sorry I got a bit freaked out. If I can help you I will. Why don't you tell me or Sophie what it is that you need help with?'

The shrill ring of the house phone broke the silence and Annie knew that the man had left, along with Sophie. Maybe now that she knew about him he would be brave enough to come back and tell her what he wanted. She ran into her bedroom to grab the spare handset, feeling much better. Picking it up she carried it downstairs so she could go and retrieve her sleeping baby from the car.

'Hello.'

'Annie, it's Derek. I hope I didn't disturb you?'

She didn't think she'd ever been so pleased to hear his voice.

'No, you didn't. How are you feeling?'

'Much better apart from this name that keeps swirling around in my head and won't go away.'

'Mine?'

'How did you guess?'

He laughed, making her feel slightly less guilty about bothering him when he wasn't well.

'There's something going on here that has been terrifying me, but I think I have it sorted out or almost sorted.'

'Well, seeing as how I'm cooped up in this stuffy bedroom on bed rest until Joan is home, maybe you could tell me. I'd like to help if I can.'

'Oh, Derek, you're far too kind. I don't want to bother you.'

'OK, well, let me tell you what I think and then you can see I already know some of it.'

Annie didn't answer so he continued.

'I have a feeling that you've had a spirit invading your personal space, getting a little too close and spooking you. I also know that you've been having some dreams, which, shall we say, are a little too realistic. Am I close?'

'You are very close. I have. These dreams feel as if I'm there when it's happening – watching. And the person I'm watching knows I'm there. He can sense me, but he can't see me. Not yet anyway. I'm terrified that he'll discover who I am and come looking for me.'

'Is this person dangerous?'

She was torn. She didn't want to upset him too much, but he already seemed to know.

'Yes, he's a killer.'

Derek sucked in his breath. 'Annie, how does this keep happening?'

'I wish I knew and then I could stop it. I'm so fed up of living my life looking over my shoulder.'

She stared down at Alfie who was still asleep in his car seat.

'Well, I think the good news is that unless this man is psychic as well, he won't be able to find out who you are.'

Annie exhaled, not realising she'd been holding her breath. 'What if he is?'

'You would have known about it by now. It's a very rare gift that thankfully not many killers possess. The bad news is I think you may have passed your gift on to that cute little baby of yours and that is why things seem to be taking a different direction than normal. Are you finding it a struggle to connect with this spirit in your house?'

'Yes, normally I can see and hear them. I don't seem to be able to at the moment.'

'Alfie is acting like an amplifier for this man.'

'Oh God, that's terrible. Does that mean he's seeing what I'm seeing in these dreams?'

'No, he wouldn't understand them. His brain isn't developed enough, thankfully. But what is happening is he's acting like a booster signal – a bit like those boxes you can buy to improve your broadband.'

'What am I going to do, Derek? I don't want this kind of life for him.'

'I'm afraid there's nothing you can do at the moment. When he's older and things have progressed, then we can look at putting in place some blocks and strategies to help him cope. For all we know he might grow out of it. Not all babies of psychic parents have the same gift that their parents do. He could grow up just a little bit sensitive, but not a full-blown medium.'

'I hope you're right, Derek. What do I do in the meantime?'

'I'm not sure. I haven't had a lot of experience in this kind of thing. I'll ask a few of my friends from the group and see what they think. Just keep out of it as much as you can. Where are these murders happening?'

'Barrow.'

'Then don't go to Barrow unless it's desperate. Try and keep calm when you're around Alfie. Maybe you could try sleeping in a different room to him? That could lessen the bond.'

Alfie squirmed, his face going bright red. He opened one eye and let out a high-pitched scream. Annie tucked the phone under her ear with her shoulder and leant down, unbuckling him and picking him up. He was screaming louder than their burglar alarm.

'I'm sorry, Derek, I'm going to have to go and feed the little man; thank you so much.'

'No problem; call me if you need me and I'll be in touch.'

'Bye.'

'Be very careful, Annie. Bye.'

But the line went dead and she never heard his last warning. Derek lay back against his pillows, replacing the phone in its handset. His stomach was churning and he had an awful feeling in his chest – very similar to the first time he'd ever set eyes on Annie Graham. She'd been in the audience at the spiritualist church where he was a guest speaker when he'd had to deliver the message to her that she was in grave danger. He just hoped it was him being overly sensitive and not a warning from beyond, because he wasn't sure how many lives the very lovely Annie Graham had left.

Chapter Eighteen

Will drove as fast through the windy lanes and roads as was safe, thankful it was still early enough that they weren't full of tourists driving fifteen miles an hour while taking in the views. When he finally got onto the A590 to Barrow, he put his foot down. He regretted not having the chance to speak properly with Annie. As soon as he got a minute he would phone Lily and ask her to go check on her. Lily loved having things to do, and if she could lure Annie out of the house and get her to go shopping, that would give her a break.

He'd never seen her looking so tired and pale; maybe they needed a holiday. Could you take babies on planes to hot countries? He didn't have a clue. He would ask Adele. She would know this stuff. Being a parent was very new to him, not to mention scary. He'd never felt anything like the love he felt for that little guy who was a combination of him and Annie. He'd never even considered being a parent would be so brilliant, even though the sleepless nights weren't much to shout about.

He couldn't wait until he could take Alfie to play rugby; Will loved it and had only given up because he spent more time off the pitch with injuries than he did on it. It just wasn't a sport for a man his age. Not that he was old; he was just a bit too old to be getting elbowed in the groin and stamped on every Sunday morning.

Before he knew it he was on Abbey Road – one of the main roads into town, with a view of the hospital he was all too familiar with because of Annie's run-ins with violent men. He drove past Abbey House Hotel, which was a beautiful sandstone building. He finally reached the traffic lights and the turn for Park Drive where he could access the public park. He pulled into the car park where there were an assortment of police and the CSI van. Debs was suited and booted, all raring to go. He nodded at her.

'Morning. Have you done the preliminaries?'

'Not yet, thought I'd wait for you.'

Brad, who had been first in the office this morning, came sauntering over with Adele, who had been coming in as he was leaving and he'd asked her to go with him.

'Boss.'

'Brad, what have we got then?'

'One of the homeless guys who'd taken to sleeping under the bridge – it's a right mess. There's blood everywhere. Some of the ducks and that huge fucking swan over there, which keeps going for everyone when they try and get near the body, are covered in it. They must have been paddling in it.'

He pointed to a swan whose white feathers were tinged pink and bright red. It was flapping at the side of the lake next to the body under the bridge.

Will ran a hand through his hair. 'Bollocks.'

'Exactly.'

'What are we going to do? Is there any way to chase it off?'

Adele shrugged. 'I've asked the guy who runs the boathouse if he can lend us a boat so one of us can maybe go on the lake and shoo the swan away.'

Brad started laughing and Will glared at him.

'Have you got a better idea, Brad?'

He shook his head. 'Call the RSPCA or that woman who deals with birds?'

'We can't wait hours for someone to come. Brad, you go and get a rowing boat and test your skills. You can row over and try and chase it away.'

'Ha-ha, good one, boss.'

Will stared at him. 'I'm not joking. I want you in a boat and ready to go in five minutes.'

Brad stopped laughing and frowned. 'Why is it always me?'

'Because Stu's no longer with us and you are. Stop moaning about it. You know how to row a boat, don't you?'

Brad turned and walked off, not even answering him, and Adele laughed.

'Are you always so hard on him?'

'No, but he has this way of annoying the shit out of me with his insensitive personality and it's far too early for this. It's warm now. If we can't get to the body soon it's going to stink even worse than what it does now and I'm certainly not going out in a rowing boat.'

He winked at Adele who laughed again. 'No, me neither. Should I ring the RSPCA just in case?'

'Better had; we need to close the park. There are far too many entrances and ways to look across here and see that bloodbath. I don't want to lose any evidence or have families coming here to feed the ducks and being greeted by the blood-soaked swan and a body under the bridge. Have we got any witnesses?'

Adele pointed to a scruffy-looking man in his late fifties sat on a bench with a half-empty bottle of Lambrini tucked between his feet.

'Meet Mr Ian Gibbs – best friend of the victim, one Billy Marks. Apparently they had a bit of a falling-out over some woman last night and he left Billy here on his own about nine o'clock. He returned about six this morning to say sorry and share his bottle of Lambrini with him and found his body and that angry swan.

He keeps mumbling about a freaky clown he saw as he was leaving the park by the entrance on Abbey Road.'

Will looked across at him. He didn't look as if he was covered in dried blood, but he could have been somewhere to get changed, then come back feeling guilty. This was the second time he'd heard a clown mentioned. He needed to look into that as well.'

'Let's have him in then.'

Will waved over one of the officers who was standing trying to shoo the birds away from the scene.

'Because he was the last to see the vic, I want him bringing in for questioning. Can you do the honours?'

The officer looked over at the smelly, dirty, drunken man and grimaced. 'Yes, sir.'

'All you need to do is get him booked in. He's not in a fit state to question yet. We'll let him sleep it off, then he can have a shower and a hot meal. One of us will be back in time to do the rest.'

'No problem.'

'Thank you.'

There was a loud splash and a lot of squawking coming from the lake and Will turned around in time to see Brad, who was standing up in the boat, waving an oar at the swan. He leant too far on one side and tipped the old wooden rowing boat. It all happened in spectacular slow motion as Brad tried his best to balance himself out and failed miserably. Adele gasped and Will grinned as there was an even bigger splash when he hit the water and actually screamed.

'Fucking bastard bird.'

Will had to turn away. Every officer, PCSO and person allowed in the area was now watching Brad and laughing behind their hands. Brad was now sat in the not so deep lake covered in slime, algae and bird shit. It was at this point that the photographer who Will disliked with a passion managed to capture the shot of the century, which would grace the local paper and the nationals in the next twenty-four hours.

Will buried his head in his hands. 'I don't believe this. You couldn't make it up.' He shouted at the nearest officer, 'Get that bloody photographer out of here now!'

The swan, which had finally given up its watch, swam away to the far side of the lake and Will thought it must have realised that if Brad got hold of it he'd wring its neck and not think twice about it, because it was swimming pretty fast.

Walter woke up and moved his head to see if it still felt as if it was going to explode. It hurt but not like it had earlier. He stood up and found that he could walk without feeling dizzy and he actually felt hungry for the first time today. He opened the fridge door, remembered he still hadn't been shopping and slammed it shut.

He went to the drawer in his bedroom, pulling out the sock he'd hidden his emergency twenty-pound note in. Taking it out, he tucked it in his pocket. That would be enough to buy some junk food from the corner shop to put him on until tomorrow. He pulled his jacket on and ran his fingers through his hair, then left.

It was surprising how much better he felt now he didn't have the weight of that stupid clown costume lying heavy on him. It all felt as if it was a bit of a dream. None of it seemed real. The smell of Mrs Batta's latest concoction filled his nostrils and his stomach groaned as he walked through the communal entrance. He wondered what it would be like to go in her flat, sit down and eat a proper home-cooked meal. It had been so long.

He reached the corner shop, which was full of kids buying bags of sweets and cans of pop. A couple of them were chased out of the shop by the miserable bloke who ran it and Walter had to hide his smile to hear them outside, calling him an old fart. He picked up a basket, filling it with crisps, chocolate bars and cans of Coke. He studied a packet of bacon, but the thought of cooking it made him put it back. There was a packet of microwave sausages on the shelf, with a bright yellow reduced sticker, and he picked it up. Could you really microwave a sausage? He didn't care. For a quid he'd give it a go.

He grabbed a loaf of bread and four cans of Stella and took his basket to the counter. The grumpy bloke scanned his stuff and held out his hand for the money without so much as a please or thank you, which really pissed Wally off. He hated rude people; it didn't take much to say please, did it? He passed him his money then held his hand out for his change, scowling the whole time. As he went outside, the two kids who'd been chased out approached him.

'Hey, mister, will you go in and get us our fags, please?'

Wally looked at them. How old were they? Eleven, twelve?

'I don't think you're old enough to smoke, are you?'

'Nah, but what difference does it make to you if we kill ourselves?'

Wally shrugged. None, he supposed. He held out his hand for their money and they passed over a five-pound note, just like that. Christ, he'd have to have done a paper round for a full month when he was their age to get that.

'Ten Lambert & Butler, mate.'

Wally had no idea if this was enough money, but he went inside and asked for the cigarettes. The owner gave him the packet and very little change. Wally went out and handed them over.

'Thanks, mister, I'm dying for a fag.'

He stared at the boy. 'You're welcome.'

Then he turned and walked away. They might have been cheeky and too young but at least they had manners, which was more than the shopkeeper did. He smiled to himself as he crossed the road and walked past the entrance to the park, which was sealed off with blue and white police tape. A PCSO was standing there guarding the entrance and he felt his heart skip a beat. What if she knew it had been him who'd done it? He felt his skin get clammy and his head began to throb once more.

The PCSO looked at him and Wally nodded, smiling. She smiled back and Wally kept on walking. He needed to get home because he would be safe there. He also needed to do something about this crushing paranoia. As he finally reached the front door to the flats he breathed out a sigh of relief. After letting himself into his flat he locked the door behind him.

Turning around, he saw the clown suit hanging from the coat hanger on the back of the door where he normally kept it. He dropped the bag of shopping. His mouth opening in shock, he looked around. This couldn't be real, could it? How the fuck did that get back here? Someone must have followed him when he took it to the park. They must have watched him dump it and then waited for him to leave before they put it back.

There's only one problem with that scenario, Walter: how did they get in? You locked up behind you. You went back for it and didn't even know, just like you killed the man in the park. You have no idea why you're killing strangers, do you? He shook his head and ran to check the bedroom and bathroom windows. No, someone must have got in through an open window. But both windows were shut and not only that, locked tight with the small key.

His heart racing and the blood pounding in his head, he went back into his living room. Maybe he'd just hallucinated and it wasn't there at all. He walked in and felt his legs give way from underneath him. There in all its bloodstained glory was the clown suit. Hanging there as if it belonged and had never been moved. He didn't know what to do or what was going on, but he couldn't take his eyes off the suit.

Summer 1950

Colin didn't go back to the circus; he didn't want to be there on his own. None of the others would help and it wouldn't be the same. He had nowhere to go and when he'd left the hospital he had wandered around the market in the town. The circus had stopped in for the next two days. He'd slept in the park and been glad it was warm; if it had rained he would have been in trouble. He didn't know what to do now. He couldn't go home because he didn't have one. He had been lost and confused when the woman who owned the fruit and vegetable stall had spoken to him. She had been watching him the last two days as he'd wandered aimlessly.

'Here, what's up with you, lad? You look as if your world has been torn apart.'

He thought about it then nodded. It had. She held out the biggest red apple he'd ever seen and smiled at him.

'Go on, take it. You look as if you could do with a good meal and a hot bath. Have you no one to take care of you?'

He took the apple, turning it around in his hand and marvelling at how colourful it was. Then, realising what she'd said, he shook his head.

'I'm on my own and I don't know where I am or where to go. Thank you for the apple. I'm starving.'

She watched as he bit into the apple and the juice ran down his chin. He reminded her of her son Freddy; he'd been called up and gone to war to fight those bloody Germans and hadn't come home. It had almost finished her off not being able to say goodbye to the son she had idolised since the day she'd first set eyes on him. He'd been such a good boy – always ready to help her – and he'd often work the stall for her if she was having a bad day and couldn't get out of the house.

She didn't know if she was going to regret this, but maybe this lad had been sent to find her for a reason. She could help him; not much, but she could offer him a room to stop in and some food and clothes. In return he could run the stall for her. It was getting harder. Her bloody fingers and knees ached from the moment she woke up until she went to bed and then if she

185

got any sleep it was a bleeding miracle. She held out her hand towards him.

'I'm Maggie Wilkes and this is my stall. I'm after a helper if you're interested and in return I can give you a room and lodgings. I can't pay you much, though.'

He took her hand and shook it. 'I'm Colin. I was going to be a clown until they dropped a pole on my head and my friend got put in prison.'

Maggie stared at him with her mouth open. 'Well, dearie me, I'm afraid this won't be as exciting as circus life, but it will be something until you find your way again. What do you say?'

He smiled at her, nodding his head up and down. 'Yes, I say yes. Thank you, Maggie.'

The cell was sparse. He didn't mind it, though. It was better than many other places he could be. He'd never regained his speech after the accident in the circus and whenever they had asked him if he was guilty he'd shrug. He didn't know what was going to happen, but he knew it was going to be bad. He'd kind of resigned himself to his fate. He couldn't speak; he couldn't stand straight without getting terrible headaches because of the damage the huge wooden pole had caused that awful day. And if he couldn't work the circus there was no point in living anyway.

They'd asked him what his favourite meal was yesterday and he'd drawn them a picture as best he could and even that wasn't brilliant. When the guards had opened the door earlier and brought a tray in with a roast chicken dinner on he'd scoffed the lot, dribbling gravy down his chin. They'd even brought him ice cream for pudding so he wasn't complaining. As he'd spooned the last mouthful of the cold pudding into his mouth he'd looked up to see a priest standing there.

The man asked him if he could come in and pray with him, but he'd given him a silent laugh and shaken his head. He hated church – always had and if they thought that, by buttering him up with a nice dinner, he'd listen to the priest, they could think again. As he lay on his bunk with his hands crossed behind his head he thought about that day in the ring when everything had been perfect until those coppers had turned up. He heard the heavy key the prison warden used to open the metal gate turn in its lock. He sat up to see what was going on and was surprised to see four guards and the priest.

'Come on, lad, it's time.'

He wondered exactly what it was time for? Maybe they were going to let him go back to the circus. He stood up and two of the guards stepped forward, shackling his arms. He let them, not wanting to fight and put them in a bad mood. They hated it when he fought with them. They took hold of an arm each and walked him out of the cell. In a few steps they were behind a wall and he was standing on what looked like an uneven wooden gate.

A brown hessian sack was pulled over his head and he panicked. Why were they doing this? It wasn't fair when he couldn't even speak to ask them. He couldn't breathe as he felt something heavy placed over his head, around his neck, and tightened. Straining to get the sack off his head he felt his feet go from under him as he fell down through the hole in the trapdoors. He felt the rope go taut and then nothing as his neck snapped and he was left dangling like a life-sized marionette.

Chapter Nineteen

2016

Annie couldn't stand feeling so helpless and scared. She had to find out more about the clown suit and what it meant. She wouldn't go to Barrow. She'd steer well clear of the town, but it didn't mean she couldn't do some internet searches. She sat down at the computer. At least it would keep her mind busy. Rocking Alfie in his bouncer with her foot, she was trying to eat a mug of soup with one hand and type into Google with the other.

The loud crunch of tyres on the drive made her pause. She turned her head, managing to spill bright red tomato soup all down her T-shirt. There was a police car outside. *Shit – Jake.* Standing up she tried to wipe the splodge of soup, making the stain spread even more. She walked to the front door, opening it before he hammered on it with his huge fist and woke the baby up.

'What's up, Miss Graham? You rang?'

She felt her cheeks burn as she tried to think of a convincing reason for asking Jake to call and couldn't.

'Nothing really. Are you hungry?'

'What do you think my answer to that will be?'

She laughed. 'Yes, because you're always hungry.'

'Correct. Did you really only want me to come here so you could fat-feed me?'

She opened her mouth, not quite believing what she was hearing. 'Fine, go and get something to eat somewhere else. I do not fat-feed you.'

He grinned. 'If I blame you, Alex can't shout.'

He looked down at the stain on her chest. 'If all you have to offer is a tin of tomato soup I'll pass. I'm thinking more of a bacon and egg sandwich with a sausage thrown into the mix and some mushrooms. All washed down with a huge mug of tea.'

'Christ, if I'd known you wanted an all-you-can-eat breakfast I wouldn't have bothered.' He pulled a face and she shook her head. 'Emotional blackmail.'

'Payback for making me drive over to see you on a boiling hot day when there are hundreds of tourists driving like twats on these windy, scenic roads. You know I still haven't forgiven you for making me transfer up to the Lakes when you went and got yourself up the duff.'

She walked into the kitchen and pulled everything out of the fridge that he'd asked for. He was lucky she had stocked up for Will.

'If you were in Barrow you'd probably be on crappy scene guard at the park. Driving slow behind tourists is probably the better of the two options.'

'True. Did you hear about that?'

She didn't know whether she wanted to or not. Before she could answer Jake continued filling her in on every last gory detail. She was glad her back was to him so he couldn't see the look on her face as she set about grilling the bacon and sausages.

'Will might not be home for hours. Why don't you drive through and go see Alex? I worry about you and Alfie stuck in this house in the middle of nowhere for days on end.'

'I'm not supposed to go to Barrow.' She could have kicked herself, but it was too late now.

'Why?'

'Because.'

'Because what?'

'Because I've been having some weird dreams about whoever is killing people and Derek told me to steer well clear.'

She finished making his sandwich and turned around, placing the plate in front of him. She looked at his face to see if he was going to make fun of her.

'Derek, the weird medium guy from the Ghost House?'

She nodded.

'How is he? It's been a couple of years since you almost got him killed.'

She crossed her arms and glared at him.

'I didn't mean that. It wasn't your fault really. It's just you haven't mentioned him for ages.'

'Well, I didn't want to involve him, but he rang me because he said he had a feeling he should. I don't know what to do, Jake. I'm scared because in these dreams I feel as if I'm there when the killer is.'

'Is what?'

'You know.'

'No, I don't know.'

'When he's killing his victims. I dreamt I followed him; only he knew I was watching him and told me he did.'

Jake chewed the huge mouthful of the sandwich he'd just taken and seemed to contemplate what she was saying.

'The real-life killer figured out you were following him in a dream and now you're scared shitless?'

She nodded.

'Annie, this is a whole new level of freakiness even for you. Does he know who you are?'

'No.'

'Hallelujah for that one. What are you going to do?'

'Keep out of Barrow and hope Will finds the killer pretty quick.'

'Have you told the golden boy all this?'

'Yes, and he freaked out.'

'And that's why you rang me last night. I'm sorry, Annie. Are you and Will OK now?'

'Yes, I think so. He's not very happy about it, though.'

Jake laughed. 'I'm not being funny or taking his side, but do you blame him? It's not as if you haven't got a crap track record at this weird attracting serial killer stuff, is it?'

She sat down on the chair opposite him and sighed. 'No.'

'Look, if you want my advice, keep the doors locked, your phone charged, and yes, you better keep out of Barrow. I can't see there's any way this sicko can find out about you. Can you not take a sleeping tablet so you don't dream?'

'What if I dream even more and he follows me in my dream and I can't wake up to warn everyone because I'm zonked out? I'd rather keep my wits about me and not sleep much.'

Jake's phone rang. He answered it and even Annie could hear Cathy their inspector's voice in the background barking orders at him. He held the phone away from his ear so she didn't deafen him. When she'd finished her mini rant he simply replied, 'Yes, boss.' He put his phone back into his pocket.

'All's not well back at the station. I'm supposed to be at a meeting with the local councillors and I forgot.'

Annie laughed. 'How could you forget something so important?'

'Because I got that mysterious text from you and decided I better come and see you were all right. I worry about you more than I've ever worried about anyone in my entire life, even though you're a pain in the arse.'

He stood up, wiped his mouth with the back of his hand and took his plate to the sink. Then he crossed to where she was sitting on the bar stool and wrapped his huge arms around her, squeezing tight. 'Ring me if you need me. I love you.'

She squeezed him back. 'I will and I love you more.'

He kissed her cheek then walked to the front door. As he went outside he turned to her. 'I think you'll be all right this time, kid. It's just a dream and unless you're like that girl from *A Nightmare on Elm Street* you'll be just fine.'

She rolled her eyes. 'Thank you, Jake; I'm so glad you reminded me all about that film. That's such a relief.'

She waved at him and shut the door, locking it. She wondered if she should have told him because now she'd inadvertently made three people aware that she could follow this killer in her dreams and it could be dangerous for any of them.

She sat back down at the computer and began to read the pages that her search had brought up. The killer clown Tufty was a man called Gordy Marshall who had been arrested after a child's body had been found in some scrubland near the circus. She shivered. How awful – the poor kid must have been terrified. Clowns were scary when they were nice, never mind one that was evil.

She read several similar articles and then she found another that talked about the trainee clown who had been running away from the police the day Tufty got arrested. There had been an accident and both Tufty and the kid had been involved. She had to read back over the article to see if she could find his name: Colin Lister. Both of them were hit by a falling circus pole, which seriously hurt Tufty and injured Colin.

She sat back feeling glad that the clown had got a little bit of comeuppance for what he'd done to the poor kid. It was like something from a film script; in fact she was surprised no one had ever made a film about it. She typed Colin's name into the search engine and was surprised to see an article from a couple of years ago with a photo of an elderly man, smiling and holding a bunch of flowers for one of his carers at the residential home he lived in.

Annie didn't know if this was the same Colin, but he would be around the right age. He looked quite fit and agile for his age. He didn't have a yellow skin tone or sallow cheeks. Maybe he was still alive. She googled the name of the nursing home to find that it was situated on the outskirts of Grange-Over-Sands, which wasn't too far away.

She sat up. Was this too good to be true? Probably, but Grange was nowhere near Barrow so that was a good sign. She could go and visit him, try to find out if this was the same Colin from the circus and then find out what happened to Tufty's clown suit. Of course it could all just be a coincidence and she could find out that he had never been to a circus in his life. But it wouldn't hurt just to go and speak to him, would it? This way she was helping Will without him knowing she was helping him, and it would give her something to do. She picked up her phone and dialled the number of the home.

'Good afternoon – Meadow Field.'

'Oh hello, I was wondering if you could help me? I'm looking for a distant relative called Colin Lister and the last I knew he was a resident there.'

'Can I ask your name?'

Annie was flustered. 'Annie Graham.' She didn't want to give her married name in case they checked up on her.

'Well, I'm not supposed to give out residents' information over the phone, but I can confirm we do have a resident of that name living here.'

'You do? Oh, that's marvellous. Would I be able to come and see him? He won't know me, but I'd like to say hello while I'm in the area and introduce myself to him.'

'Of course you can. We don't have visiting times; it's open hours. Would you like me to tell him you'll be calling?'

'Erm, yes, if you like. That would be great, thanks. It will be in the next couple of hours.'

'I'm sure Colin will be thrilled. He doesn't get any visitors. It will be a nice change for him. Goodbye.'

She hung up and Annie wondered what she'd just let herself in for. Her cheeks were burning. She didn't do lying and she felt bad, but if she could just find out a bit more about that awful costume it might help Will to catch the killer before he killed again.

Will sent Brad home to get changed, because he stank and the smell coming from him was worse than the blood around the victim, which was now being dried up by the sun and attracting every insect within a three-mile radius. Debs had almost finished taking all her samples and the body was ready to be moved up to the hospital mortuary.

The swan – much to everyone's relief – had kept away and let them get on with what needed to be done. The entire park had been sealed off while the search team was assembled and they figured out the killer's way in and out. Will had a fleeting thought: what was it Annie had said? She had followed the killer into the park in her dream. She would know which entrance he'd come through and save them hours of searching.

He was torn. If he asked her it would make their life so much easier. But they would want to know how she knew, and then she would be dragged into this whole investigation. It also occurred to him that she might even be able to identify the killer. Bollocks, why didn't she have the ability to produce amazing poems or bake cakes to die for? Why did she need to have a sixth sense that seemed to bring her in contact with dangerous killers and their ghosts?

He walked back to the car, wondering what he should do. After taking off his suit jacket and tie, he undid the top few buttons on his now-damp shirt. He got in, started the engine and turned the air conditioning on full blast to cool himself down. His head was thudding with the heat and he leant back, pressing it into the cool leather headrest. He closed his eyes.

He had two victims, no known connections, different sexes; the only similar thing was they were around the same age. As far as he knew they didn't know each other. The killer hadn't left any visible clues although the DNA and scrapings from underneath Pauline Cook's fingernails were being fast-tracked so they might come through today with a match.

God, he hoped so. He just wanted whoever had done this in custody so they couldn't hurt anyone else. They could deal with the why and what for once they'd caught him. A loud knock on his window made him jump. He saw Adele standing there looking just as hot and flustered as he'd been. He pressed the button to let the window slide down.

'Everything OK, Will?'

He nodded.

'The undertakers are here. They're ready to move the body.'

'Good, that's good. What about the clean-up team? Has anyone requested one? We can't leave all that congealed blood there. It's a health hazard.'

'Yep, I believe that was done a couple of hours ago. They're on standby once the scene has been cleared.'

'Thanks, Adele, I appreciate your help.'

'No problem, that's what I'm here for. Task force are ready to go. Apparently Hobbs said they always come in and out of the Abbey Road entrance so they're going to start from there and make their way back to the scene.'

'Sounds like a plan.'

He got out of the car, still wondering if he should have just simplified everyone's life by calling Annie. They walked the short distance from the leisure centre car park across to the bridge and down the steps. The familiar sight of the undertakers' silver 'Private Ambulance' met him. It was parked on the grass verge as near to the bridge as possible. The two undertakers were leaning against it waiting for the go-ahead.

Will made his way towards them, giving the area one last look around. He stuck his thumb up and nodded for them to get on with it. He wanted to be out of the sun and in his office with the fan blasting cold air onto his face. At least the hospital mortuary was always cool – another bonus of always being the detective in charge of the latest murders. He felt tired in a way he never had before, as if his entire body and bones were weary. And they were, because he was weary of dealing with so much death and violence.

As the undertakers left the scene with a police car following behind, Will decided he needed a cold shower and an ice-cold drink. He turned to Adele.

'Come on, we've done our bit. The uniforms and PCSOs can keep the scene guard on until the searches have been done.'

The look of joy on her face made him smile. They walked back to his car in silence, both of them too hot and knackered to make small talk. As he started the engine and the air con came on full blast, Adele closed her eyes and sighed. 'Thank God. I don't know what's worse, working a murder scene in summer or winter. What do you think?'

'I think I'd rather not work one at all to be fair, but if I had to choose it would be winter. I can't stand being this hot and the smell is always a hundred times worse in summer.'

Adele nodded in agreement. She still didn't open her eyes. 'What I would give for an ice-cold glass of anything alcoholic to numb the pain and take away the stress.'

Will chuckled. 'I wouldn't say no either; however, the best I can do is one of those slushy type drinks from Costa. Would you settle for one of those?'

'Oh God, yes, please; the tropical one tastes just like Malibu and pineapple.'

'Right, two of those it is then. I wonder if Annie knows about them. She's partial to a Malibu and pineapple now and again.'

'Well, if she doesn't you should take her one home with you or take her for one. They make a nice change from coffee in this heat. How is she anyway? You've been a bit quiet today. Is everything OK?'

Will debated about telling her what had happened last night

then changed his mind. He knew Adele wouldn't gossip but he didn't want to upset Annie in case it did find its way back to her. Jake had so many ways of finding out information. He wouldn't hesitate to tell her if he thought Will was talking about their marital life more than usual.

'She's fine, thanks; just a bit bored of being at home, I think – and doesn't know what to do with herself.'

'It must be difficult living where you live; I suppose she's quite isolated from everything.'

'Yeah, it does have its advantages, though. She can't get into too much trouble in the middle of nowhere.'

Adele smiled. 'You've had a tough couple of years. It can't be easy for either of you, trying to get over what's happened.'

'It's been the best time and probably the worst time of my life. I never imagined I'd ever meet anyone who makes me feel the way I do about Annie. Yet we've had so much scariness to deal with at the same time that it's unbelievable.'

'Well, hopefully things have settled down now you both have Alfie and she isn't working.'

'It has; it's been wonderful. But the time is going by so fast. He's already eight months old and she'll have to decide if she's going back to work soon. I know she's just as torn as me. She loves working and likes to be independent. I would never take that away from her. I just don't want her working this job unless it's in the offices, but that's not Annie's style. She'd hate it cooped up in one place.'

'I can't blame her. As much as I sometimes hate this job I couldn't imagine doing anything else. Could you afford it if she didn't work?'

Will laughed. 'Yes, we could. She doesn't need to work at all. I'm surprised no one has filled you in on all the gory details of my life yet.'

'Ah, I've heard bits and pieces, but I prefer to hear them from the horse's mouth and not gossip.'

'Brad.'

'I couldn't possibly say.'

'We're not millionaires, if that's what you've been told. Well, not yet anyway. My dad is quite well off, though, and I'm an only child, so I suppose, one day that I'd rather not think about, it could come to that. For now, let's just say I can more than take care of everything.'

'What about you? Do you really need to work?'

He looked at her. 'What do you mean?'

'If you're fortunate enough to be able to support the both of you, why on earth are you doing this job, Will? It's mentally draining, depressing and you looked as if you were worn out before.'

'I don't know; it's not something I've ever really thought about. I used to love this job, but since Henry Smith and Heath Tyson it's kind of lost its appeal. I don't know what I'd do with myself if I couldn't come to work, though.'

'Then maybe that's how Annie's feeling – that she's scared to do anything else. If I was you I'd be thinking about setting up some kind of business where the two of you could work together and forget about this place. You've done your best for the people of Barrow. You caught killers and almost died doing this job. Maybe it's time you started something new.'

'Like what?'

'I don't know; maybe you could set up a consultancy business, become private detectives. There must be something better than this. Don't tell me you don't worry every time you leave her on her own, because you must be terrified. I would be.'

Adele stopped talking, clearly worried she might have over-stepped the mark. She opened one eye and looked across to Will, who was trying to think of a way he and Annie could start again – something different. He looked at her and smiled.

'Thanks.'

'For what?'

'For making me stop and think that there's more to life than this. It's a great idea and I'm going to try and think of something Annie will agree with.'

'You're welcome. Now take me for my tropical slush before I die of heat exhaustion.'

Chapter Twenty

Annie dropped Alfie at Lily and Tom's house. She didn't want to take him with her and get him involved in what she was doing in any way, shape or form. She knew it wasn't dangerous; for all she knew there were six thousand Colin Listers in England and he wouldn't have a clue what she was talking about. She kissed Alfie as she passed him over to Lily.

'Thank you; I'll be a couple of hours at the most.'

'Sweetie, you can be a couple of days for all we care. We love having him, don't we, Tom?'

Tom grinned. 'We certainly do. It keeps Lily's mind off interior design.'

Annie laughed. 'Ah, I'm glad to be of some use then.' She winked at Tom and ran back down the steps to the car to get the changing bag out. She handed it to Tom who was still waiting for her. Lily had disappeared into the huge house with Alfie.

'Tell me to mind my own business, Annie, but you're OK, aren't you?'

'I'd never tell you to do that, and yes I'm fine, thank you.'

'What about that son of mine? Is he keeping all right?'

'He's fine. Did you hear about the murders?'

Tom nodded. 'Unfortunately. Can I just ask you – whatever

you're doing has nothing to do with them, does it? I worry about you both so much and now there's that gorgeous baby as well.'

'I promise I'm not getting involved. Will would kill me himself. I'm just helping out with a little bit of background research. I'm not going anywhere near Barrow.'

He breathed out a sigh of relief. 'Good. Anyway, have you been thinking any more about that business idea?'

She smiled. 'Yes, I have and it sounds better by the minute. I just need to discuss it with Will. He's so busy at the moment we haven't had the time.'

'Well, tell him to make time. It's very important for you both.'

'I will, see you later.' She waved and he waved back. She felt awful lying to Tom. In the space of an hour she'd told two lies when normally she never did. What was wrong with her? Technically they weren't massive lies and she wasn't getting involved in Will's case. She was just trying to find out where the hell that clown costume had come from and who had bought it so Will could do the business and catch the killer before anyone else got hurt. That wasn't a bad thing; it was good, and it wasn't dangerous.

She was going to an old people's home not a prison or psychiatric hospital. She drove away. It would only take her thirty minutes, if that, to get to Grange as long as the traffic wasn't too bad. It helped that she knew which retirement home it was. She'd passed it many times going to the quaint seaside town, which once had the best open-air swimming pool she'd ever been to when she'd been a kid.

As she turned into the drive of the once-grand house that had been converted into a retirement home, she wondered if she was getting too involved. Could this be dangerous? A minibus full of elderly people, all with white hair and smiley faces, drove past her and she waved. They all waved back and she told herself no, it wasn't dangerous and she was being far too cautious.

She parked her car, applied a thin coat of nude lipstick and spritzed herself in Chanel. She didn't want to look or smell like the normally flustered mother she was. There were cameras around the building's perimeter and she wondered if they were there to keep an eye on the old people or the people coming into the home. Grange was quite an affluent area and there would more than likely be quite a few wealthy pensioners living here.

The reception area was huge and grand. There was a crystal chandelier that she would have loved in her own house. It was far more modern than she'd anticipated, though she wasn't quite sure what she'd been expecting. The desk was unattended and she took a seat on the leather sofa opposite it. She didn't want to appear too eager or rude.

After a few minutes a smartly dressed woman came striding towards her. 'Sorry, there was a bit of an emergency. Can I help you?'

Annie recognised her voice from the phone call earlier. 'Yes, I rang up about an hour ago, to see if I could speak with Colin Lister.'

The woman held out her hand. 'So you did. Annie Graham, is it?'

Annie took it and shook it. 'Yes, that's me.'

'I've told Colin you were calling. He was a bit surprised to be honest. He didn't think he had any family left that were still alive, but he's looking forward to meeting you.'

If ever Annie had felt guilty, now was the time: not only had she lied about being related, the poor bloke might have got his hopes up that he wasn't all alone. Oh God, what was she going to do about it?

'Come on, I'll take you down to his room.'

For a fleeting moment she almost turned around and ran back to her car. This was awful. But she couldn't do it to him. The least she could do was to go and see him and come clean about her reason for wanting to visit. She followed the receptionist down a long corridor, her stomach churning. The woman stopped and knocked on a white door with the number thirteen on it. Annie was quite surprised they had a number thirteen – most older people were superstitious. The door opened and the man whose picture she'd seen in the paper stood smiling at her.

'You must be Annie. Come in. It's lovely to meet you.'

The receptionist smiled at Colin. 'Should I arrange to get some tea brought down, Colin?'

He nodded. 'That would be lovely, Kate; thank you.'

Annie smiled. He held out his hand to shake hers and she took hold of it. She had not expected his grip to be so firm or him to be so young-looking for his age. He stepped back and she followed him in, admiring the room, which was light and airy. He had some black and white prints on the wall – all scenes from circus life – and she felt a tiny spark of hope.

'I like those. Do you like the circus, Colin?'

He nodded. 'I loved the circus. It was my favourite place in the whole world once upon a time. Please sit down. Kate won't be long with the tea and then you can tell me more about yourself. I was surprised. I didn't think I had any family left.'

Annie sat down in the chair he was pointing to. The door opened and a girl who only looked about seventeen came in balancing a tray of tea on one arm while trying to hold the door. Annie jumped up and took the tray from her before she gave herself third-degree burns.

'Thank you, Lindsey,' Annie said, looking at the girl's name tag.

She smiled. 'You're welcome.' Then she disappeared, letting the door slam behind her.

Annie watched as he poured out two cups of tea, adding the milk.

'Sugar?'

'No, thank you.'

He passed her a cup and she took it from him, not realising that her hands were trembling until it began to rattle and she had to put it down on the table that was between them.

'I'm so sorry, Colin; I have to tell you I'm not really a relative and I feel terrible for lying. It's just they put me on the spot when

203

I phoned and I didn't think they would let me come and see you if I told them we didn't know each other.'

Colin absorbed the information as if he was thinking really hard about it, then he smiled at her.

'I already knew that, dear. I have no family. I was an only child, but I'm intrigued, so would you like to tell me why you're here?'

'This is a bit complicated and a bit of a tenuous link, but I'm a police officer and there have been some serious incidents in Barrow. I believe the offender has been wearing a clown suit.'

'How can I help you with that? What sort of incidents? If you want me to be frank with you, dear, then you'll have to tell me exactly what kind of incidents you're talking about.'

She had no idea if she was doing the right thing, but the murders had been all over the news. The only thing that hadn't was the clown suit.

'This is between you and me, Colin.'

He nodded.

'There have been two murders. I did some research into vintage clown costumes and one came up that looked very similar to the one we think the suspect wore. Did you ever work at a circus, Colin?'

'I did, a very long time ago, and not for very long – much to my dismay.'

'Did you ever work alongside a clown called Tufty? He wore a black and white stripy clown suit with a big ruffle around the neck and had three tufts of hair on his head.'

She pulled a piece of paper out of her handbag with a small picture of the newspaper article showing a picture of Tufty that she'd printed out before she left. She handed it to him.

He paused then nodded.

'I did and he was such an amazing clown. He was so funny and taught me everything that he knew in such a short space of time. He completely changed my life.'

She felt her breath exhale, not realising she'd been holding it in.

'Boy, that was a long time ago. I was seventeen when I met Gordy Marshall, who was better known as Tufty. I can't tell you anything at all; when I was younger I didn't manage very well with social situations. My mother was a drunken slop, who didn't ever help me with my schoolwork or in fact any part of life. I don't really know what happened back then; it's all so long ago.'

'I'm sorry. I don't want to stir up memories for you and upset you. It's just I'm trying to trace what happened to that clown suit. So, you know?'

He shook his head. 'I don't know if I do. My memory isn't what it used to be. I think it might have been left at the circus. One of the other clowns might have kept hold of it or maybe whoever got Gordy's caravan. I'm sorry I can't be of much help to you.'

Annie smiled. 'Don't be sorry. I shouldn't have bothered you. I just wondered if you knew; to be honest, it was a bit of a long shot.'

They both sipped their tea. Annie put her cup down and stood up. 'Thank you for seeing me. I'm sorry if I've caused you any upset.'

He looked at her as if he was searching for something in her face; maybe she reminded him of someone from a long time ago, but she felt a little bit uncomfortable.

'I'll see myself out.'

'Thank you for calling, Annie; it was nice to see you. I don't have any visitors. If you ever find out what happened to the suit, would you come back and let me know? I'd forgotten all about those hot, sweaty, long days. They were amazing: the smell of the greasepaint and the animals. You know, the lion tamer could actually put his head in the lion's mouth. The crowds used to love it. I used to love it.'

She picked up the piece of paper she'd handed to him and scribbled her phone number on it.

'If you do remember something, please could you give me a ring? I don't live that far away. I can be here in thirty minutes – and thank you for your time, Colin.'

She walked out of his room, leaving him staring at the newspaper article about the arrest of Tufty the clown. Luckily for her, she could see the receptionist at the opposite end of the corridor helping an elderly lady along. Annie walked even faster to get out of the doors before the woman stopped to question her super-short visit.

Once she was outside and back in her car, she reversed and drove away as fast as she could, unaware that Colin was watching her from his bedroom window and smiling. She'd brought back all sorts of memories for him that he'd managed to push to one side and forget about. He hadn't thought he would survive outside of the circus, but he had.

He'd found a way and a place in life where he'd got along just fine. He'd helped out on the fruit and veg cart owned by Maggie Wilkes for a few months until the undertaker opposite had asked him to help out one day because he needed someone strong – and he had. Never looking back, he still missed the circus, but he'd learnt that there were other ways to live your life, even if they hadn't been anywhere near as much fun.

Wally went back to bed and slept for hours. This time, when he woke up, he felt almost human again. His stomach groaned. He was starving and needed proper food. He would order a pizza to be delivered with what little money he had left and while he was waiting he would go to the Co-op and buy an evening paper to see if there was any mention of a body being found. If he was really lucky they wouldn't find one and it would be a huge relief; although the coppers were pretty crap so they might not find it for days.

He tried to push it from his mind because if he thought about it too much the sickness came back, taking away his appetite, and he really wanted pizza. He didn't walk past the park or he'd have seen the PCSO still standing at the entrance in front of the blue-and-white-striped police tape that was stretched across to stop anyone from entering the crime scene.

There was a large crowd of teenagers outside with their skateboards and younger kids waving their mobile phones around, wanting to go in, searching for Pokémon to catch. Instead he went in the opposite direction, towards the nearest shop for his paper and a breath of fresh air. He actually felt different, as if he'd spent the last few days in a haze and had woken up. It must have been that suit; maybe it was haunted by whoever wore it last, and whoever it belonged to must have been an evil, sick fuck.

He picked up the paper and a large bottle of cola, not even looking at the headlines in case it made him break out into a cold sweat and have a panic attack in full, public view. He managed to make it all the way back home and was through the gate when he heard a car screech to a stop outside. He turned back to see the pizza delivery guy rooting through the red insulated bags on the back seat of his car.

Wally hurried inside the entrance and opened his door, ready to take charge of his hot, greasy, cheesy feast. The communal front door banged behind him and he smelt the food, which in turn made his stomach gurgle loudly. The guy with the pizzas followed him.

'These yours, mate?'

Wally nodded.

'Fifteen pounds ninety-eight, please.'

He added the please as an afterthought and Wally bit his tongue. Stepping inside his flat he placed the paper on the corner of the sofa then turned around, handing the money over and taking the warm assortment of boxes from him. He kicked his front door shut with one foot and turned around as he walked into the living room. He knocked the paper off the chair and it fell to the floor.

Wally had forgotten all about the suit until he saw it then, in all its bloodstained glory. He felt his fingers lose their grip on the boxes as they slid from his grasp and landed on the floor. He looked down at the huge headline on the front page of the paper: 'Body Found in Park'; then he looked at the suit, which was on the coat hanger on the back of the door. He felt his stomach lurch as the room began to spin once more. As he fell to the floor, everything went black. His head hit the pizza box, which, luckily for him, broke his fall and stopped his head from hitting the cold, concrete floor and smashing his face in.

When Wally eventually fluttered his eyelids, he wondered why he was lying on the floor. He shifted his head, feeling the crumpled cardboard underneath him. His body was stiff and he could feel the coldness creeping through his clothes and making his skin numb. He pushed himself up, then opened the pizza box. It was a bit cold now, and pieces of stringy cheese were stuck to the lid. His stomach groaned and he wondered if he'd passed out because he was ill.

He sat up, leaning against the back of the threadbare sofa where he ate the pizza. He didn't look at the paper and he didn't turn around to see if the suit was still there. Right now he needed fuel to make his body work properly and that was all he cared about. The churning in his stomach made it hard to stomach the pizza, but he bit more off and chewed it slowly.

When he had eaten almost three-quarters of it, he pulled the box with the French fries in near to him and ate the ones he could salvage that hadn't been squashed into the floor when he'd fallen. When he could physically eat no more he still didn't move, groaning now because he was too full. If he turned around and saw the suit he was liable to throw up everything he'd eaten. What he did was pull himself to his feet and go to the bathroom to look at his face because his nose was sore and his cheek was smarting.

It took him a couple of attempts to grab the pull-string, but he caught it and yanked it hard enough for the light to fill the room. He looked into the mirror and grimaced. No wonder his nose was sore. It was crusted with dried blood around his nostrils. His cheek had the beginnings of a dark blue and black bruise, filling almost the full side. He prodded it with his finger, the pain making him flinch.

After running the towel under the tap and wringing it out, he sat on the side of the bath and pressed it against the side of his face. What was he going to do now? Just how had that suit come back? He didn't understand and none of it made any sense. Why couldn't he remember going back to get it? When his face was too numb to feel the pain he stood up, had a pee, then took a deep breath and opened the toilet door. He hoped he'd imagined it and that it wouldn't be there, but he stared at it in horror. It was hanging there in all its glory for the world to see what he had done.

He forced his trembling legs to walk forwards, towards the costume. He was going to pull it down off that hanger and burn it. It wouldn't be able to come back if it was a pile of charred ash. As he stood just inches away from it he reached out his hand to grab it, but snatched it back. He couldn't do it; he was shaking so much. He was afraid of a costume. It was ridiculous. How on earth could that even be possible?

He backed away from it until his calves pushed against the sofa and he fell back onto it. Not once looking away from it, he wasn't sure if he was on some huge trip, or whether his antipsychotics had been a faulty batch and not working properly. He might be coming down with something and hallucinating.

As if he'd reminded himself of how ill he'd felt earlier, the pain in his head came rushing back and he lay down on the sofa – never taking his eyes off the suit until it hurt him to keep them open. Then he turned on his side, away from it. Feeling sleepy, he hoped that when he woke up this would all turn out to have been a bad dream. That there would be no stripy, bloodstained suit that was able to come back of its own accord to watch him and give him orders.

It was too unreal to make any sense of and he wondered if he was delirious; maybe he was or maybe he'd had a full mental breakdown and couldn't distinguish between his dream or waking state? All of these were better options than the one he had. He wanted his sneaking suspicion to be true. It was much easier to believe that the suit was haunted and telling him to kill. Even though the reality was it had nothing to do with the costume.

Colin got dressed, choosing clothes that didn't stand out in the crowd. No checked shirts or bright jumper today. Instead he opted for a pair of dark-brown trousers, black T-shirt and jacket. He picked up his camera, put it around his neck and walked along the corridor to reception.

'Afternoon, Colin, are you going out?'

'Yes, I think I am. It's too nice to be stuck in here all day. I'm feeling a bit restless to tell you the truth. I'm thinking of getting the train to Ulverston and having a wander around, if that's all right?'

'You could get the train to London as long as you're back before they lock up for the night. You know what the night shift manager is like.'

Colin winked at her. 'I do. She's stricter than a nun running a home for tearaway boys.'

He turned and walked away. She laughed at him and carried on scrolling through the latest round of everyone's holiday photos on Instagram. He always felt such a sigh of relief when he was outside the building. As he caught sight of his reflection in a car window he paused. Was that old man staring back at him really him? Where had his life gone in such a flash?

He smiled to himself and carried on walking in the direction of the train station. If he got a move on he might even make the next train and not have to hang around the platform for forty minutes or more. He liked going on the trains. He'd never gone on them as a kid and they reminded him of his short time with the travelling circus.

He really wished that policewoman hadn't come to visit him. He'd been doing all right the way he was. Not thinking about his past life, which was so different to his life now, and it was all so long ago. He preferred to remember the good things that had happened back then and not the bad or the sad. Now he was feeling unsettled again, thanks to her, and he'd have to do something to get rid of it; only he wasn't sure exactly what it was that would restore the normality in his life. For now, a wander around the town and some photography would have to do the trick.

Chapter Twenty-One

Colin had got off the train at Barrow, so absorbed in his memories he'd completely missed the Ulverston stop. He'd seen the headlines of the paper on the billboard outside the station café about a body being found in the public park and had decided to have a walk up Abbey Road to the entrance of the park. It was gory, he knew, but he hadn't seen anything so exciting for years. Of course the body would be long gone and he wouldn't get anywhere near the park to look, but he had nothing better to do with his time.

As he'd wandered to where he could see a crowd of youngsters gathered, he'd stood on the opposite side of the road for a short time. Then, walking a bit further up, he found a low wall to perch on and take the weight off his feet. He heard a door slam behind him; he didn't turn around to see who had come out. It was none of his business, and then he heard a voice whisper, 'The clown did it, the clown did it, the clown did it.' Over and over the tall, skinny man from the auction house who Colin had asked about the clown suit walked past him with his head bent down, muttering the same words. Colin watched him.

The man was the same height as Gordy had been only much slimmer. When Colin was about to get up and go on his way, the man came back. This time his muttering was louder and he was much more agitated than he had been minutes ago. 'The clown did it, the clown did it.' Colin turned and watched as the man avoided looking in the direction of the park opposite and then rushed back in through the front door, leaving it open.

Colin knew that he should ignore it. The man was unhinged. It was plain to see and he could be dangerous. Only he couldn't ignore it. What had he meant: the clown had done it? He pushed himself up and walked through the open front gate. He walked into the communal hallway of the flats and saw the door of the flat furthest away close.

He had no business being here. What he should do was go and tell the police officer standing across the street that there was a man acting very suspiciously in here. He walked towards the front door, stepped outside and then paused as his mind flooded with a multicolour slideshow of his life when he'd been truly happy.

Will went into his office, closing the door behind him; he needed some space to think things through. He also needed some help. It was unfair to expect him to run with both cases. Adele had made him think with her suggestion of packing it all in and going into business with Annie or even finding another job.

He sat down with a piece of paper and tried to write a list of all the things he was good at. In between chewing on the end of his pen, he managed to write down sex, solving murders, being a dad. What else was he good at? He screwed his eyes up while he tried to think of something else. Was he a good husband? He thought he wasn't too bad; then he remembered last night and the fact that he hadn't had time to talk to Annie properly. He'd begun to write that down but then put a big black line through it. No, he wasn't a good husband if he didn't even find the time to find out what was scaring his wife so much.

He tried to think what else he could do. This was so bloody hard. He could do odd jobs around the house, but preferred not to. He couldn't paint landscapes or write books, and poetry was definitely out of the question. He could set up a private detective agency, but it would still take him away from home and possibly bring him into contact with dangerous people, which meant putting Annie in danger. And besides, if he was going to do something like that he may as well stay where he was. This was too hard. He would have to ask Annie what she thought he was good at. God help them if she said sex, solving murders and being a dad.

There was a knock on the door and a much cleaner, sweeter-smelling Brad with still-damp hair opened it. 'Boss.'

Will sat up, pushing the piece of paper he'd been writing on underneath a frayed brown file on his desk. 'Brad.'

'What did you want me to do?'

Will paused as if he was really thinking about it. 'Learn how to row a boat for starters.' He couldn't help himself and started laughing.

Brad frowned at him. 'You might be laughing now, but you won't when I come down with bird flu and pass it on to you lot. You pack of wankers, not one of you came to help me.'

This made Will laugh even harder. There was some shouting outside and a loud thud, making him stand up. Brad turned to see what was going on and Will heard him mutter, 'Fuck.' Will followed him out to see what the commotion was, just in time to see two of the uniformed officers punching the living daylights out of each other. Brad ran and grabbed one and Will the other, pulling them both apart.

A red-faced Shona was standing there, looking as if she wanted the floor to swallow her whole. In seconds Will had assessed the situation and figured out that Shona had obviously been seeing both of the younger coppers and they'd found out. Will dragged his copper into his office and Brad dragged his along the corridor so they could both calm down before the chief super realised what was going on and came out of his office to suspend the pair of them. Adele took Shona off to the ladies' to compose herself.

Will slammed his door shut. He took one look at the miserable expression on the young lad's face and felt sorry for him.

'Look, I don't particularly want to know what this is all about because I have a pretty good idea, but you can't go around fighting like that in the station of all places.'

He felt a bit of a hypocrite. When he'd first starting seeing Annie, he and Jake had had a similar set-to because Jake didn't want Will breaking her heart and Will did have a reputation as a bit of a playboy.

'Sorry, Sarge, it won't happen again.'

'No, it won't, because next time you might end up with the super breathing down your neck. I suggest you both apologise to each other and let Shona get on with fucking her own life up and not your careers. Do I make myself clear?'

He nodded. Will pointed to the door. He was definitely getting too old for all this drama. The officer left and Brad came back along the hall, grinning. Obviously he was glad that at least the gossip about his embarrassing tumble into the park lake hadn't lasted long. This would keep the gossips busy for weeks. Brad sat down at his desk, waiting for Shona to come back so he could take the piss out of her. Will didn't know what was worse, working with an office full of twenty-year-olds or being out chasing killers.

The phone on his desk rang and he picked it up. The tone of the voice on the other end told him everything he needed to know without even getting to the details.

'Are you sure? Yes, I'm on my way.'

He grabbed his suit jacket from the back of his chair and shrugged it on, sipping the last of his coffee, then throwing the paper cup into the bin. He went to look for Adele who was on her way out of the ladies'.

'Are you good to go? There's another body.'

The look on her face just about summed up how he was feeling at this very moment: pissed off with a huge sprinkling of tired and a stress migraine to add to the enjoyment.

'Where?'

'That block of flats on Abbey Road opposite the park where they tasered that poor woman a few days ago. They don't know if it's suspicious yet. It could be a suicide, but the victim is wearing a bloodstained clown suit and the officer on scene can't see any open wounds.'

'Really?'

'Really.'

'This isn't some kind of wind-up?'

'After today I no longer possess a sense of humour. No, it's not a wind-up.'

She sighed loud enough for the pair of them. Will turned to Brad, who was actually sitting playing some stupid game on his phone.

'Brad, turn that off and get yourself up to the mortuary. Take Shona with you. I want a full report on my desk about Billy Marks. See if they're ready to do the PM. When you get back start getting me every piece of background information we have on the system for him. He's old-school and will have a record as long as my arm. I want all his associates printed off and the most recent ones spoken to.'

'Where are you going?'

'There's another body.'

Even Brad's face paled at the thought of the workload three sudden deaths in the space of a couple of days were going to cause. Adele followed Will. 'At this rate, the amount of time we're spending coming in and out of the station and working crime scenes, there's no need to go to the gym. I've never walked so much since I joined the job and was a patrol officer walking the beat.'

Abbey Road was one of the busiest roads in the town and it was a good job the flats were situated on a stretch of it with four lanes for the traffic; otherwise they would have caused pandemonium. Will parked behind the police van. There was an empty ambulance just in front of it. The two paramedics came out of the shabby-looking front door. One of them, who'd also been present at Pauline Cook's house, shook her head.

'Does it look suspicious?'

'It looks super weird is how it looks, so yes, I suppose you could say it's suspicious.'

He felt his stomach heave at the thought of having to face another body so soon. 'Is it bad?'

'Nope, he's relatively fresh. Still warm. We got an emergency call to say someone had stopped breathing. We got here and the flat door was wide open so we went inside and that's when we saw him lying on the sofa with a plastic bag over his head.'

Will felt a spark of hope that this was going to turn into a suicide and not a full-blown murder investigation. Not that a suicide was much better. It was still a tragic waste of a life and terrible heartbreak for the family. He was just being selfish and thinking about how much easier it would make his life. The officer who'd come to the job after the ambulance had phoned it in. He was standing at the entrance to the flats.

Will turned to Adele. 'We better suit up, just in case.'

She didn't say a word and followed him back to the boot of his car to pull out a full set of protective gear.

'You're going to have to restock, boss; you're almost out of everything.'

Will nodded. 'You'd think that in a bad year you'd maybe use two or three of these things, not three in the space of a week.'

'When I told my sergeant I wanted to transfer to Barrow he actually laughed and said that if I was after an easy life I was fooling myself. I thought he was talking bollocks, but now I realise he was telling the truth. Seriously, it can't be this bad all the time, can it?'

Will didn't know what to say; no, it wasn't usually. It did, however, go through phases – for want of a better word – where it would be manic and then calm down for a couple of months.

'I'd like to say no, but I'd be lying. It's not like this all the time;

however, it is like this quite often. I bet you'll be withdrawing your transfer request as soon as possible after this.'

She looked at him. 'Nah, believe it or not, as knackered as I am, I like working with you, and the rest of the team aren't too bad either if you allow for them all being half my age.'

They went into the block of flats. At least it wouldn't smell if he was fresh, which was a huge relief. Will was expecting to go upstairs to the flat they'd visited the other night after the serious domestic. He thought that either she'd finished the job off or he'd killed himself.

As he walked up the stairs he heard the officer shout to him, 'It's downstairs, boss, the bottom flat on the right.'

Will turned around and realised it was the flat he'd knocked at with the strange, jumpy man. What was his name? Screwing up his eyes he tried to remember but couldn't. At least he had his details in the back of his pocket notebook that he'd left in the car. He'd have a look when he came back out.

Adele waited for him to lead the way and then followed him inside. The paramedic was right; Will had never seen anything like it in his life and he'd seen some strange stuff. The scrawny guy was lying straight out on the sofa dressed in a black and white satin clown suit, which was indeed covered in what looked like bloodstains. He would need Matt to confirm this, though; for all he knew it could be tomato sauce. The stains were dried and not fresh.

Over his head was a clear polythene bag that had been fastened with a black tie wrap – the sort he had a garage full of back home. He stepped closer and took out the miniature tablet. The only thing he used his for was to take photographs. Once he'd remembered his password and opened the damn thing up he took a couple of snaps. He wanted to show Annie. Hadn't she said something about a clown being at Pauline Cook's house?

Adele, who hadn't spoken up until now, looked at Will. 'Is there a circus in town?'

He shrugged. 'I wouldn't have a bloody clue.' Tucking the tablet back in his pocket he noted the bruises on the man's face, but he couldn't see any other injuries. Stepping away from the body he turned to look around the flat. He couldn't see anything of any value; in fact it was a shithole. There were no signs of any forced entry. The victim could have left his front door open, hoping that someone would come along and find him, save his life. He wanted so much to say that it wasn't suspicious, but he couldn't. It didn't sit right; it was all out of sync.

'Come on, let's wait outside for Matt. I need to know who phoned it in. I can't say that it's suicide; as much as I would love to, it's not right. There's something strange about this and I have alarm bells ringing in the back of my mind.'

Adele smiled at him grimly. 'I agree; it's odd.'

They walked out, leaving the man where they'd found him. Will suddenly remembered his name: Walter Lacey. While they waited for Matt to arrive they began to knock on doors to see when the last time was his neighbours had seen or spoken to him.

Chapter Twenty-Two

All the way home Annie couldn't shake the feeling of being watched, which she put down to the ghost of the young man in her house. She felt gutted that she'd found out no information whatsoever about that clown suit to pass on to Will. She was going to go home and try her best to help the man in her house to move over to the light. She didn't want any spirits hanging around and upsetting Alfie, who could probably sense him just as much as she could. Her phone rang and she pressed the button on the steering wheel, allowing her to talk.

'Annnie, please don't come get this precious baby yet. My friend is on her way from Manchester and she hasn't seen him yet.'

Annie laughed. 'Well, I've finished now and was on my way, but I can go home and get sorted out. Actually that would be perfect; thank you, Lily.'

'My pleasure. See you later.'

She ended the call and Annie wondered if Lily had a sixth sense she didn't even know about. Most people had it. They just never tapped into it. She always seemed to know when Annie needed some space and time to get things done – either that or she was just very perceptive.

Parking outside her house, Annie looked up at her bedroom

window. It was a habit she couldn't break after her close encounter with Betsy Baker. No matter how many times she did it, the thought that someone would be staring back down at her was always at the back of her mind. She got out of the car and walked across to the garage that doubled up as a storage shed. There was a large box full of candles, and next to it one full of light bulbs. She hated the dark and living out in the middle of nowhere if there was a power cut wasn't the most fun thing to endure on your own.

After pulling out four white church candles she took them to the house. She would roll the rug up and light the candles in the lounge, then tell him he needed to go to the light. It wasn't something she'd had to do before, but she'd watched it being done on the television so it couldn't be that hard, could it?

As she moved Alfie's baby bouncer and toys off the plush rug and rolled it up, she wondered if she should phone Derek to get his advice. She wasn't scared of the spirit who had somehow found his way here, but she did find it unsettling that he couldn't speak to her. She bent down to get a box of matches from the side of the wood burner and began to light each candle. As she lit the fourth one her mobile rang. She glanced at the coffee table to see who it was and didn't recognise the number. As much as she wanted to ignore it, she was unable to. She snatched it up and answered.

'Is this Annie Graham?'

'Yes, speaking.'

'It's Mrs Brown from the vicarage. I'm afraid I have some bad news.'

Annie felt her knees go weak and sat down onto the sofa.

'It's Father Trelmain; he collapsed and has been rushed to the hospital. They think he's had a heart attack.'

'Is he alive?'

Annie was biting her lip and had her fingers crossed. She was terrified of what the elderly woman on the other end of the phone was going to tell her.

'Yes, but he's in a bad way.'

'Which hospital?'

'Westmorland, I think. It was all a bit of a blur to tell the truth. He gave me such a shock. He was rushing out of the rectory towards the church and there was such a clatter. I ran outside and he was on the floor. Some of the workmen from the church had already phoned for an ambulance and had put him in the recovery position. It was so awful. He looked grey and he grabbed my hand and whispered: *Annie*.'

'Thank you for letting me know, Mrs Brown.'

She ended the call and ran out of the house to her car. She loved Father John. He was like the dad she'd never known. She felt terrible; he hadn't looked well when she'd called in to talk to him a few days ago and all she'd done was go on about her life. She should have insisted he went to the doctor's then. She should have taken him herself.

Before she set off she rang Will, who didn't pick up, which made her so mad with him she didn't leave a message. She didn't even know for sure which hospital they'd taken Father John to. She rang Westmorland, who told her they had a limited A&E running and he was more than likely to have been taken to Furness General Hospital in Barrow.

Annie set off driving, hoping that Will could get back to her before she reached the outskirts of Barrow. It didn't matter that she'd promised him she wouldn't set foot anywhere near Barrow. What mattered was that she was there for John when he needed her.

Teatime at Meadow Field residential home was always manic. Nurse Andrea Wallis, who was dishing up the medication, looked to the table that Colin usually sat at to get his tablets. She was surprised to see his seat vacant. She caught hold of the arm of the auxiliary who was walking past.

'Emma, please can you take this down to Colin – is he not feeling well?'

Emma shrugged. 'I don't know. I'm on the other side of the corridor. Jenny is doing Colin's side.'

Andrea looked around for Jenny and couldn't see her. 'Please, just go down and check on him for me. I'd go, but I can't leave the medicine trolley.'

Emma took the small plastic pill pot from her, went out of the doors and walked towards Colin's room. She knocked, waiting for him to call her in. He didn't. She knocked again and opened his door a little.

'Colin, it's teatime. What's the matter? Not like you to miss a meal.'

She was greeted by silence. Opening the door wider she stepped inside. His room was empty. She checked the small en suite, which was also empty, and turned around and went back to the dining room.

'He's not in his room.'

Andrea frowned. 'Where is he then?'

'If I knew that I wouldn't be working here, would I? I'd have known which six numbers to pick on the Euro.'

'Mind the trolley.' Andrea rushed out to the reception area. 'Have you seen Colin?'

'He went out just before dinnertime; said he was going to Ulverston for a stroll. He promised he'd be back before you started your shift. Is he not here?'

'No, he bloody well isn't. Why didn't you tell me this before at the handover?'

'I didn't think. He goes out all the time. He's probably missed the train, that's all. He'll be here soon.'

'When does he ever miss the train? I'll tell you when: never. Was he OK when he left? Did he seem himself?'

'I think so; he didn't look any different.'

'Has anything happened that I should know about?'

'He had a visitor this morning – some woman who said she was a distant relation visiting the area.'

The nurse's face paled. 'Who was she? What did she want?'

'For Christ's sake what is this – the Spanish inquisition? He's a grown man in case it escaped your notice. I think he's bloody well mature enough to decide if he wants to speak to long-lost relations or to go out of this sodding place and get some fresh air. He's probably in the pub pissed as a fart. *Because that's where I would be if I had to live in this mausoleum day in day out, waiting to die,*' she muttered under her breath.

Andrea didn't take any notice of her. She was too busy dialling the police to report him missing.

Jake was sitting at his desk staring at the attachment he'd just opened that had come from Will. It was a photograph of a dead man lying on his sofa in a clown costume and was one of the weirdest things he'd seen in a while. He replied to Will's email, asking him what was going on.

The whole time he was playing with the huge salad in front of him while waiting for his reply. He'd eaten all the chicken and a minute portion of coleslaw. He'd never been fond of rabbit food. He was also bloody starving and cursing Alex for not chucking in a couple of doorsteps of bread. The rest of the station was empty. A car accident on the A590 by Newby Bridge had meant all the staff except him had been deployed to it. He heard Cathy laugh behind him.

'Jesus, that's a sorry excuse for your dinner. It's almost as bad as mine.'

'Why, what you got?'

'I did have a wholemeal salad wrap that tasted like shite with no butter or mayo on it. Are Kav and Alex in cahoots about what to feed us? Because I can't take much more of this. I need stodgy, greasy, fatty food to keep me going in this shithole.'

Jake laughed. He felt better about the state of his lunch. If Kav had Cathy on a healthy eating kick, things must be bad.

'What do you say that me and you go down to the pie shop and get a couple of pies and cream cakes? I won't tell Alex if you don't tell Kav.'

Jake stood up. 'I'd say that was a fucking brilliant idea, boss.'

She nodded her head. 'Me too; come on, I'm foaming at the mouth.' They left the station and got into the van that Jake was driving. The pie shop was only a few minutes down the road, but neither of them wanted the pleasure of foot-patrolling through busy Bowness. It was too full of tourists and Jake didn't think Cathy would cope if they got stopped every thirty seconds to get asked for directions, boat sailing times or to have their photographs taken.

He stuck his hazard lights on and parked on the double yellow lines outside the delicatessen that also sold pies and cakes. He even made it to the door before his radio crackled into life. He listened as the control room asked him to go to Meadow Field in Grange as he was the only available patrol.

'Is it urgent?'

'It's a grade two. There's a missing patient who hasn't been seen for several hours. The nurse sounded pretty upset so I'd suggest you get there sooner rather than later.'

'Roger.'

He quickly asked for an assortment of pies and cakes then rushed out to the van.

Cathy looked at him. 'If you'd have come out of that shop empty-handed I'd have eaten you.'

'Steady on, boss; you know I'm a married man.'

Cathy stared at him, waiting for him to put the pies on the dashboard, then she punched him in the arm.

'Filth, Officer Simpson. Pure filth.'

Jake laughed. 'Did you hear that shout?'

'I did and, seeing as how I'm bored, I'll go with you to keep you company. I haven't been to Grange for ages. It will be a nice run out and that way I can eat my pie and cake before you do.'

He set off driving along the busy road, not having to blue-light it because it wasn't a grade-one job, but going faster than he normally would.

Chapter Twenty-Three

When Annie finally arrived at the hospital she parked on double yellow lines, abandoning her car and not caring if she got a ticket. She needed to see John. He had a sister who had died last year. Annie was the closest thing to family he had. She rushed into the emergency department and asked for him.

'Who are you?'

'I'm his daughter.'

She felt terrible. That was three blatant lies in the space of one day, but they would never let her in if she told them she was his friend and she couldn't do that. She couldn't go home without seeing how bad he was for herself. She gave John's details to the receptionist so they could book him in and then she gave her own details. The nice man smiled, not even raising an eyebrow when she gave John's address as the rectory. He pointed to the hard blue plastic chairs.

'You can wait out here, or go into the relatives' room. It's up to you. I'd go into the relatives' room if I was you. The chairs are comfier and it's more private.'

Annie knew from experience just how hard those blue chairs were, but she'd take a chance. She didn't want to be hidden away and forgotten about in the relatives' room; if they took him down to intensive care or theatre she would see him go past.

'Thank you, I'll wait here. Can you tell him I'm here?'

'I'll tell the nurse.'

Annie went and sat on the chair facing away from the exit. She pulled her phone out to see if Will had tried to ring her back and realised it was dead. Shoving it back in her pocket she decided she'd ring Will again as soon as she knew what was happening. She'd left her handbag and purse in the car and didn't have any loose change on her for the payphone.

After what seemed like forever a doctor called her name and she stood up. She held the door open for her and Annie followed her through to the cubicles.

'I'm afraid your dad has had a serious heart attack. We had to resuscitate him when he came into the department.'

Annie felt hot, salty tears fill her eyes and the doctor reached out and grabbed her hand.

'But we've managed to stabilise him. We're going to transfer him down to intensive care shortly but in the meantime would you like to come and sit with him?'

'Yes, please. Will he be OK?'

'I'm afraid it's early days yet. This was quite a severe heart attack. The next twenty-four hours will be crucial.'

The doctor led her to a room at the end of the department. Annie could count the cubicles that she'd been a patient in. There were so many of them. She wondered how on earth Will had coped with the stress and heartbreak of it all. The doctor stepped to one side to let her in. She saw the frail figure lying on the bed, hooked up to almost every machine in the department, and burst into tears. The doctor patted her shoulder and left her to it. Annie wiped her tears on her sleeve, then walked over to the bed and bent down to kiss John's forehead. He looked so grey. She sat on the chair next to the bed and gently clasped her fingers around his hand.

'I'm here, John, and you're going to be fine. Have a sleep and then you'll feel much better.'

She sat watching the rise and fall of his chest, the whole time praying to God to look after his ever so faithful servant.

Cathy had eaten her pie and was just cramming the last of her jam and cream doughnut in her mouth as Jake arrived at the retirement home. He looked at her and she shrugged.

'A girl has got to eat. You can have yours when you come out. If you don't piss around in there it might still be warm.'

'Are you not coming in?'

'I said I'd come keep you company, not do your bloody job for you.'

He shook his head at her and got out of the van. 'Don't you dare eat my cake.'

'Would I do that to you?'

Slamming the door shut he walked towards the entrance and muttered, '*Yes, you bloody would.*'

The receptionist and a nurse greeted him at the door.

'Sorry to have called you out. I'm Andrea Wallis – the nurse in charge tonight.'

Jake looked at the clock above the reception desk. It wasn't even half past five. If he thought his working hours were shite, hers were abysmal.

She explained what had happened and he nodded his head as he listened.

'So Colin goes out on his own and uses the trains quite frequently?'

'Yes.'

'But he's always back by four o'clock. The trains could be running late; you know what they're like.'

'We've already spoken to the staff at both Grange and Ulverston stations and they're not. They've been very helpful. They said they would get the CCTV footage ready for an officer to look at of the times Colin would have got the train and where he would get off.'

Jake was impressed. That was one of his jobs ticked off his list.

'Has anything happened to upset Colin? What is his mental health like at the moment?'

'Well, he had a visitor this morning, which is very unusual for him because he has no family that we're aware of and he never has anyone coming to see him.'

'What was he like after they'd gone?'

'Fine, he seemed his usual self. Very upbeat and happy. He's not a depressive type of man. He doesn't take any medication except for heart tablets and painkillers for his knees, which sometimes give him some trouble.'

'Can I take a look at his room? I know this seems ridiculous and I'm not insinuating that you wouldn't have already done this, but I have to ask. Have the staff checked the entire building: toilets, bathrooms, other residents' rooms, kitchens, gardens, to make sure he isn't in one of them?'

'Yes, the entire building has been searched. There are two staff out checking the gardens as we speak. I've also checked our CCTV and he's not come back through the front doors. We only have him leaving.'

She led him down to Colin's room. Jake was hoping the bloke would be curled up in his bed fast asleep. He followed the nurse in and almost sighed. Colin definitely wasn't in his neatly made bed. He looked at the vintage circus prints on the wall and noticed a box on the bedside table. He picked it up and took the lid off to see a stack of black and white photographs, which he picked up and began to look through.

They were actually very good considering their age and he smiled to see pictures of a circus tent with a row of clowns outside. The next one had only two clowns on it and was much clearer. There was something about it that jarred his mind. He stared at it. Why did it look so familiar? And then he realised exactly what looked familiar. He typed Will's number into his radio keypad and waited for it to ring.

'Go ahead.'

'It's Jake. I'm at Meadow Field nursing home in Grange. There's something here I think you should take a look at.'

'What are you talking about? Jake, I've got three bodies stacked up at the morgue. I haven't got time to come to Grange.'

'Well, I think you better make time because I've just found some old photos in one of the resident's bedrooms and they're of a clown wearing what looks like the exact same suit as your latest body.'

'On my way.'

The nurse looked at him, her mouth open, all the colour drained from her face.

'Shit, not Colin's body – sorry, that sounded wrong. A body has turned up wearing a similar costume to the one in this photograph. It's a young lad.'

'Oh, thank God for that. Oh no, I don't mean that. It's terrible someone is dead, but I'm relieved it's not Colin.'

Jake knew what she was trying to say. He just wished he knew what all of this meant. He crossed to the window that looked out onto the car park and knocked on it to catch Cathy's attention. She held her hands up and pointed to the paper bags still on the dashboard, which made him smile: guilty conscience. He beckoned her in and she shook her head, so he typed in her number on his radio.

'What, Jacob?'

'Boss, I need you in here, please.'

'You're a pain in the arse, Jake. I haven't touched your cake.'

'Good or I'd be putting in a grievance. Please, I need some advice.'

She rolled her eyes at him, but opened the van door and jumped out. He walked out of the room to greet her in the corridor. He told her what he'd found and she looked at him.

'What are you thinking?'

Cathy looked at the nurse who was still hovering.

'Could you give us a minute, please?'

'Certainly.'

She walked off back towards the huge lounge where it looked as if they'd rounded up every resident and had them contained.

'I don't know. Will sent me a photo of the sudden death he'd been to before. The guy was wearing some freaky black and white stripy clown suit. I've just been looking through Colin Lister's photos and there's a stack of them from back in the day – taken at a circus – and there's a clown on them wearing what looks like the same suit.'

He bent down and fiddled around with his tablet to see if he could get the email open to show her. He finally managed to get it open and passed it to her.

'Yes, I agree that's a freaky outfit to wear to kill yourself in; maybe he has some kind of clown fetish.'

Jake went back inside Colin's room and picked up the photo he'd put on the small bedside table. He handed it to her. She studied it and looked at the photo on the tablet.

'Well, I can definitely say it's not the same person.'

Jake looked at her. 'Of course it's not the same fucking person. I'm not saying that.'

'Then what are you saying? Yes, the costumes look similar; however, I'm not an expert on clown suits. Maybe this is like a common one among them. The dead guy probably bought it off eBay.'

He rolled his eyes at her, wishing he'd left her in Bowness.

'Don't you think it's kind of weird, though? A body turns up wearing a clown suit and this old guy, Colin, who was probably in the circus, has pictures of clowns wearing a similar suit and has gone missing?'

'You watch too much television, Jake. This is real life not *The X-Files*. Do you think we have a seventy-year-old serial killer on our hands who likes to dress his victims up as clowns before suffocating them? Come on, that's pushing it even for you.'

'He's in his eighties actually.'

Cathy started to laugh – her too-loud, raucous, belly-shaking laugh – and Jake joined in. It was infectious, until the nurse came back in to see what was happening, stopping them both in their tracks.

'Is everything OK?'

'Yes, sorry. Have you got a recent photograph of Colin we can distribute to officers in Ulverston and a description of what he was wearing?'

The nurse nodded and disappeared again.

'You're a bad influence, boss.'

She nodded. 'And you're a cock, but I love you even though you are.'

'You say the nicest things. Will's on his way. We can see what he has to say. If he thinks it's a load of rubbish we can get on, can't we?'

'Aw, you called in reinforcements; maybe you're not such a cock after all. With a bit of luck he'll want this and you can take me back to get some indigestion tablets. Bloody pies kill me off every time I eat them.'

They wandered back up to the reception area to sit and wait for Will. The nurse passed Jake a photo of Colin, which he photographed and added as an attachment, sending it to the control room to distribute to officers who would be attached to the incident log and sent out looking for him. One of the auxiliaries brought them two mugs of coffee and a plate of biscuits, which put a smile back on Cathy's face.

She leant over and whispered, 'I'll let you off, Jake. At least they have decent biscuits.'

Chapter Twenty-Four

Adele gave Will directions off her phone. His satnav had frozen in time and space. He hoped to God that there was some kind of link between this missing man and the latest body. It would give them something to go off, which was better than the nothing they had at the moment.

'Do you think there will be some connection?' Adele had read his mind.

'I hope so.'

She nodded. 'Me too, we could do with a break. Take the next left, then it's the first on the right.'

She stopped the annoying voice of the woman who was giving her directions, looking as though she was tempted to chuck her phone out of the window. Will pulled up outside the retirement home and Adele whistled.

'If my kids ever farm me out to a home, then I want to end up somewhere like this. It's beautiful.'

'It's not bad, is it?'

They got out of the car and walked in to see Jake and Cathy sitting there, nursing mugs of coffee.

'Thanks for this, Jake.'

Cathy sat up. 'Not sure there's much to thank him for yet.'

Adele held her hand out to Cathy who took it and shook it.

'Well, if you don't need me I'll go and wait outside. It's all a bit much like police work to me.'

She winked at Will and went outside. Jake took him and Adele down to Colin's room.

'I haven't touched anything except the tin box the photos were in. I've left those on the bedside table next to it. It's probably a huge coincidence, to be honest, but it just felt wrong if you know what I mean?'

Will knew exactly what he meant. Pulling on a pair of latex gloves he went inside to look at the photographs. He held the close-up of the two men up to his face. It definitely looked like the same suit as the one Walter Lacey had been wearing – or, if not, one very similar. He passed the photo to Adele, who studied it. Will flicked through the others.

He looked at the pictures on the wall and noticed a piece of paper that had fallen behind the armchair. He picked it up, unfolding it. It was a photocopy of a newspaper article with a close-up of one of the clowns in the photo and the headline 'Tufty the Killer Clown'. He read the article, which told him that the clown had been hanged for killing a woman, his own parents and a child. He passed it to Adele, who scanned it.

'Shit, this is all too weird. It has to be connected somehow.'

'We need to find this Colin Lister. It seems as if he is the key to all of this because I can't make head nor tail of it. There's definitely some connection. I just don't know how or what.'

Will went to find Jake. 'Have you got some evidence bags in the van?'

'Yes, loads of them.'

'I just need a few for now.'

The nurse, who was looking flustered, came out of the lounge.

'Can someone tell me what is happening? I can't keep our residents cooped up in here all night. Some of them want to go to the toilet.'

'If I'm honest, at the moment I can't really tell you much except that there are some items of interest in Colin's room that may be pertinent to a murder investigation that is currently ongoing. I'm afraid I'm going to have to get our CSI to come and photograph them in situ. I can't let anyone in or out of his room. Have you heard from Colin?'

Shocked, she didn't know what to say so shook her head. Jake came back in clutching some bags and passed them to Will.

'Colin had a long-lost family member visit him this morning out of the blue.'

Will looked at the nurse. 'Do you have a record of who it was? We will need to speak to them as well.'

'We should do. We normally keep a list of who comes in and out.'

She went behind the desk and looked through the book. There was nothing written on the page for today. Then she noticed a scrap of paper next to it with Colin's name written on it and, underneath, a name she wasn't familiar with.

'Yes, here it is. An Annie Graham.'

Will actually felt his heart skip a beat and his legs trembled. Jake shook his head.

'Are you sure it says Annie Graham?'

She passed him the paper and he showed it to Will, who was feeling the familiar ball of dread forming in his stomach.

'It doesn't mean it was her, Will. There's bound to be more than one Annie Graham in England, and besides, she's not Graham anymore, is she? She's Ashworth.'

Will felt the pressure of the blood as it rushed through his brain and shook his head. He took out his phone. He had two missed calls from Annie. He dialled and got voicemail. He shook his head and Jake pulled out his phone and rattled off a text, sending it to her with his fingers crossed.

'Do you have any more details about her: address, phone number?'

'There's nothing here, I'm sorry. Just a name.'

Jake looked at the camera above the entrance.

'Can you check the CCTV, please. We need to know what she looked like.'

She went behind the desk and began to fiddle with the camera's hard drive. Adele – who had figured out that the Annie who had them in such a flap was more than likely Will's wife – was on her radio asking for a patrol to go and check their home address. The camera started to play and after a few minutes that felt like hours to Will he watched his wife, his Annie, walk through the doors of the home into the reception area.

Jake whistled under his breath. 'What the hell is she doing here?'

Will looked at him. 'If I knew that I'd tell you. She never mentioned any of this.' He remembered their argument and how she'd needed to talk to him and he'd rushed off to work. What was she doing visiting Colin Lister? She didn't even know him and had never mentioned him to Will ever. His phone rang from an unknown number and he answered it to hear Annie's trembling voice on the other end.

'Oh, Will, it's terrible. I'm at the hospital.'

'Annie, are you OK? Who is with you?'

'I'm fine. It's John; he had a massive heart attack.'

Will stuck his thumb up at Jake, who mouthed: '*Thank fuck for that.*'

'Which hospital? I'll be there soon. Annie, what the hell were you doing visiting Meadow Field to see Colin Lister?'

'Ah, you found out about that. Did they phone the police and report me?'

'For what?'

'For lying to get in to see him. I knew it was a bad idea. I was just trying to help you.'

Will sat down on a chair. 'I haven't got a clue what you're talking about. I'm here because he's gone missing.'

236

'Oh no, has he? He's a lovely chap. Look, my money's about to run out; my mobile is dead. I'm at FGH. I'm going to come home now. There isn't much I can do at the moment.'

'No. Don't you dare leave that hospital until me or Jake come and get you.' The phone went dead. *Annie, for once in your life, do as you're told.*

Jake was already out of the doors. 'I'll go get her and bring her home. Cathy can babysit her. As long as Annie feeds her she'll be fine.'

Will was grateful that, this time, Annie wasn't being held captive by some serial killer who wanted to slit her throat.

'Thanks, I'll carry on here for now.'

Adele looked at Will. 'Jesus, my heart is racing. Thank God she's fine.'

He couldn't suppress the laughter. 'Welcome to my world, Adele. I love my wife more than anything, but she has a habit of getting mixed up in more disasters than you could imagine.'

'You can say that again. How come you're not grey or bald?'

He shrugged.

Chapter Twenty-Five

Colin had wandered for miles; he was tired now and sat down on a bench. What a day he'd had. He looked at his watch and felt bad. He'd promised the nice receptionist he'd be home before the night shift started and he wasn't. Still, he was a fully grown man. He could stay out if he wanted to. He didn't have to answer to the staff at the home. He only did it for an easy life.

He didn't have one of those phones all the kids had; he didn't like them, much preferring proper telephones. He'd been intending to call the home, but he'd walked for miles and not come across a single phone box. It was madness. When he was younger they were on every street corner and surely there must be more people than him who didn't possess one of those tiny boxes of technology.

He hadn't realised just how tiring today had been until now, when he'd sat down. That man from the auction house had lied about Gordy's old suit. He had known there was something shifty about him when he'd talked to him after the auction. The way he'd behaved wasn't normal – when he'd been muttering to himself.

Colin had panicked when he'd gone inside and seen the man wearing that old costume. He'd turned around and left the flat, not bothering to close the door behind him. He'd rushed out onto the very busy main road and begun walking as fast as he could to look for a phone box. He'd looked for such a long time. All he wanted was for someone from the home to come pick him up and take him back to his boring, but safe, life.

Annie went back to the intensive care unit to say goodnight to John and to make sure the staff had her phone number. She made the nurse who was looking after him promise to phone her if he woke up or if he took a turn for the worse. There was no way she would let him be on his own if the time came. He promised her that he would and she bent down to kiss John's cheek. 'I have to go now, but I'll be here when you need me. They have my number. I love you.' A tear fell from her eyes and ran down his cheek. She gently wiped it away.

Then she forced herself to leave. She was going to ask Jake if she could stay at his until John was out of danger. She'd go home, pick up Alfie and get some things. About to get in her car, she remembered what Will had told her: she had to wait until he or Jake came to pick her up. Well, that was a pretty stupid idea. She had her car here. She couldn't just leave it. A police van turned the corner and she saw Jake behind the wheel. He pulled up next to her.

'Taxi for Ashworth.'

'I don't know what's going on, but I've got my car.'

'Strict orders from your husband – you're to come with me. Your car will be fine. The parking guys go home at four. We can come back for it after. Come on, I'm in a rush.'

Annie rolled her eyes, but opened the van's passenger door and got inside.

'Care to spill the beans? What on earth were you doing at Meadow Field?'

'Have you found Colin Lister? I feel really bad. I found an article in the paper about a killer clown back in the Fifties.'

'I saw it. You left your new best friend Colin a copy.'

'Well, you know I've been having these terribly vivid dreams about being there when the victims were killed. And the killer wore a creepy clown suit just like the one in the article. I searched the internet for a Colin Lister and his name popped up. I didn't think it would hurt to go and speak to him. I didn't mean to upset him that much that he'd do a runner.'

'Don't blame yourself, kid. He'll be fine. Will's off on one because I found black and white photos of someone who I think is a younger Colin Lister wearing that same suit. Will went to a sudden death earlier and the victim was dressed in an identical suit.'

He passed her his tablet to show her the photo of the dead man. Annie took it from him and gasped.

'Oh my God, I'm ninety-nine per cent sure that's the guy from my dreams. Did he kill himself?'

'No idea; that's for Will to figure out. We panicked when we saw the stuff in Colin's room and the nurse said an Annie Graham had been to visit him. You know, at this rate you're going to kill Will off, because he looked as if he was going to have a heart attack. Oh my God, Annie, I'm so sorry. How is John? I was so caught up with everything I forgot.'

'He's stable for now.'

Jake turned out of the hospital entrance onto Dalton Lane and drove along until he reached Abbey Road. Once he was on Abbey Road he began the drive back to Grange. They passed a bench where there was an old man huddled over. Annie turned her head to look at him.

'Stop the van. I think that's Colin.'

'What?'

'You have to go back. I'm pretty sure you just drove past him back on that bench.'

Jake swore under his breath, then did a sharp turn around the mini roundabout and drove back towards the bench. As he stopped, Annie opened the door.

'Annie, don't get out.' His voice was lost on her because she'd already jumped out and was crossing the road to get to him.

'Fuck, Will is going to kill me.' Jake followed her.

The elderly man on the bench looked tired and confused.

'Colin, it's Annie from this morning. Are you OK?'

He looked at her – wondering who on earth she was – when it all came back to him and he smiled.

'Ah yes, I do remember you, my long-lost relative.'

'Colin, this is my friend Jake. Would you like us to take you back to Meadow Field?'

The man paused then nodded his head. 'If you wouldn't mind, that would be lovely. I'm so tired I don't know how I even got here.'

He went to stand up and Annie leant down, taking him by the elbow, which caused Jake to wince. He shook his head at her and she frowned. She helped Colin to cross the road to the van. Jake opened the cage doors ready to put him in.

'Get a grip, Jake, we can't make him sit in that all the way back to Grange.'

Jake bent down and whispered in her ear, 'He's a murder suspect, Annie. We have to.'

'You are not putting an eighty-year-old man in the cage. I'll sit in the back with him.'

'Jesus, you don't know what he's capable of.'

Annie looked at the frail man standing in front of them. 'Not very much by the look of him.'

She opened the sliding door and helped Colin up the high step. Sitting him on the seat she fastened his belt.

'Annie, you sit up front with me or Will is going to kill the pair of us.'

She did as she was told, slamming the sliding door shut and getting in the front. Jake was on his radio informing control he had the missing man with him and was taking him back. Jake's radio rang. It was Will.

'Can you take him to the station and book him in, Jake? We need to talk to him.'

'Wish someone would make up their bloody mind where I'm going.' He looked into the rear-view mirror at the pale, crumpled old man. 'Actually, I don't know if that's a good idea. He looks exhausted and not very well. It might be better to bring him back and get any medication he needs; otherwise Smithy will only send us straight up the hospital and you know how long that will take.'

'Sorry, yes, you're probably right. Is Annie with you?'

'Yes.'

'Is she safe?'

'Yes.'

'Thank you.'

They drove back in silence, Colin lost in his thoughts and Annie wondering how this elderly man was involved in this mess. As Jake drove faster than normal to get them all back, she tried to piece it all together. Annie felt the familiar icy cold air on the side of her neck and shivered. What was the boy doing here in the police van? She looked behind her, not seeing him, but she could sense he was near.

Good Lord, could today get any weirder? She was just about done with it and wanted to pick Alfie up from Lily's house and give him a huge cuddle. Jake managed to get through the traffic much quicker than a normal car and before long they were at the turn-off for the home. The air in the van turned from too warm to icy cold in seconds. She turned around. Colin had perked up now they were almost back, which made her feel marginally better.

'I'm so glad to be home. Thank you, officer, for the lift. I honestly had no idea how I was going to get back. You can smooth things over for me with the night nurse? She's a bit of a dragon.'

Annie turned her head and smiled at him. 'You're very welcome, Colin.' She felt slivers of ice grip her arm and a raspy voice whispered in her ear, '*He isn't Colin.*' The jumble of thoughts that had fogged her mind all the way back cleared and it was there, so obvious she couldn't believe she hadn't seen it before.

She turned to look at the man behind her, who had also sensed the change in the atmosphere. They were so close. Annie could see Will, Adele and Cathy waiting at the front doors for them to arrive, along with two nurses – such a beautiful sight, a lovely welcoming party. The man looked at her and she whispered, 'You're not Colin Lister, are you? Your real name is Gordy Marshall – or do you prefer Tufty?'

He gave a brief laugh. 'I said to myself this morning after you'd left that you'd be trouble; I knew it. All these years I've lived my life as poor, hapless Colin, lived happily ever after until you had to come and spoil it.'

He stood up, bracing himself on two legs. Using all his strength he lifted the red iron battering ram, which had been by his feet and which they used to break doors down. He swung it at Jake's head and the crunch made Annie squeal. It clipped the side, knocking him straight out. The van veered to the left as Jake slumped onto the wheel, blood pouring from the deep wound on the side of his head.

Annie screamed in frustration as she tried to grab the wheel and turn it, but Jake's weight was pressed against it. It was careering towards the huge fir tree she'd admired this morning and there was nothing she could do to stop it except brace herself for the impact.

Will, who was watching in horror, realised what had happened and shouted at her to jump out of the van, but she couldn't hear anything except the pounding of her heart as the tree trunk came into view. Curling herself into a ball she wrapped her arms around her head, praying the airbag would activate and save both her and Jake from the brunt of the impact.

She shivered as she felt a sudden coldness envelop her. It felt as if she'd been wrapped in a protective ice pack, and then there was the terrible sound of metal crunching as the van ploughed into the tree and she was thrown forwards into the blackness.

Will ran after the out-of-control van, closely followed by Cathy, Adele and the nurses. The sound as it slammed into the tree was horrendous and he knew then that if any of them got out of it alive it would be a miracle. He wasn't going to lose her like this. After everything they'd been through she wasn't dying in the front of a police van and leaving him a widower and Alfie without his mum.

He reached the van and struggled to open her door; it was jammed and would only open a little. He could see her crouched over, blood everywhere, and he felt as if his world had just ended. Then she groaned and he sprang into action. There was steam and smoke coming from the front of the van, but he didn't care. He yanked the sliding door open to see the old man trapped under a seat that had dislodged.

Will ignored him and leaned over to unclick Annie's seat belt. He pulled the headrest off the seat, leant over and grabbed her under the arms. Dragging her with all his strength he managed to pull her over and they both landed in a heap on the ground. Adele took one arm and he had the other. Between them they carried her to a safe distance, then went back to help Jake.

Cathy had managed to get his door open, but he was a dead weight and she couldn't get him out. Will pulled his friend with all his might until he tumbled out of the door to the ground, landing in a heap on the grass. Cathy grabbed his feet and Will his armpits and they half carried, half dragged him to where Annie was.

The nurses were trying to get Colin out, but there was a whoosh as the tank exploded and the force of the explosion blew them back. They screamed at the sight of the old man in the back of the van, unable to free himself and about to be burnt alive. Will and Adele grabbed them to stop them going back to help him. There was nothing they could do for him now.

Adele had radioed for ambulance and fire brigade. The van had gone up in a spectacular fashion; it was burning well. Cathy was sitting on the ground nursing Jake's head in her lap. His tanned face had lost every inch of colour and the wound on his head was bleeding profusely. A nurse came running out of the home with some towels and a first-aid kit. She bent down and pressed a towel against Jake's wound to stem the bleeding.

Annie groaned and Will knelt down next to her. She was battered and bruised, with a cut above her eyebrow, but she was alive. He hugged her tight, smothering her head with kisses.

'Jake?'

'He's OK; well, he's breathing and unconscious and bleeding a lot, but he'll be fine.'

She looked at the van. 'That wasn't Colin Lister.'

'Then who the hell was it?'

'Gordy Marshall – Tufty the clown. He was the killer from the Fifties. When there was an accident at the circus he must have told them that Colin was Gordy. He'd been badly injured and couldn't speak. Poor Colin couldn't read or write properly so he couldn't tell them what had happened. Oh my God, they hanged an innocent man and Gordy Marshall got to live out the rest of his life in freedom. He got away with murder and framed poor Colin.'

'How do you know this?'

'Because Colin tried to show me what had happened: the dreams, the cold spots, the heavy breathing, because he couldn't speak. Colin came to me to help him.'

Will tried his best not to be freaked out. If it had been anyone else telling him this he would have put it down to concussion. But it was Annie, who could speak to the dead even though he didn't particularly like it, and he believed her.

'Colin helped me. He saved me and Jake.'

She crawled over to Jake and reached out to hold his hand, which was icy cold; then she smiled.

'Where are you, Colin?'

Cathy stared at Annie. 'Who is Colin? Is that not the dead guy in the van who attacked Jake?'

She shook her head. 'No, that wasn't Colin; that was Gordy Marshall. Colin was a kind, gentle soul who suffered the worst miscarriage of justice – and he just saved Jake's life, and mine.'

She looked over to the van that was now well alight, the smell of burning fuel, rubber and flesh filling the air. Turning to one side, in the distance she could see the outline of the cumbersome, shy young man who had come to her for help and had ended up saving her. He smiled at her and lifted his hand to wave.

'Thank you, Colin.'

He shook his head. *'Thank you, Annie.'*

She began to cry, huge heaving sobs of relief and emotion because he could talk again. A break in the clouds opened as a beam of brilliant white light shone down on where he was standing. He looked up towards it and smiled. Annie nodded her head, smiling back, and then he was gone – to a much better place. His soul was free. Annie made up her mind she would do her best to clear his name and make sure that people knew an innocent young man had lost his life in a terrible case of mistaken identity. Jake let out a groan and opened one eye.

'What's that stench? Am I dead? I feel as if I'm dead. Oh God, I'm bleeding.'

He looked up to see Cathy's face peering down into his.

'You did eat my cake. You've got guilt written all over your face.'

She laughed. 'You stupid bugger; no, I didn't. You probably burnt it to death. Thank God you're alive.'

He tried to turn his head and see where Annie was. He saw her tear-stained face and shut his eyes. 'Aw, are you really crying over me, Annie Graham? That's sweet.'

She bent down and kissed his cheek. 'Yes, Jake, I'm crying over you.'

'Good, now you know how it feels.'

An ambulance turned into the drive and Will waved it towards them. Annie stood and watched as they loaded Jake onto the stretcher and into the back of the ambulance. Cathy followed.

'I'll go with him.'

Will smiled and Annie stuck her thumb up.

Adele turned to them. 'I think you should take Annie and follow. It would be wise to get checked out. I'll stop and sort this mess out.'

'Do you mind? Thank you, I really appreciate this.'

'My pleasure, Annie. It was lovely to meet you. Maybe next time it will be under better circumstances.'

Annie laughed. 'I certainly hope so. Thank you.'

'You're welcome.'

Adele watched the ambulance drive off, followed by Will's BMW, and let out a sigh. What an end to a long week. At least everyone who mattered was alive.

Chapter Twenty-Six

Annie knocked on Jake's front door and was greeted by Alex. He bent down and kissed her cheek.

'He's in the living room being a drama queen. If he asks me to get him one more glass of water I'm going to scream.'

She laughed. 'He's milking it for all he can get then?'

Alex arched his eyebrow and she followed him inside. Jake was sitting reading a story to Alice. He had a big bandage around his head and she was glad to see he had a lot more colour in his cheeks than the last time she'd visited. When he noticed her he pretended to faint.

'Pack it in. I haven't got any spare Oscars for you. Are you driving Alex mad?'

He pointed to his chest. 'Me, driving him mad? He's lucky I'm alive. I almost died and he's moaning about getting me a glass of water.'

Annie laughed again. 'Trust me, Jake, you need to get over it. I'm afraid you're old news now, so man up.'

'Ouch, you two are harsh.'

'Yeah, it's called tough love.'

Alice looked at Jake. 'Man up, Daddy.'

Jake, who was so shocked to hear her speak three words, pointed to Annie.

'My daughter's first sentence, thanks to you.'

Then he started to laugh and Annie, who'd been mortified, joined in. She kissed him on the cheek.

'Sorry, Jake, and thank you again for being there for me. I love you.'

'Yeah, you proper love me? I'll let you off then. Have you found out what to do about the real Colin Lister's wrongful execution? I can't stop thinking about him.'

She nodded. 'Me neither. That poor boy must have been so scared. I've made a start; I made an application to the senior Justice Minister to get him the royal prerogative of mercy.'

'The what? I've never heard of it.'

'No neither had I – at least not by its official name. It's a post-humous royal pardon for the miscarriage of justice for execution by hanging.'

'Wow, get you. Annie, I'm impressed. Let's hope they do it.'

'I'm sure they will. How could they not? It might take a very long time, but at least we know the truth and Colin's at peace now. I can't stop. I'm on my way to the hospital to see John. I just wanted to make sure you were coping.'

She smiled at him and kissed the top of Alice's head. 'Bye, clever girl.'

Alice waved at her. 'Bye, lever girl.'

Annie drove away. She couldn't wait until Alfie could talk. They were growing up so fast. As she reached the hospital, this time she managed to find an actual parking bay and paid for a ticket. She was hoping they were going to let John come home today. She'd phoned Mrs Brown earlier, who had all but moved into the rectory ready to look after him. It was quite sweet really. As much as he moaned about his housekeeper she was a good woman. When she got to his ward she almost squealed to see him fully dressed and sitting in the chair by his bed.

He smiled at her. 'Well, if it isn't the lovely Annie Graham I see before my very own eyes.'

'You look so much better. Have they said you can come home?'

A cloud passed over his face and his expression darkened for a second. He nodded. 'Yes, they've had enough of me. The sister said she was glad to see the back of me.'

Annie laughed. 'Good, let's get you home where you belong. Mrs Brown will be over the moon.'

He rolled his eyes. 'She may well be, but I might not.'

'Don't be so mean. Someone needs to look after you.'

He stood and she picked up his overnight bag that she'd brought in for him a couple of days ago. She'd packed it with everything he could possibly need including his faithful, faded Rolling Stones T-shirt, which he was wearing now. They walked slowly out of the ward, Annie with her arm looped through his. She hadn't told him about Gordy Marshall – not wanting to burden him with any extra worry – and he'd been very good and not asked her how she'd got the purple bruise across her cheek and the cut above her eye.

As they stepped outside into the fresh air, he inhaled deeply. 'I will never again take the sun on my face or the fresh air in my lungs for granted. Thank you for everything, Annie.'

'You're welcome; it's the least I can do.'

They walked to her car and she opened the door for him. He brushed her hand away when she leant in to fasten his seat belt.

'I'm not an invalid just yet.'

She grinned and walked around to the driver's side. 'Come on, let's get you home; then I have to go to work.'

As she walked into the station, Annie vowed to herself she would never take her friends for granted again. It had been quite a shock to be the one on the other end of the drama. Watching from the sidelines had been terrifying and it had made her one hundred per cent sure that she was doing the right thing. She knocked on Cathy's office door.

'Come in. Have you brought food?'

Annie smiled as she pushed the door open and passed her a carton with a huge slice of fresh cream cake inside. Cathy nodded her head in appreciation. Annie also passed her a crisp white envelope.

Cathy arched an eyebrow at her. 'Is this what I think it might be?'

Annie shrugged. 'That depends on how bad you want to get shot of me.'

'There is nothing I would want more. Don't get me wrong; I love you, kid, but my stress levels are almost back to normal.'

Cathy ran her finger along the inside of the envelope and pulled out the letter. She read it and Annie was pleased to see a small tear form in the corner of her inspector's eye. Annie blinked back her own tears, but they weren't of sadness; they were of relief. She had a new adventure to concentrate on. She should be getting the keys for the shop near the Lakeside where she was going to set up a café and bookshop. Will and Kav had agreed to do the decorating once the keys were hers. Cathy stood up and walked around to where Annie was standing. She pulled her close and squeezed tight.

'I accept your resignation. You're a bloody good officer and I'll be sad to see you go, but you're an even better friend and I'd much rather see you living your life and not having to live in fear. You're doing the right thing, kid. When I retire I'll have a part-time job working for you.'

Cathy winked at her and Annie hugged her back. 'You and Kav are always welcome; you know that.'

'Always?'

'Yes, always.'

Annie turned and walked out, the lump in her throat making it difficult to talk. As she stepped out into the fresh air she smiled. This was a beautiful place to live and she was going to start living her life with no regrets, but most importantly no fear.

251

Will looked up from his computer as Adele walked into his office carrying two mugs of hot coffee. He pushed aside the printouts and files that covered the desk to make some space.

'I'm confident the DNA evidence will come back and prove that Walter Lacey was responsible for the deaths of Pauline Cook and Billy Marks. Annie has been doing lots of research into Gordy Marshall aka Colin Lister. I believe it was Gordy Marshall who killed Walter Lacey; hopefully there will also be DNA evidence to prove this. He'd got away with murdering his parents, along with Colin's mother and the little girl who Colin was hanged for. All this time he got to live out the rest of his life not caring that he let an innocent man die. Who knows how many more deaths he could have been responsible for over the years?'

Adele passed a mug to Will and sat down. 'I've got a headache just trying to get my head around it all. I suppose we'll never know how many people Gordy Marshall murdered. Were there any suspicious deaths at the nursing home?'

'I've got Shona and Brad looking into it. I'm hoping there weren't. This is a big enough mess without adding any more to it.' He gestured at the papers. 'There is one good thing, though. Guess what Annie was going to do this morning?' He looked down at his watch and smiled. 'In fact she should have already done it.'

Adele shrugged. 'I don't know; you'll have to tell me.'

'She was going to see Cathy and hand in her resignation.'

'Really, that's brilliant news. You must be so relieved.'

'I already feel ten years younger; maybe now we can live a relatively normal life. No more looking over our shoulders, no more worrying about what she's doing and who she might be getting involved with. You never know who the face behind the mask is, how many seemingly ordinary people have turned out to be sadistic killers. Well, no more. Today is a very good day, Adele.'

Debs was the only CSI in the large office. After pulling on a pair of latex gloves, she opened the brown paper evidence bag with the clown costume inside. It needed to be dried out fully before it could be sent away to the Forensic Lab in Warrington for testing. She cut off the green tag from the drying cabinet door, writing down the information into the evidence book. Then she pulled out the costume to hang it inside.

Placing the evidence bags next to it for continuity, she couldn't stop staring at it. There was something so mesmerising about it. She heard her name called from out in the corridor and snapped out of her daze, repulsion filling her mind as she released the bloodstained sleeve she'd been holding. She slammed the door shut and resealed it, this time with a yellow tag.

Tugging off her gloves, she turned to walk out of the office. As she reached the door a voice whispered, 'I'll be waiting for you.' Turning around to see who had spoken she felt her heart miss a beat. There was no one except for her. Closing the door behind her, she heard the soft click as it locked, and she shivered.

Acknowledgements

I'd like to say a huge thank you, as always, to my brilliant editor, Victoria Oundjian, for her patience and guidance. Also thank you to Helena Newton for the copy edits. And to the rest of the HQ digital team for their hard work in making this book what it is, the wonderful design team for my scary clown cover. I love it.

I owe a huge debt of thanks to my wonderful readers who have taken Annie Graham into their lives; it's wonderful to hear from you. The emails, messages, comments and chance meetings, usually when I look like I've been dragged through a hedge, are amazing and mean a lot to me. It's your kind words which make this writing life worth all the hard work.

I have to say a huge thank you to Claire Benson for always being so patient when I'm asking her the weirdest of questions.

A very special thank you to Justin Hawkins from the Criminal Cases Review Commission for taking the time out his very busy schedule to speak and enlighten me on the subject of pursing the royal prerogative of mercy.

A very special thank you to my newest character, Adele Dean, who is the amazing real-life Adele Dean. Adele bid for the chance to become a character in this book to raise money for the fabulous charity group Lookin' Good and Feelin' Great. These truly amazing ladies are making a huge difference to cancer sufferers in the Furness area. Adele, what started out as a small character has turned into a main one. I hope you like her; I think she's pretty cool.

A very special thank you goes to Gail and Paul O'Neill, who just happen to be the most lovely, supportive friends anyone could ask for.

I'd like to thank my husband, Steve, and my children, Jessica, Joshua, Jerusha, Jaimea and Jeorgia, for always being there, for supporting me when I'm having a bad writing day or some kind of computer emergency. A very special thank you to my beautiful grandchildren, who are far too young to read these books, but I hope that one day they will enjoy them. Gracie, Laurence, Donovan and Matilda, you make my heart overflow with love – you are all amazing. A special thank you goes to Tom and Danielle for being such wonderful additions to my family.

It's been hard since I lost my gorgeous dad to stomach cancer last September; he was my whole family's rock and there is a huge hole in all of our hearts. My mam is amazing and if you read these acknowledgements, Mam, please know that I love you so very much.

Love always
Helen xx

Want to return to where it all began for Annie Graham?

THE GHOST HOUSE

After years on the police force, Annie Graham never expected that it would be her personal life leaving her physically and emotionally scarred.

While on a break from work, trying to put the pieces of her life back together, the role of caretaker to a beautiful, crumbling mansion in the woods seems like a good escape.

But something about the house puts her on edge, and her suspicions are confirmed when she finds the diary of former resident Alice. The house holds a dark connection to a series of terrible murders committed over one hundred years ago.

And when a search for a missing girl turns into a hunt for a serial killer, Annie fears that history may be repeating itself. But as the past collides with the present, has Annie's unofficial investigation put her in the killer's sights?

Discover the haunting and gripping Annie Graham crime series

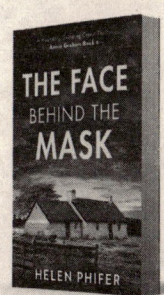

Dear Reader,

We hope you enjoyed reading this book. If you did, we'd be so appreciative if you left a review. It really helps us and the author to bring more books like this to you.

Here at HQ Digital we are dedicated to publishing fiction that will keep you turning the pages into the early hours. Don't want to miss a thing? To find out more about our books, promotions, discover exclusive content and enter competitions you can keep in touch in the following ways:

JOIN OUR COMMUNITY:

Sign up to our new email newsletter: http://smarturl.it/SignUpHQ

Read our new blog www.hqstories.co.uk

X https://twitter.com/HQStories

www.facebook.com/HQStories

BUDDING WRITER?

We're also looking for authors to join the HQ Digital family!

Find out more here:

https://www.hqstories.co.uk/want-to-write-for-us/

Thanks for reading, from the HQ Digital team